RAZOR ROCKS

PARADISE CRIME MYSTERIES BOOK 13

TOBY NEAL

Book Cover Design by ebooklaunch.com
Formatting by: Jamie Davis

CHAPTER ONE

DETECTIVE SERGEANT LEILANI TEXEIRA clutched the dashboard of her partner Pono's jacked up purple truck, affectionately nicknamed Stanley. "Can you slow down?"

"No." Pono changed gears. The cop light on the dash strobing, Stanley roared forward even faster as they zoomed down Highway 30 toward Ma'alaea Harbor, whipping around a line of rental cars.

Lei shut her eyes. "Bruddah. Getting killed on the way to the harbor won't find your cousin any faster, and besides, if we get in a wreck, Tiare will kill us both."

Pono's formidably competent wife, Tiare, was not to be messed with. Her partner's big brown hand tightened on the chrome skull that marked Stanley's shifter, but he eased up on the gas pedal.

Lei sat back in her seat. "I know this is hard—but whatever's happened has already happened. You gotta stay objective about the case, or Captain Omura will pull you off of it."

Pono scowled, his pidgin thickening. "It's my cuz. Not jus' any kine cuz—dis my uncle's oldest boy Chaz Kaihale. We been close since small kid time."

"I know. Chaz is good people." Lei touched Pono's tense bicep, her fingers lightly brushing the slash of a scar where a tribal tattoo of interlocking triangles had been torn by a meth dealer's bullet. *She'd been so terrified when the man who was her brother in everything but name had been shot . . .* "Tell me again what you know. Let's get a plan before we meet with the Coast Guard."

Pono blew out a breath and put both hands back on the wheel. The truck slowed to a reasonable rate at last. "Chaz called me from sea. Remember, he's a captain and goes out with a couple of guys to crew luxury boats for Dream Vacations Luxury Yachts. Anyway, I wen get one call from him yesterday; he stay yelling. 'Pono! You gotta help us! Get pirates coming!' and then damn if the phone didn't cut off." Pono flexed his fingers. "Ho, I was laughing. I thought Chaz was pranking me cuz it was April first! But when I tried to call back, the call nevah go through. So I'm thinking, eh, he pranked me, but even with the satellite phone, half the time his calls get cut off." Pono glanced over at Lei. Even with his favorite Oakleys hiding his eyes, she felt his pain. "Turns out, the call was legit."

"You couldn't have known! I mean, it was April Fools' Day!" Drifts of wayward curls, whipping in the breeze from the partly open window, lashed Lei's face. She bundled her hair back with a rubber band she spotted encircling the gearshift.

"I should have tried harder to find out what was going on. Chaz, he one prankster, but I should have called the ship-to-shore radio at least . . . anyway, I did nothing. Then, just now, I get a call from that Coast Guard guy we worked that Molokini case with— Aina Thomas. Remember him? He called my cell, telling me they found the yacht my cuz was captaining washed up on the reef off Lana'i. No one on board, but get bloodstains." Pono speeded up again.

"No, Pono, no . . ." Lei's stomach lurched under the sensible black polo shirt she wore with jeans and athletic shoes. "You didn't tell me anything but 'go get in the car, we got a case involving my cuz.' This is big, if it's *pirates*. If it's *murder*."

"I know."

"Are you sure Thomas was calling you as an investigator? Maybe he was calling you as a witness, because you and Chaz are close. He found your name listed somewhere in Chaz's phone or something."

Pono's mouth just tightened, and Lei had her answer—*Pono wasn't thinking right now.*

Lei needed to take charge. She dug a Maui Police Department ball cap out of the backpack, loaded with investigation paraphernalia, resting at her feet. She tugged the cap down low and tight on her head, and took out her phone. "I'll call Captain Omura and brief her with what we know. And let me take the lead when we talk to Thomas. We got dis, partner."

LEI HADN'T SEEN Petty Officer Aina Thomas in several years, not since they'd shared a gut-wrenching case involving the murder of a beautiful young marine biologist in the waters off of Molokini atoll. A lot had happened since she'd been briefly attracted to the handsome Coast Guardsman, including the rescue of her husband, Michael Stevens, from foreign kidnappers, and the birth of a daughter.

Wind, characteristic of the area, whipped the palm trees as they pulled into the marina parking lot of Ma'alaea Harbor. Lei hopped down off the chrome step of the lifted truck, patting her weapon in its shoulder holster and straightening her jacket over it, checking that her badge was clipped onto her belt.

"We go!" Pono boomed, his usual mellow attitude gone as he slammed his door. Lei jogged to keep up as they moved along the waterfront, the ocean glimmering in the distance. The clang of wind-whipped rigging and the squeak of boats at their moorings made a strange kind of music.

Lei spotted the Coast Guard craft at the end of the pier, and hurried to get in front of her partner.

A quiver of purely personal nervous tension sharpened Lei's voice as she hurried toward the nattily uniformed young man standing on the dock in front of the powerful rigid-hulled Coast Guard *Defender* Zodiac. "Petty Officer Thomas. What have we got?"

"Sergeant Lei Texeira and Detective Pono Kaihale." Thomas's voice was brusque. His crisp navy uniform still looked really good on his trim, athletic frame. "Long time. I see you came with your partner, but I only called Pono. As a witness, to be interviewed."

"That may be what got this going, but Captain Omura has authorized us to investigate the missing persons and signs of foul play you've discovered on behalf of the Maui Police Department. So, going forward, this will be a joint investigation." Pono's body heat simmered just behind her; her partner was barely containing his anxiety, and it felt like a thundercloud at her back. Even without seeing Pono's expression, Lei knew he'd be as intimidating as hell with his arms crossed over his bulky chest and those inscrutable Oakleys hiding his worried eyes. "Why don't we go to your conference room in the Coast Guard building, where we can speak privately?"

Aina Thomas had a face much like her own: tawny brown skin, a few freckles across the nose, the tilted brown eyes of mixed Japanese-Hawaiian and Portuguese, curling dark hair buzzed military-short. Other than his hair, seeing him was like looking at a twin brother.

Thomas shook his head in negation. "We need to get back to the wreck. We can brief you on the way. Follow me." He spun with precision, and headed for the ladder leading up onto the deck of the Coast Guard *Defender*.

Lei glanced around as she ascended the ladder onto the rigid-hulled inflatable twenty-five-foot craft. Two giant Honda outboards idled harshly; as soon as she and Pono were on board, a crewman handed them life vests, and Thomas ushered them into the cramped quarters of the small forward cabin. "We can talk in here. It's about thirty minutes to the wreck."

"Wow, this thing really rips," Lei said. "It's usually an hour from Ma`alaea to Lana`i on the ferry."

Thomas's quick, triangular grin reminded her of why she'd found him so attractive. "You have no idea. Grab onto something."

Lei caught hold of a support stanchion on an inside wall just as the boat surged forward, spinning away from the dock and violating the usual inside-harbor speed limits. Pono jostled against her until they both found seats on a padded storage bench against one wall.

"Why don't you tell us what you wanted to talk to Pono about?" Lei shouted over the noise of the engines. "It must be pretty urgent if we didn't have time to talk about it somewhere quieter—and more private." She indicated the Guardsman driving the boat with her head.

In answer, Thomas handed the man a set of earmuffs. "It's ear protection and a comm unit," Thomas told them. The Guardsman put them on, his eyes front and full attention on driving the speedy craft.

Thomas removed a touchscreen tablet from a drawer and sat in one of the two bolted-down captain's chairs, swiveling to face them. "I called you because we suspect foul play. I called Pono because of his relationship with Chaz Kaihale, the captain. We think Kaihale may be involved with whatever went on."

"Why you say that about my cousin?" Pono rumbled, fierce with defensiveness for his family member. "He's a good man. Never been in any trouble."

"Because Kaihale's nowhere to be found, nor are the passengers . . . and the boat was robbed. Stripped of the passengers' valuables, parts, anything that could be sold. Usually these kinds of hits are an inside job," Thomas said. "Otherwise, we're talking pirates, and that seldom happens in Hawaii for a number of reasons I won't get into right now. It's a good thing the ship hung up on the rocks, or we'd have nothing to investigate at all; I saw a hole in the hull other than what the rocks made, and I think the perps tried to sink it."

Pono folded his thick arms and opened his mouth to defend his cousin some more, but Lei held up a hand. "Guys. Let's agree at this point that this shipwreck seems like a crime scene and move forward without assumptions for the moment. So, Aina, did you notify the police on Lana'i yet?"

"I did. Sergeant Gary Miller was on duty and said he'd be going down to the beach to meet us."

"I'll get ahold of him." Lei took out her phone and routed her call to the on-island officer through Captain Omura. Maui County consisted of five islands of varying sizes: Maui, the main island, Kaho'olawe and Molokini atolls, Moloka'i, and Lana'i. The two atolls were uninhabited, and officers rotated out to Lana'i for shifts, while larger Moloka'i had its own police force.

Lei knew Miller from other cases. It would be good to have backup on-island from the energetic young black man, though the Lana'i police station was tiny with little investigation resource equipment. They'd have to process all evidence on the main island of Maui.

Once Lei had established contact with Miller, she put away her phone.

The Guardsman driving the *Defender* turned his head. "Ship ahoy. We're here." Lei's pulse picked up with the familiar hit of adrenaline that made being a cop so addictive.

CHAPTER TWO

THE YACHT WAS BEAUTIFUL—OR it had been, before it drifted into the jagged formation known as Razor Rocks. Pure white from stem to stern but for a delicate scrolling design along its hull in pale blue, the *Sea Cloud* was a sleek, graceful shape heeled over to one side, caught on the rough black lava protruding from the churning surf like the teeth of a monster. A gaping hole near the bow allowed surf to surge in and out belowdecks.

Lei surveyed the craft, Pono a warm bulk beside her. A stiff breeze hit, and she tugged her ball cap lower as she leaned over the metal rail, peering at the remains of the yacht.

Thomas appeared at her elbow. "Lana'i folks nicknamed this spot Razor Rocks, because so many boats have died out here. Like I said, if this one hadn't run aground, it would have sunk from the hole they put in the hull and we wouldn't have this crime scene for you to investigate, at all."

"Good thing I grabbed my kit," Lei patted her backpack. "How can Miller get out here to join us from the shore?" Lana'i rose in a golden hump directly ahead, fringed by its skirt of barrier reef, the edge of which was marked by Razor Rocks.

"We have a tender boat." Thomas gestured to a small mini-inflatable lashed to the stern of the larger craft. "We have to use that to get close enough to the wreck to board it, anyway. Petty Officer Sanchez will go get Miller while we get started and we can all regroup here when you're done collecting evidence. We need to get moving. The tide's coming in, and there's a danger the craft will come off the rocks." As they spoke, two Guardsmen unfastened the tender and launched it.

Lei was glad she'd worn her thin windbreaker parka over her regular clothing as she climbed down the short ladder onto the tender, taking a seat in the bow. Pono looked a little green around his brown complexion as they motored through the chop, the inflatable loaded heavily with Lei, Pono, Thomas, and Sanchez at the tiller.

They reached the *Sea Cloud*. The yacht's deck was slanted at an angle by how steeply it had heeled over, and there was no visible way to climb onto the slick side. "How are we supposed to go on board?" Lei asked.

Thomas held up a grappling hook. "We'll use this to pull ourselves up to the main entrance hatch. Then we should be able to get inside just fine—I did it before."

Lei bit her lip, exchanging a glance with Pono, as the Guardsman tossed the grappling hook up. He had to make several casts to catch it on the metal railing surrounding the main hatch leading into the interior of the yacht.

He tugged the hook, checking how secure it was. "I'll go up first, then give you two support getting on board. Sanchez can help from below."

Sanchez's help seemed unlikely given the movement of the tipsy inflatable as it bobbed against the side of the grounded yacht, as surf surge banged it to and fro.

Getting up to the hatch proved to be every bit as nerve-wracking and physically taxing as Lei had been concerned it would be, but finally the three of them stood in an open bay, canted at a tilt, facing a door with shiny brass fittings that led into the interior.

They gloved up and Thomas opened the door, hooking it back to stay ajar. "I'll take you to the navigation room first. That's all I needed to see before calling for an investigation."

They made their way to what had been the highest point of the yacht, an upper level cockpit with room for two crew members and a large instrument panel. Lei, Pono and Thomas flicked on flashlights to shine around an interior rendered dim without power.

Thomas shone his beam over a blood smear on the instrument panel. "After we ascertained the craft was abandoned and I saw this, I searched for the crew and passenger manifest. Every boat over a certain size needs to keep a log of who's on board and contact numbers, in case of emergency."

He reached under the instrument panel and pulled out the manifest. The black laminated book was stored in a heavy Ziploc bag. He slid a thumb along the edge to open it, and removed the book.

"Who else was on board?" Pono asked.

"Your cousin was captain, and he had two crew members aboard, plus the family of five who chartered the yacht." Thomas tapped the front page of the manifest. "Faifale Honopua was crewing, and Priscilla Gutierrez, cook and maid. The guests on this cruise were the Peterson family. Patrick Peterson of Enviro Enterprises dot-com, his wife, Emma, and their three daughters, Joanie, Adelia and Sarah."

"No sign of any of them, eh?" Pono rubbed his bristly mustache in a habitual way that told Lei he was troubled. He hated cases involving children.

"Nope." Thomas slid the book back into the plastic sleeve designed to keep the damp out. "We'll take this with us, but as you can see, everyone had a photo of their ID attached, per protocol. I've already run the parents' names. They are from Seattle, and there are no missing persons alerts out on any of them, nor do they have any outstanding warrants. That doesn't go for the crew, however." Thomas's jaw bunched as he addressed Pono. "Did you know your cousin has liens on his house and car? That he's got a bench warrant out on him for back child support?"

Pono scowled. "He's been going through a nasty divorce, I knew that much. The wife, she was cleaning him out. But I nevah know how bad it was."

"Honopua also has a record," Thomas said. "Petty theft, a gas station robbery. No weapons or violence. And Gutierrez is an illegal alien. I ran her ID and it came back invalid."

Lei took the logbook from Thomas. "I'm going to need this." She stowed it in her backpack. "Now we know why you suspected Pono's cousin, but we shouldn't be trying to solve the case and discuss suspects right now. We're here to search this ship and find any clues or evidence we can, while we can. I for one am worried this thing is going to come loose from the rocks."

As if on cue, the yacht gave a loud groan. The deck shuddered beneath their feet. Thomas frowned, hooking his radio off of his belt and hollering into it. "Sanchez! Are you getting Miller? Drop him off at the main craft and get back here to pick us up, ASAP. This vessel is unstable!"

Lei was already moving, her gaze roaming the cockpit for any further signs of anything out of place beside the blood smear. "Pono, can you take a picture of that blood trace? I'll collect a sample."

Her partner nodded, taking the MPD's Canon camera from her hand to shoot several photos of the area, while Lei opened a swab packet. She quickly labeled it and scraped a bit of the blood off with the swab, bagging it. The trio headed down the sharply slanted ladder to the main deck.

The three of them stayed together, roaming through the deck area. The living quarters and galley showed signs of disruption, with overturned furniture, broken light fixtures, and open cupboard doors. Pono began photographing the mess, but Thomas shook his head. "This all could've happened after the boat ran aground. Hard to tell what might have been related to the actual incident. Let's go check the living quarters more closely. Our team just made sure they were empty last time I was on board; we didn't take time to look around."

Lei was in the lead as they entered one of the cabins. "This must've been where the girls were staying." Feminine clothing spilled out of a built-in wall unit. Three of the four bunk beds were mussed, with covers tossed back and pillows on the floor.

Lei mentally batted away an image of the girls' bodies, floating drowned in the sea. *Hopefully they were ashore, at worst being held hostage or kidnapped for ransom.* She would have to check into the Petersons' financial situation and connections, see if there was anyone who stood to gain from the family's disappearance.

"Guys, especially keep an eye out for any phones, laptops or tablets. Kids this age live online." Lei pulled open the drawer of the desk and grabbed up a pink satin diary, decorated with a little clasp and padlock. "I'll take this. See if one of the girls was keeping a log of their journey."

Pono rattled through the clothing in the wall unit, his mouth pinched. His own children, Maile and Ikaika, were approaching the same age as these girls.

Thomas appeared in the doorway. His golden-tan face had gone pale. "I think you both need to see something in the main cabin."

CHAPTER THREE

LEI AND PONO walked into the main cabin behind Thomas. Lei covered her mouth with a hand, muffling a gasp.

The bed's white comforter was rumpled; blood spatter spread over one side, and ran down from the edge in a macabre waterfall that ended in a large pool that had soaked into the nap of the royal blue carpet covering the floor.

Lei moved forward and squatted to examine the area. As she leaned in close, that too-familiar burnt iron smell flared her nostrils. The blood had set, but not yet dried. A skin on the surface was undisrupted even by the movement of the yacht as it trembled under the waves' battering.

"That's a life-threatening amount of blood right there," Pono spoke from behind his busily clicking camera. "This is a murder scene."

"This happened less than a day ago," Lei said. "The victim bled out here." She stepped carefully around the pool, scanning the bed with her flashlight. "Let's go over the whole bed. I'll search for hairs, fingerprints, anything we can lift from here." Lei was already combing over the bed, leaning down just inches from the silky white comforter with her flashlight and a pair of tweezers.

"Agree that this looks like a kill scene. But it's always hard to solve a murder without a body. Aina, can you do a more thorough sweep through the cabins? Check all storage units, the refrigerator, anywhere big enough to hold a body. Hopefully they didn't just chuck the vic overboard."

"I bet they did." Pono shook his head. Tiny pearls of sweat gleamed in his black buzz cut even though the room was humid and cool. "The ocean is a handy dumping ground."

"Yeah, but I don't see a blood trail going out onto the deck," Lei argued. "Unless they wrapped the body in something, it would have been messy getting it out of here."

Thomas poked his head out of the bathroom. "Shower curtain's missing." He jangled the empty rings. "The curtain was likely plastic. They probably rolled the body up in that and dumped it. But I'll keep searching."

Suddenly the yacht gave another moaning shudder, and the room abruptly tilted. Lei gave a cry as she crashed into Pono, grateful that he caught her with one arm as he grabbed a wall with the other. Thomas, hung up in the doorway of the bathroom, yelled into his radio. "Sanchez! Where are you? We need pickup!"

"On my way, sir!" Sanchez's voice fizzed with static.

"We'll be topside, waiting." Thomas hung the radio back on his belt and addressed Lei and Pono. "We need to get out, now. I'll work on getting the boat sealed up enough to be towed back to the harbor, where we can investigate it more safely."

"Just a few more minutes." Lei pulled herself up and hurried to scramble around the room, checking for any other signs of disturbance. Kneeling to look under the bed, she spotted a plastic handle fillet knife. "This is likely the murder weapon." She bagged the knife and slipped it into her backpack along with the bloody evidence swabs.

The shriek of rending metal and plastic tore the air around them, and the floor shifted dramatically, canting to the right. Lei tumbled onto Pono a second time as her partner landed against what had been a wall, and was now the floor. Thomas rolled down to crash into both of them as any furniture that wasn't bolted down smashed around them.

"Abandon ship!" Thomas yelled. Lei would have smiled at the corny line if the situation hadn't been so dire. "Anyone hurt?" The Guardsman hauled himself upright on hands and knees, giving Lei a hand.

"We're fine! But we're not going to be in a minute!" The craft was definitely moving, loosed from the rocks somehow. Perhaps their weight, moving around, along with the tide, had lifted the yacht off the rocks . . . and now, the thing was sinking, and quickly. Water poured in through the doorway, a terrifying waterfall. "We need to get out of here!"

Pono was the first to reach the doorway, now almost horizontal above them. He reached back and hauled Lei up beside him. The two of them were able to pull Thomas up through the opening. Water gushed in, seemingly from all directions, making climbing through the wreckage and fun-house tilted rooms a challenge.

Don't panic, just focus on getting out. Place each hand and foot carefully . . . you can't afford to slip. Lei used the metal doorways to draw herself out and up, heading after Thomas toward the exit through which they'd come.

She'd made sure her backpack straps were tight, and she was grateful for the flotation device she still wore under it . . . but none of that would do much good if they sank while trapped inside.

They finally reached the entry door and burst out into fresh air. Lei glanced around, registering the nearby Coast Guard craft, the bobbing tender, and the startling fact that the yacht was now barely clearing the surface of the water.

"Sanchez!" Thomas gestured frantically to the man in the tender. "Toss over the grappling hook!"

Sanchez drew abreast of them, one hand on the tiller and the other on the grappling hook with its attached rope. The inflatable was only four or five feet below, almost close enough to risk jumping for. She inched toward the hull's edge and a clear spot where she could jump away from the yacht.

She registered the horrified faces of the watching Coast Guard crew even as the *Sea Cloud* abruptly heaved over and sank in a violent wash of swirling water and bubbles.

Lei hardly had time to draw a deep breath, as chilly water hit like a blow and abruptly closed over her head.

She kicked out, stroking as hard as she could towards a surface that must be above . . . but as hard as she tried, she couldn't seem to reach it.

Lei opened her eyes and looked up at the surface, in spite of the stinging water.

That mercury-like silvery ceiling was farther away than ever.

The pull of the sinking yacht was taking her down with it.

CHAPTER FOUR

LIEUTENANT MICHAEL STEVENS pushed a hand into his hair, clenching a fistful of the dark locks and giving a tug to express the frustration he was feeling. "I understand. Thanks. Let us know if anything changes." He banged the handset of the departmental phone down. "Damn it."

"Still no luck?" Brandon Mahoe, his partner, glanced up from the other side of the desk they shared on the quiet third floor of Kahului Police Station. The junior detective had made steady progress as an investigator under Stevens's leadership, and their partnership had continued for the last couple of years.

"Nope. We can't find anywhere for Lei's grandpa Soga to go after his operation."

"Why isn't Lei making these calls, LT? Just curious."

"Captain Omura told me Lei's pulled a high-visibility joint investigation with the Coast Guard. She won't be able to work on much of anything personal until that settles down." He sat back and sighed. "And here's something to remember: when you're married, you're a team. We share everything, no matter whose relative it is."

"I get it. I was just asking."

"Soga's our kupuna, the kids' great-grandpa. The fact that we can't find an assisted living for him is a huge problem."

Eighty-plus-year-old Soga Matsumoto had been living independently at the home he owned on O'ahu, participating in his Buddhist temple and repairing and creating the beautiful paper lanterns used in Honolulu's annual floating lantern festival, when he'd fallen and broken a hip. Soga had made it through the replacement surgery with Lei by his side, and she had flown home to work while he recovered at a convalescent hospital.

Soga loved his life on O'ahu, but had agreed to move to Maui to be closer to them and his great-grandchildren following his recovery. Stevens had been as happy as Lei with the plan to bring her only surviving family member from her mother's side closer to home—but a care home was proving hard to find.

"What about your cottage?" Mahoe said.

Stevens stifled a stab of annoyance—Mahoe was a good kid but way too opinionated about Stevens's personal business. "Can't. Our parents are in there." Wayne, Lei's father, and Ellen, Stevens's mom, had fallen in love. They'd been living on the property in the little *ohana* cottage, an arrangement that worked great since the older couple provided much of their childcare.

Mahoe must have read Stevens's expression. "I was just thinking out loud. You know my mom's a nurse. She's often mentioned the shortage of housing and care on Maui. She'd love to start a group home or something for elders, but we don't have the seed money needed to get it going."

"Too bad. I'd totally trust your mom to take care of Soga." Stevens glanced at the clock and closed the folder where they'd been storing information as they worked their way through the available facilities on the island. "I'm not sure if we're going to be able to bring him over to Maui if we don't find something." He powered down his computer. "I gotta go. I have to swing by the store on the way home."

"I'll close up here," Mahoe said. "Finish up our notes and send the report in."

"Thanks." Stevens and Mahoe had just wrapped up their latest case. A brief breather before another investigation that was likely to suck them in to late evenings and early mornings was to be taken advantage of, and Stevens made the most of opportunities to spend extra time with the family.

"See you tomorrow." Stevens shrugged into his jacket just as the scanner on the office's credenza belched out emergency codes for an ocean rescue of officers in trouble off the coast of Lana'i.

That had to be Lei and Pono! Stevens's gaze met Mahoe's. "There aren't any other joint cases with the Coast Guard right now!"

The younger man stood up, grabbing his weapon harness off the nearby hall tree. "I'll go with you to the harbor; we'll find out what's going on."

They hauled ass down the stairs and out of the building as Stevens called Dispatch on his radio for an update. "The Coast Guard hasn't given us an update," Iris told him. "But they're all over it with rescue protocols. Relax, Lieutenant, I'm sure Texeira and Kaihale are fine."

"*You* relax, Iris. That's my wife you're talking about!" Stevens barked as they jumped into Stevens's ancient brown Bronco. He turned the key and the engine, recently rebuilt, roared impressively into life. "Here. Talk to your boyfriend." He tossed the radio to Mahoe.

Iris, a dainty Chinese girl with nerves of steel and not much of a sense of humor, had been going out with Mahoe for over a year. "Hey baby," Mahoe said. "We're headed down to Ma'alaea to see if we can assist. Tell us more about what's going on?"

"The Guard called in that an intentionally damaged yacht had washed up on Razor Rocks off Lana'i. While the investigators were on board, the yacht came loose from the rocks and sank."

The truck surged forward as Stevens swore, his heart leaping into overdrive, his foot dropping hard on the accelerator.

Iris went on, imperturbable. "I asked for more details. The communications officer said that their man, Petty Officer Aina Thomas, who's the main Coast Guard crime investigator, along with Lei and Pono, had all reached the exterior hull when the boat abruptly went down. They'll have swum to safety by now, most likely."

"Then why hasn't the Coast Guard called with an all-clear?" Mahoe asked.

"I don't know. I'll try their communications officer again," Iris said, and the radio went dead.

This time Mahoe was the one to swear. He flicked on the portable cop light and put it on the dash, grabbing the sissy strap as Stevens wove through traffic.

Stevens's vision narrowed to just the road and obstacles in front of it. His heart sounded like bongos and his breathing—he wasn't even sure he *was* breathing.

Lei was everything to him. To their family. *She couldn't be gone.*

CHAPTER FIVE

AFTER THAT QUICK glance at the surface Lei clamped her eyes shut, drawing all her focus inward and swallowing down the quick breath of air she'd been able to grab. Swallowing made it last longer, and so did remembering her scuba lessons. *The undertow of the sinking craft couldn't hold her if she was floaty enough.*

Her bulky backpack, loaded with an SLR camera, backup weapon, the big paper manifest, handcuffs, flashlight, nightstick, pepper spray and more, was what was dragging her down. She had to get rid of it, and lose her shoes too. *But the evidence she'd collected would be gone . . .*

Her mind's eye filled with flashes of her loved ones: Michael Stevens, crystal blue eyes intent as he bent to kiss her; Kiet, laughing as he ran to her, sun on his shining black hair; Rosie, her dimpled grin finally filled in with pearly baby teeth; her father Wayne; her mother-in-law Ellen; their beloved Rottweiler, Conan.

She couldn't drown. *She was needed.* The case would get solved somehow, the backpack retrieved by divers. She had to live. Nothing was more important than that.

Lei continued to sink as she struggled to get out of the backpack's tight straps, tugging and pulling. The straps seemed to be caught on her inflatable vest and the cotton jacket underneath.

She couldn't get the pack off!

Her arms were held down, tangled in her jacket and the straps . . . and she was still sinking.

Lei's diaphragm spasmed, trying to draw breath.

She wouldn't let it, couldn't . . . *no please oh God, not this way, I don't want to die this way . . .*

And suddenly, hands were helping her.

Stripping the pack off. Grabbing her, turning her, pulling her by the back of the inflatable jacket.

Lei thrashed, releasing valuable air, kicking frantically, trying to help, but probably hindering.

She wanted to take off her shoes, but there was no more time.

No time, *no time no time* . . . Black dots were closing in around the red behind her eyes, but finally Lei was free of the pack.

A hand caught one of her flailing ones, tugging her upward.

Aina Thomas. Had to be.

He'd come back for her.

Thomas was a waterman through and through, and with his Coast Guard training, he could hold his breath much longer than she or Pono.

Lei kicked with all her strength as Thomas towed her upward.

They broke the surface just as Lei sucked an involuntary breath, catching water in her mouth. The seawater burned like liquid fire all the way down her throat into her lungs. She floundered, coughing and retching, fighting the weight of her clothing, shoes, and lean body mass.

Lei felt a stinging tug as her rescuer towed her by the hair. The position lifted her face clear of the water and tilted her onto her back. "Just relax. I've got you." Thomas's voice, a little breathless but confident.

Lei focused on breathing, and let him pull her through the choppy waves.

Where was Pono? Was her partner okay?

"Lei! Holy crap, seestah, you wen give me one heart attack!" Pono's bass voice boomed above her; they'd reached the side of the Coast Guard craft.

Lei shut her eyes and smiled, too worn out to do anything but go limp as a dozen hands caught her, lifting her up onto the sun-warmed deck of the Coast Guard craft.

Someone took off her shoes.

Someone else put a pillow under her head and covered her with a thermal blanket.

"Lei! Talk to me, girl!" Pono sounded frantic and way too loud, right in her ear. Lei hauled her heavy eyelids open enough to see his looming shadow, handily blocking the sun.

"I'm fine," Lei croaked, and promptly rolled onto her side to retch and cough, as Pono thumped her on the back.

Pono settled her back. "I just swam straight up. Couldn't believe you weren't right behind me with Thomas. Then he sucked a few breaths and went back down . . . longest minutes of my life."

The Guardsman who doubled as a medic pushed Pono back and knelt beside Lei with his kit. "I'd like to check you out, Sergeant, if you don't mind. You've probably got a little hypothermia and water inhalation, but I'd like to make sure that's all there is."

Lei nodded, shivering and miserable. The man applied a stethoscope to her back and asked her to take some deep breaths, which set off another round of retching and coughing. Her eyes watered and her nose ran. Meanwhile, the Coast Guard craft had lifted into a vibrating roar, and Lei felt the huge rigid-hulled inflatable slamming through the rolling waves of the rough Au`au Channel as they headed back toward Ma`alaea Harbor.

Finally, Lei was able to curl up and rest, shivering in her wet clothes under the crinkly silver blanket. Pono bent over her with his cell phone. "Someone here wants to speak to you."

Lei took the phone with a trembling hand and applied it to her ear. "Texeira," she croaked.

"Sweets, are you okay?" Stevens was yelling in his fright. "You sound awful!"

"I'm fine. Just got checked by the medic, here. I sucked some water getting away from the sinking ship. Throat hurts, but I'm okay." Lei flashed to the strangling hold of the heavy backpack holding her arms down, dragging her in the wake of the ruptured yacht. "One of the Guardsmen came back for me, thank God. Aina Thomas. He saved my life." She turned her head, searching for the Guardsman. She spotted him inside the boat's cabin, talking to the crew. "I probably wouldn't have made it if he hadn't come back for me. That backpack . . ." her throat closed.

Pono plucked the phone out of Lei's fingers. His pidgin was heavy in his agitation. "Your wife been t'ru one heavy kine t'ing an *bumbai*, she need res'. I tell you what wen down." Her partner, his soaked pants and wet shoes leaving prints on the deck, told the story with much hand gesturing as he walked into the lee of the cabin out of the wind. Lei curled up tighter and shivered in her silver thermal blanket.

Thomas, done with whatever report he'd been making, came out of the cabin and squatted next to Lei. He was still wearing his wet uniform, but wrapped in a crinkly blanket too. He peered at her, brown eyes crinkled at the corners with worry. "Our medic tells me you're okay—but how are you feeling?"

Lei slid a hand out of the warm nest formed by her blanket to squeeze his arm. "Alive, thanks to you."

He cleared his throat. "Oh, you'd have got to the surface without me. The will to survive is incredibly strong."

"No." Lei shook her head. "I wasn't getting out of that pack without help. It was pulling me down like an anchor."

"Just doing my job." Thomas patted her shoulder awkwardly. *Whatever attraction they'd once had for each other was definitely gone.*

"But now, the evidence, and the crime scene, are both on the bottom of the ocean." Lei shut her eyes, suddenly weary. "We're going to have a hell of a time with this case, now."

CHAPTER SIX

LEI CONTINUED to hold Stevens's hand as he punched in the code to the gate opening into their home in verdant, green Haiku on the east shore of Maui. A high wooden fence around their two-acre property wasn't a guarantee of safety—they'd been attacked by a pyromaniac even with it in place—but that sturdy barrier still gave Lei a sense of security, of a private world. It also kept their kids, and their Rottweiler, Conan, safely contained inside.

A twinge of sadness made Lei close her eyes, remembering Keiki, her first Rottweiler. The loving, battle-scarred old girl, Lei's companion for more than ten years, had passed away peacefully from old age a year ago. Keiki was buried on the property with a hand-carved petroglyph, engraved by one of their Hawaiian friends, marking her resting place.

Conan, much younger, was already barking a deep-throated welcome on the other side of the gate as it rumbled open.

"I didn't say anything to the family about what happened to you," Stevens squeezed Lei's hand as they drove forward. "No sense worrying our parents or Kiet, since you're fine."

"Good," Lei agreed. "I'll ditch this blanket. I'm sure Thomas wants it back, anyway." She stripped off the silver thermal covering, bundling it up and stuffing it behind the Bronco's seat as Stevens navigated the winding gravel driveway leading through a property rich with fruit trees and marked by two separate dwellings. "Easy enough to explain that I had to go swimming for a case."

"And you wouldn't even be lying." Stevens's crystal blue eyes crinkled at the corners, but tension still bracketed his mouth from the stress and drama of picking her up at the Ma`alaea dock. "Sure glad that Coast Guardsman went back for you, or this would be quite a different homecoming."

He parked the truck in front of their open garage, cluttered with the kids' toys, gardening implements and tools, and a mountain of laundry piled on the washer at one end. The house was simple, a new stucco and cement block rectangle with a fire-retardant metal roof, but they slept well in its sturdy structure. Lei loved every square inch of it, since they'd built it themselves with the help of friends.

"I need a hug." Lei shivered in her damp clothes, reaching over to Stevens. "I don't ever want to get that close to drowning again."

"Amen to that," Stevens said gruffly. "I almost had a heart attack when I heard what happened."

They held each other for a long moment. Lei wriggled over the gear area to rest her cheek on Stevens's chest, reaching up to encircle his neck with her arm. She made a little sound of need and tipped her face up towards her husband's. Stevens bent his head to kiss her.

For just a moment, they shut out Conan's barking, war whoops from Kiet and a little friend of his as the boys ran around the yard, and the sound of eighteen-month-old Rosie howling in tantrum mode from Wayne and Ellen's cottage.

Lei shut her eyes and sank into the kiss, into the warmth and love of her husband's arms. Gratitude suffused her. *Nothing was guaranteed. Every day was a gift.*

"Ew, gross, Mom and Dad!" Seven-year-old Kiet yelled

outside Stevens's window as his friend giggled. Conan barked loudly on Lei's side, clearly worried something was wrong.

Stevens let Lei go with a sigh. "To be continued." He touched her nose with a finger. "Divide and conquer, ok? You go get Rosie and relieve poor Mom, I'll deal with the boys."

"Deal." She pressed another quick kiss on his jaw. "We have a date later. Much later, when everyone's in bed."

Lei got out of her side, calming Conan with a soothing voice and pets on the head. Stevens got out of his side, grabbing each of the boys under an arm and carrying them off as they shrieked with glee.

Ellen appeared on the porch of her and Wayne's little plantation style cottage, with its border of *ti* plants and red hibiscus. The cottage had not burned in the fire that destroyed the main house, and retained the charm that was such a part of those vintage structures.

Her mother-in-law seemed frazzled, her silver-blonde hair in disarray and food smeared on the shoulder of her blue smock. "I was getting ready to call for reinforcements, beg Wayne to come home from the restaurant or something. Our girl has been super cranky today."

"She's teething. I'm *so* sorry I forgot to give you the frozen washcloths I made last night. She loves to chew on them." Lei hurried up the wooden steps to scoop the toddler, hiccupping miserably, into her arms. "Oh, sweetie, what a grumpy face you have!"

Rosie looked as frazzled as Ellen. Her silky brown curls were a sticky mess and her face was crumpled and shiny from wailing. She burrowed her wet face into Lei's neck and popped her thumb into her mouth, quieting at last as Lei hugged Ellen with her free arm. "You deserve a grandma-of-the-year medal!"

"I do, don't I?" Ellen made a mock 'Scream' face with her mouth wide and hands cupping her cheeks. "Thank God the kids have school and nursery care . . . I'm only good for a couple of hours of hard-core parent duty!" Her gaze swept Lei, and she frowned. "Your clothes are all wet. Did you fall in the water or something?"

"Sure did. I'll get both of us into a hot shower. That ought to distract baby girl here," Lei said. "Give Dad a hug for me, will you?"

"I will. I'm getting cleaned up and meeting him at Ono Grindz for a date," Ellen said. "We're going to the movies."

"Oh, what I'd give to go to a grown-up movie!" Lei exclaimed. "I don't think we've been out in the eighteen months since Rosie was born."

"Well, we'll have to fix that situation. But not until that tooth comes through, right, sweetie?" She caressed Rosie's hair. "I'll see you tomorrow, darling."

"Bye!" Lei waved and prompted Rosie to wave too. Carrying the baby, she hurried across the yard. Kiet's friend was being picked up, so Lei greeted the boy's mom and they talked story for a few minutes until Rosie began fussing again, and she was finally able to get inside the house and into the shower.

The big, tiled walk-in shower was large enough for Lei to carry Rosie in with her. She played with the baby under the warm water, cooing to her, soaping both of their bodies and hair, loving on the fussy baby until Rosie was giggling and relaxed. It was early for her bedtime, but when Lei got out and wrapped them both in towels, her daughter was soft and sleepy, resting her head on Lei's chest, her eyes at half-mast. Lei admired Rosie's long lashes as she blotted the extra water out of the baby's hair.

Carrying the sleepy toddler, she held a finger to her lips, cutting Stevens off from commenting as she tiptoed through the living room past Kiet, intent on his daily dose of Cartoon Network. Stevens nodded, waving his spatula at her. He was stir-frying something that smelled delicious, and her stomach rumbled as she passed him, carrying Rosie to the kids' room.

Lei put a diaper on the baby, and then pajamas. She settled

Rosie in her crib, turning on a white noise machine and lowering the blinds. Rosie promptly rolled over, hiking her little padded butt in the air, and plugged her mouth with a thumb.

Lei tiptoed into the master bedroom and dressed in her favorite old pair of pj's. On her way back to the kitchen, Lei draped a lightweight Hawaiian print quilt, created by Rosie's godmother Esther Ka`awai, over the baby. She hovered a moment, smoothing the quilt over Rosie's back and savoring the sight of her sleeping child —then she shut the door gently, casting her eyes heavenward in thanks that the baby had gone down so easy.

Lei came up behind Stevens in the kitchen, sliding her arms around his chest from behind and snuggling her cheek against his shoulder blade. She breathed in the smell of his clean body and shirt—*he'd found time to shower, too.* "Thing One is down. Only Thing Two to go." They'd come up with those *Cat in the Hat* nicknames after Rosie came along.

They both glanced over at Kiet, snuggled with Conan on the couch, his gaze on the TV. The little boy's hair gleamed in the soft light, and his slender arm seemed tiny draped over the Rottweiler's sturdy side. "Gotta get some food into him," Stevens tossed the beef stir-fry one last time. "Can you check on the rice?"

Lei lifted the lid of the cooker. "Almost done. I'll set the table."

They were a team. A team fixing dinner, a team caring for their children and their home, a team solving crime at work.

But later on, in the privacy of their bedroom, they were passionate lovers whose souls connected through their bodies.

Lei fell asleep in her husband's arms, thankful again for how far they'd come . . . just to be exactly where they were.

CHAPTER SEVEN

LEI WALKED into the morning team meeting at Kahului Police Station, still scrunching gel into damp, wayward curls. At least she'd managed to find a clean set of clothes, and her backup weapon was oiled and loaded. A woman had to have priorities—and hers had been getting Kiet to school on time and Rosie settled at nursery care, while Stevens dealt with the dog and prepped food for dinner when they all got home.

Captain Omura had beaten Lei to the conference room and taken the head chair at the battered Formica table that had seen too many team meetings to count. "You seem recovered from your ordeal yesterday, Texeira."

"I am, thanks. It was scary, but no lasting damage." Lei sat beside the immaculately dressed woman affectionately nicknamed the "Steel Butterfly." Omura's shining, bobbed black hair, classy makeup and red lacquered nails were perfect, as usual. "I owe my life to Petty Officer Aina Thomas."

"I read the report. Scary, indeed." Omura blinked, hiding emotion. "I'm glad you're okay."

Pono pushed the door open with an elbow, both hands occupied with a pair of MPD coffee mugs. He handed one to Lei. "Figured you hadn't had time to grab a cup."

"Thanks, partner. And you remembered creamer." Lei peered in at the tarry brew and stirred the chunks of dissolving powder with a red straw stick Pono'd thrown in. "Too bad that fancy coffeemaker's acting up."

Lei's good friend Sophie, a tech investigator based on O'ahu, had gifted their department with a new Keurig coffeemaker for Christmas. Lei had enjoyed the smooth, tasty stuff until the machine had disappeared. "Unfortunately, those pod refills cost too much for our budget," Omura said. "It's in the storage room at the moment."

Lei opened her mouth to volunteer to chip in for more of the coffee pods, when Becca Nunez, their crime scene tech, walked in ahead of Aina Thomas.

Nunez was new to Kahului Station; she'd only been there a year, and she carried her computer tablet against her chest like a breastplate. A recent grad from University of Hawaii's forensics program, she wore her hair in an edgy cut with a bright magenta streak in the front, and was fond of goth—today she wore a chain mail mesh necklace.

Thomas took a chair across from Lei. "I see you're feeling better."

"Totally fine. Thanks again for the rescue." Lei lifted her mug in a toasting gesture.

Captain Omura already had her laptop open. She drummed her glossy fingernails across the metal keys, making an impatient sound. "Let's get started. Time is of the essence with all of these people missing. I'll call our man on Lana'i to join in." She connected the video call, and shortly, they greeted Gary Miller.

The young black man waved, grinning, from his communication window on the Captain's laptop. "Hey all. I was sorry to miss all the drama yesterday. I was waiting on the beach for pickup from the Coast Guard tender boat, and just before it reached me, the guy turned around and hauled ass out to the wreck! Then I saw it go down." His expression sobered. "Looked intense."

"Did you have a chance to do those sweeps, checking for survivors coming up on the island?" Thomas asked.

"We are short-staffed at the Lana`i Station, as you know, but we have a civilian neighborhood watch group. Great folks. We rousted all of them to patrol the beaches. No one has seen anything," Miller said. "Any survivors of the wreck must have taken off on another boat."

Thomas leaned forward to speak to the group. "We called out our big cutter, the *Independent*, yesterday. They came out to support us as we dove the wreck after we took Lei and Pono back to Ma`alaea. We also sent patrols all around the different channels and bays on Lana`i, looking for signs of any people or craft that might have come ashore. Nothing. We've also been diving for any bodies near the wreck. So far, nothing."

Omura steepled her fingers. "So, what do we know? Texeira, go to the board and summarize for us."

Lei got up and went to the whiteboard on one of the walls, uncapping an erasable marker.

Thomas turned to Captain Omura. "Our divers went down to the wreck as soon as they were able and the yacht had settled on the bottom. Fortunately, it's not too far down, only forty feet or so. Unfortunately, any crime scene trace that would have been useful was lost. We did, however, recover Lei's backpack."

Nunez inclined her head. Tiny silver skeletons swung at her ears. "The backpack is in the lab drying out, Lei. The evidence bags inside were paper, so that was a mess, but the blood samples you retrieved were sealed in plastic, so they're still good. The fingerprints you picked up were on gel, and that degraded in the water, so we're at zero with those, unfortunately." Nunez took a breath. "The good news is, you'll get most of your personal stuff back, unharmed."

"I don't care about that," Lei said. "But I'm sick about that fingerprint evidence getting lost."

Pono nodded. "I've been on the phone with my cousin's family. Got his blood type. We need types for the rest of the passengers and crew. Once we rule out anyone who's not a match to the samples we collected, we can go in deeper for a DNA match."

"I've submitted the blood samples to DNA processing already, but as you know, those go to O'ahu and take a week or more," Nunez said.

"To that end, I've been on the phone with O'ahu," Omura said. "Talking to the folks from Dream Vacations Luxury Yachts and trying to find out more about the Peterson family, and who to notify that they are missing. I got the number of a next of kin, and their lawyer." She slid a folded note over to Lei. "You and Pono need to contact them, find out all you can about the family. Do a background on them. We need to figure out if this crime was opportunistic, or targeted toward the Petersons."

Thomas nodded. "We're trying to ascertain the same thing. Chaz Kaihale has motive—he's upside down on a mortgage, and has big debt . . ."

"My cuz would never do something like this," Pono rumbled.

"Pono. We get it that this is your cousin, but we have to follow the evidence. If you can't do that, can't be objective, you need to be pulled from the case. Now," Omura said.

Pono shook his head, speaking carefully. "My cousin has had some troubles. He was broke and going through a rough divorce. But he has no history of violence, or crime of any kind, for that matter." Pono rubbed the bullet scar on his arm. "He called me when the attack happened. Told me they were being boarded by pirates. I thought he was pranking me, because it was April first."

Thomas frowned. "You told me that when we were on our way to the wreck. I told you then, and I stick by it, that these kinds of crimes are usually inside jobs initiated by a crew. Granted, those are not usually perpetrated by stable, longer-term employees like your cousin and the two who were on this boat, but insiders none-theless . . . See, pirates don't really operate in Hawaii."

"Say more on that subject," Omura commanded.

"There are eight main Hawaiian islands. All of them are rela-tively close together, except for Kaua`i. We have a strong Coast Guard presence on every island, and a whole fleet keeping the waters safe. Where can anyone hide that we can't find them? Another reason we don't have pirates is that the Hawaiian Islands are so isolated—they're thousands of miles from any landmass in any direction. Pirates have to travel all that way, either by boat or plane, to get here . . . and once they do, we control the harbors and airports." Thomas sipped from his own mug, and grimaced, clearly disliking the departmental coffee. "Pirate problems tend to occur where there's little water law enforcement, and a lot of places to hide along the coast. Hawaii has some remote areas, but we can spot craft by air with choppers, or by sea with our fleet. Again, where can they go?" Thomas's jaw bunched, as did his fist. "If this was pirates . . . we'll nail them quickly."

Lei cleared her throat. "I understand what you're saying, but I'm inclined to believe that someone unknown attacked the yacht. I've known Chaz for years, have even been on a charter with him and the family. He takes safety seriously and really owns that 'cap-tain' role. Maybe it wasn't pirates, but the disarray inside the craft was consistent with some kind of an attack."

"I wish we had the yacht to go over for evidence," Nunez said. "It would tell us a lot."

"And maybe that's why the perps sank it," Pono said. "They meant for it to end up at the bottom of the sea, and for everyone to be gone. Without a body or a crime scene, who's to say what happened to the family at all?" He rubbed his mustache vigorously in agitation. "And my cuz . . . he's a handy one to blame."

"Here are the questions we need to resolve right away: was the wreck of the *Sea Cloud* an opportunistic, one-time attack on a rich-looking target by raiders from Lana`i or elsewhere? Or, is it a targeted attack on the Peterson family for some reason or reasons unknown? Or . . . is it a pirate raid, part of some larger pattern?" Omura pointed at Thomas. "You explained why pirates are uncommon in Hawaii. Have there been any other attacks similar to this on the other islands?"

"No. I'd have told you if there were," Thomas said.

Omura pointed to Lei. "I think we need to transition into who's doing what at this point. Let's make sure the Coast Guard and our team have clear roles, so no one duplicates anything. Miller, I want you to canvass and keep searching on Lana'i. Check for anyone who knows anything, any sign of where the attackers could have come ashore, any sign of the victims. Lei and Pono, I want you to dig into the family and the crew. Find out anything and everything you can about them. And Petty Officer Thomas?" She cocked her head to one side like an inquisitive bird. "You guys take care of everything to do with the boat and the ocean."

"Yes ma'am," Thomas said. "Already on that."

"Call me 'sir'," Omura said. "Get to it, everyone."

"Yes, sir," everyone said, and they got to it.

CHAPTER EIGHT

LEI SETTLED into the familiar modular cubicle that she shared with Pono in Kahului Station's main work area, while he went on the hunt for fresh coffee.

She booted up her aging computer. This process was always a pause in her workday, filled with clicking and wheezing, and suspense of whether or not today was the day the poor old thing would kick it.

Waiting, Lei scanned the area around her desk for anything needing clearing, her gaze falling on the small corkboard pinned to the sound-insulated, movable wall. She'd pinned photos of her growing family and their dogs to it, through the years.

Hard to believe how much had happened since, as an early-twenties young recruit, she'd left Aunty Rosario's little house on D Street in San Rafael, California, with Keiki as a young dog recently washed out of K-9 training, and had moved to the Big Island. Her first job as a patrol officer had been with South Hilo Station, and there she'd met her longtime partner Pono and fallen in love with Michael Stevens. After several career and interisland moves, all three of them had ended up on Maui. Lei had finally found her niche, doing the work she was best suited for: homicide investigation.

Her mouth tightened as her gaze dropped to the crisp new manila case jacket holding the documents generated by the *Sea Cloud* case. The file was already thickening with paperwork and printouts, most recently a faxed set of copies of Chaz's fingerprints and those of the other crew members. Only the Peterson girls' fingerprints were on file, submitted voluntarily by their parents to a Child Find database in case any of their children were ever lost.

How awful that those diligent parents were now missing, along with all three daughters, and those fingerprints were actually needed.

What had happened to that family and the Sea Cloud's crew?

With all eight people still missing for more than twenty-four hours, it seemed more and more likely that they were feeding the sharks.

What powerful motive could have prompted such a heinous crime? It had to be something personal, maybe some financial or other motive in the Petersons' lives . . . Or it was opportunistic pirates. Whatever it had been, she'd work her ass off to get to the bottom of it, if her damn computer would just cooperate.

"Freakin' thing." Lei whacked the side of the monitor. The device rewarded her by displaying random wavy lines. "I don't have time for this crap."

Even if she did get the computer working, she wasn't going to be able to find out much online with the antiquated software they were running—*and this case was big!* She needed answers from the mainland, from another island, and much more than basic background information, plus she needed it fast . . . they should probably involve the FBI, but the captain hadn't authorized that yet, which meant she couldn't yet bring in her agent friend Marcella Scott. Lei still functioned as the FBI's Maui contact, and having access to their superior resources had been a boon on many a case.

But her ex-FBI, tech sleuth friend Sophie would be able to get those answers. Sophie now worked for a private security firm, but still had the best skills and programs of anyone, anywhere.

Pono returned with their refilled mugs. "I made a fresh pot. It shouldn't be too bad this time." He set her mug down at her elbow. "I'd like to go interview my cousin's ex, Cheryl Ortega, and find out what had been going on between them. Find out what was up with Chaz's finances. I want to clear his name. Make sure we find another suspect."

Lei picked up her mug and stirred the swizzle stick, blending in the powdered creamer. She took a sip. "Mmm. This is much better, Pono." She set down the coffee. "I get your agenda. You and I both know Chaz didn't do it—kill a family of five, plus crew? I can't see it, no matter what the provocation. I'm not going to stand in your way on your plan, but you heard the Captain—we need to dig into the Peterson family." She frowned, worry tightening her brows. "The more time that goes by and none of the missing persons are found, the more likely we're working on the homicide of eight people."

"I can't even think about that." Pono dropped into his chair, hunching forward, shutting his eyes and massaging his temples. She'd never seen him this upset on the job—but then, nothing they'd worked on had hit so close to home. "I love Chaz like a brother. He can't be gone."

"Maybe he's not. Maybe . . . they're being held prisoner for some reason." Lei couldn't find words to comfort Pono when the outlook was this grim. She patted his shoulder. "Let's just keep working. That's what you can do to help Chaz. I'm sure his ex-wife has heard the news on the 'coconut wireless'—even if she hated him, she has to be upset by the gossip. You go your way on this. I'll go mine and focus on the Petersons. Call or text me in between, and we'll reconnect when we can."

Pono stood up. "I'll go drop in on Cheryl, then. I want to catch her by surprise, if possible." He shrugged into his weapon harness and slid on the thin parka he wore over it. "I'll keep you posted.

TOBY NEAL

And you stay out of trouble, Sweets." He pointed a thick finger at her as if cocking a pistol. "I couldn't handle it if something happened to my sistah, too."

"No *pilikia*," Lei agreed. "Got you covered, partner."

Pono gave a little salute and left, abandoning his coffee.

Lei sighed and turned back to the monitor. The wavy lines had resolved, but staring at her MPD logo and login, her jaw tightened with frustration. She pulled up the case file online, put in her earbuds, and took out her phone.

"Lei! I never hear from you these days!" Sophie's Brit-accented voice was upbeat, and she sounded right next door, not a hundred miles away on another island. "What's new?"

"All good in the hood, girlfriend," Lei said. "Other than Rosie cutting a major tooth and giving everyone hell, it's domestic bliss over here. You?"

"Ah, well, not so blissful—but I'm carrying on." Sophie's volatile love life was a source of both worry and teasing from both Lei and Marcella, as she continued to have trouble settling down with just one of the men pursuing her. "Things are lively at home. But enough of the small talk . . . I know better than to imagine that Sergeant Leilani Texeira is just calling me in the middle of the workday to socialize. What do you need?"

"Am I so predictable?" Lei smiled.

"Yes, but I love you anyway. Cough it up."

"Like a hairball?" Lei laughed. Sophie had become so much better at English, relaxed, and open in her communication than she'd been when the women first worked together in the FBI. Back then, Sophie had been intimidatingly hard to know, reserved, prickly, and usually hidden in her computer lab. "You're right. It's a case—a big one." Lei quickly outlined the situation. "I need all you can find out on the Peterson family, their company, Enviro Enterprises dot-com, and also Dream Vacations Luxury Yachts, the company operating the *Sea Cloud*."

Sophie chuckled. "You know I'm private security now, and charge by the hour . . . right? I'm pretty sure you can't afford me."

Lei set aside the banter, her voice going serious. "I know, Sophie. I'd never tap on you with *pro bono* police business if it weren't serious. Pono's cousin Chaz, who was captaining the yacht, is being considered as a suspect. A family of five with three teenaged girls has disappeared. Eight people, gone, with a heavy blood pool and signs of violence on board before the yacht went down." She swallowed. "I don't hit you up often, but I need whatever leads I can follow, like . . . yesterday."

"I remember Chaz. I met him at that baby luau for Rosie's first birthday." Sophie, too, had sobered. "I will get on this right away."

"I owe you," Lei said. "Anything you need—just say the word."

She heard the smile in Sophie's voice. "I can probably get anything I need. But not a friend like you, Lei. I'll ping you back as soon as I know anything."

Lei hung up the phone, and dug the slip of paper the Captain had given her out of her pocket. "Eeny, meeny, miney, mo . . . which to call first, the next of kin or the lawyer?"

CHAPTER NINE

STEVENS HAD BARELY GREETED Mahoe and their officemate, recruiter Kathy Fraser, when his phone buzzed with an incoming call from Iris at Dispatch. "We've got a body. The vic washed up on the rocks in Lahaina. Captain wants you and Brandon on this one. According to the first responders, there's a visible stab wound on the corpse."

"We're on it." Stevens gestured to Mahoe and tugged his windbreaker back off the hall tree he'd just hung it on. "What's the exact location?"

"Body's hung up on the rocks at the entrance to Lahaina Harbor, near the ferry dock. Responding officers have taped off the area, but there's time pressure as the boats using the harbor have schedules to keep." Iris's keyboard sounded busy.

"I take it you've called Dr. Gregory already if there's a time crunch for removing the body?" Stevens headed toward the door, lifting a hand in goodbye to Kathy. The blue-eyed brunette waved back, smiling. The diamond ring Stevens's brother Jared had put on her finger flashed in the low light coming through the blinds. *That was an excellent recent development—past time Jared married a good woman, and Kathy was great.* "Get ahold of the

Coast Guard, too, Iris. We'll want their help in managing the harbor, and in case this body has something to do with the *Sea Cloud* case that Lei is on." Stevens made for the elevator and Mahoe trotted to catch up.

"I'll call him right away." Iris was still typing.

"Good. We'll keep you posted." He ended the call as they got on the elevator. "We'll take your new truck this time, Brandon. Got a body and an impatient harbormaster in Lahaina."

"Sweet." Mahoe rubbed his hands together with anticipation. He was still young enough to be excited about a new case, but Stevens had seen too many bodies over the years to feel that same enthusiasm. He tightened his mouth on a rebuke—*the job would beat Mahoe down soon enough without his help.*

Mahoe drove a black Tacoma four-door truck with racks on top and *MauiBuilt* stickers all along the bumper. Stevens got in the passenger side and put the portable cop light on the dash as soon as his partner pulled out of the parking lot onto the busy highway.

Stevens thumbed to Lei's number on his phone. She did not pick up, so he left a message. "Hey, Sweets. We're headed out to Lahaina Harbor, where there's a fresh body washed up on the rocks. Male stabbing victim. I don't have any more details, but this sounds like it could be one of your *Sea Cloud* missing persons. I'll let you know as soon as we have a positive ID. Love you."

Mahoe glanced over. "Maybe you can pull up the cruise personnel fingerprints on your laptop while we drive. We could do a quick visual comparison at the scene, confirm it with photos if the body's not too far gone, and save time."

"Good idea." A flicker of pride warmed Stevens as he glanced at his young protégé. Brandon Mahoe had come a long way since they'd first worked together on one of the young officer's patrol cases involving petroglyphs being stolen from sacred sites.

Stevens removed a small satellite-enabled field laptop out of his backpack. He logged on as Mahoe wound through the busy traffic of Kahului and entered the highway toward Lahaina.

"I hope it isn't Chaz." Mahoe's dark brows drew together in a furrow on his forehead. "I've never had to deal with the body of someone I know before."

"Stay in this business long enough, and you will." Stevens shook his head. "Yeah, I hope it isn't either. On the other hand, if it is Chaz, he's definitely not the perp in the *Sea Cloud* case. Not that any of us who know him believe that he could be."

Mahoe didn't hesitate to use his horn as well as the dashboard light to clear the way as they careened onto the Pali Highway, that scenic stretch of two-lane road overlooking the ocean, leading around the upper left side of the figure eight that made up Maui's general outline.

Stevens opened the case file via the laptop balanced on his knees, and pulled up the two male possibilities that had prints in the system: Chaz and his Tongan crewman, Faifale Honopua. Patrick Peterson, renter of the *Sea Cloud*, was not in any databases. "I'd better call Lei's Coast Guard liaison, Aina Thomas, and let him know about this body."

When Thomas picked up Stevens's call, the Coast Guardsman's voice was rough. "We are already on our way—got a notification from 911. No rest for the weary. We've been diving all around the wreck site and projected rip current areas, patrolling for bodies. Still hadn't found anything."

"It seems like too much of a coincidence for there to be a male homicide vic in the water, in an area where it could have washed up from Lana`i," Stevens said. "I'm glad you'll be there; I hear the boats using the harbor are restless, wanting to keep to their schedules. I imagine the first responders are having trouble clearing the harbor of tourists and lookie-loos."

"We'll manage the harbor situation. No problem."

THE SCENE at the harbor was as chaotic as Stevens had anticipated. The responding officers had done their best, cordoning off the area around the body and holding back the crowd with scene tape and a few sawhorses. Still, spectators were three-deep all around the breakwater, crowding over the accessible areas. Everyone seemed to have their phones out, filming the sad sight of the man's body floating face down against the rocks near the jetty where the large white ferryboat parked.

Even as Stevens and Brandon elbowed their way through the crowd, flashing their badges, they heard the booming bullhorn of the Coast Guard as their vessel arrived. *"This is a restricted area. All nonessential personnel are to clear out of the harbor immediately!"*

The strident announcement, coupled with the serious demeanor of the uniformed men bristling with weapons as they lined the railing of a large, rigid-hulled Coast Guard inflatable, quickly dispersed the crowds.

Stevens greeted the uniformed officers and signed the crime scene log, Mahoe close behind him. He was glad he was wearing rubber-soled athletic shoes as he clambered carefully down steep boulders from the top of the breakwater and approached the body. Mahoe panted a bit behind him, carrying their heavy crime scene backpack.

Stevens squatted on a flat stone, assessing the corpse as it washed gently against the rocks: *mixed-race male, approximately 5 foot 10 and 180 pounds, black hair, wearing a blue polo shirt and tan chinos with boat shoes, one missing.*

Mahoe took the department's camera out of the backpack, photographing the body and the surrounding area.

"The vic's clothing seems like it could be a shipboard uniform," Stevens said. "I think I see an emblem on the sleeve."

"You're right, LT. Looks like one to me."

"Can you find me a rescue hook, Mahoe?" Stevens asked, as his partner finished the photographing.

"Got one right here." The call came from above. Aina Thomas, Lei's Coast Guard contact, scrambled down the rocks towards them carrying a hook on a long pole.

Thomas worked the large, blunt metal hook underneath the floating body. From his vantage point, Stevens could see what the first responders had reported as an indication of a homicide: a bloodless, gaping wound, so long that it wrapped around the part of the man's neck that wasn't underwater.

His belly, empty but for that morning's cup of coffee, tightened; a humpback whale tattoo, a distinctive piece of tribal art, was inked into the notch between the man's neck and shoulder. The humpback whale was the Kaihale family's *aumakua*, or ancestral guardian spirit. He'd seen that tattoo before, when Chaz was alive and laughing.

Stevens glanced up and around, making sure the spectators were gone. The steep boulder-strewn harbor edge was lined with concerned faces, but they were all in uniform. Hopefully no random tourists had got close enough to get a picture of Chaz's body to post online. *It would be terrible for Pono to hear the news that way.*

Stevens turned to Thomas and Mahoe. "This is Pono's cousin, Chaz Kaihale. I recognize his tattoo."

"Shit. I'm sorry. Pono seemed pretty broken up when we went out to the wreck yesterday," Thomas said. "Can you help me get him up out of the water?"

"On it." Mahoe maneuvered in beside Thomas and caught the back of Chaz's shirt, pulling the body the rest of the way out of the water onto a low, flat rock.

"Pono is going to take it hard." Stevens rubbed a hand across his face. The weariness he had struggled with on and off since his stint in South America dragged at his bones, and the beginning of one of his chronic headaches began behind his eyes, a distant but approaching drumbeat.

"At least, now we know Kaihale wasn't involved with whatever went down with the *Sea Cloud*," Thomas said.

"Small comfort," Stevens murmured.

Above them, a disturbance. "Make way! Coming through." Dr. Phil Gregory's distinctive, cheerful voice parted the crowd. "That you down there, Mike?"

Stevens turned to wave at Maui's portly Medical Examiner, gesturing for the ME to join them. "Always a pleasure to see you, Dr. G, but I hate the circumstances."

Dr. Gregory was wearing one of his distinctive aloha shirts, this one covered with bright parrots. A ball cap covered his balding pate, and he was already gloved up. His wife and assistant, Dr. Tanaka, wearing scrubs, stared down from the breakwall, her hands on the transport gurney and a worried frown on her face as Dr. Gregory clumsily navigated the sloping rocks.

Dr. G sighed in exaggerated relief as he reached the boulder where they'd pulled Chaz's body out of the water. "Whew. Made it down without adding to the body count."

"I have an ID," Stevens said. "This is Chaz Kaihale, Pono's cousin. He was captaining the *Sea Cloud* when it went down."

"Yeah, and now that we've found him, there are only seven more missing," Thomas sketched in the basic facts that they knew so far for Dr. Gregory's benefit.

"Aw, crap." Dr. Gregory shook his head. "I liked Chaz. I met him at one of your barbecues."

Stevens stood to his full height. "Now that you're here to investigate the body, I have to make some calls. Mahoe, can you document the scene and work with Dr. Gregory?"

"You got it, LT." Mahoe squatted beside Dr. Gregory. "How can I help?"

Stevens moved up and away. As he climbed up the rocks, his headache increased in intensity. The young patrol officer, a recruit named Ching, held the logbook as he signed out. Ching pointed to his vehicle. "I've got some donuts and coffee in there, LT. You look like you could use a little caffeine and sugar."

"Sure could." Stevens walked over and opened the door of the MPD cruiser. He grinned at the sight of a pink box on the front seat holding malasadas from famous Komoda Bakery in upcountry Makawao. "Whoa! You've got the good stuff here."

"And there's a container of Starbucks coffee in the back," Ching said. "I was on my way to bring all that in for a departmental meeting, when we got the call."

Stevens sat for a moment in the driver's seat, loading up a napkin with several of the fragrant, sugarcoated rounds of Portuguese pastry made daily by a dedicated family business. He poured himself a still-hot cup of coffee into one of the paper cups, then waved thanks to Ching as he walked back to Mahoe's truck. The vehicle was locked, so he walked a little further, deep under the huge, spreading branches of the famous Lahaina banyan tree.

His bad news call to Pono could wait for a minute, long enough for him to down some of the malasadas and a few sips of coffee. Seated on one of the worn benches, Stevens's gaze followed the graceful, massive arms of the banyan. The branches spread from a central hub of trunk, but were thick enough to be separate trees. Periodically, roots had grown down to support the massive, heavy lengths, which reminded him of an octopus's legs.

The cool, dappled shade and gentle breeze seemed to be pushing the headache back, as was the hit of sugar and carbs. He finished the last of the delicious treats and his coffee.

"Time for the moment of truth." He took his phone out and gazed at it. Would Pono, who'd been a friend for years, rather hear the news from him, or from his partner, Lei?

He would ask Omura how to handle it. He had to call her first, anyway.

Stevens pressed and held down the button to her speed dial, and moments later the Steel Butterfly picked up. "Lieutenant Stevens. What have you got?"

"Homicide victim, not a drowning. I have a positive ID." Stevens blew out a breath. "It's Pono's cousin Chaz Kaihale. His throat was cut."

"Oh, no." Captain Omura said. Stevens pictured C.J. pressing her red lacquered fingertips against her temples, but she would never disturb her makeup by touching her face. "Pono is not going to take it well. I'll have to reassign him, and he won't like that, either."

Stevens was Omura's second in command at Kahului Station, and over the years of work together, he and C.J. had become close. Stevens tugged at his hair, the sting somehow decreasing the pain of his headache. "I know. I'm wondering how I should break the news to him. Call him direct, or ask Lei to tell him. What do you think?"

"I will call Pono. It's my job to notify him of the death, and to reassign him." C.J. Omura never shrank from the difficult tasks of leadership, one of the things he respected about her. "I'll also offer him some bereavement time off. Perhaps his wife can convince him to take it."

"I'll call Tiare and handle that part. Ask her to persuade him to stay out of the office for a while," Stevens said. "We can tag team it. But that will leave Lei without a partner, and she's primary on this case."

"She's not without a partner. You and Mahoe are her partners, now that you pulled Chaz's body."

"True." Stevens felt energy coming back—*maybe it was the donuts and coffee, maybe it was the idea of working a case with Lei.* In all their years at the same station, they'd never been primary together on a homicide. "I'll get ahold of her next. We got this, Captain."

"Not yet. We are still missing seven people." Stevens could hear the tip-tapping of her glossy fingernails on her keyboard. "What do you think of Petty Officer Aina Thomas? He's the Coast Guard's primary crime investigator."

"Seems competent. Had already started clearing the harbor of rubberneckers when we arrived, a huge help. And he came down to the body with a retrieval hook. He seems on top of things."

"Did he say if their divers had found anything near the wreck?"

Stevens nudged a curious dog away as it dragged an elderly lady in a *muumuu* and *lauhala* hat over to his spot under the banyan tree. "He said no."

The Captain's keyboard paused, and she sighed again. "I just don't think this is the only body that's going to be washing up on our shores."

"Unfortunately, I agree." Stevens was going to have to catch up with Lei on all of this. And weren't three teenaged girls on board the *Sea Cloud?*

He didn't want to see how they'd appear after another day or two if they were in the ocean.

CHAPTER TEN

LEI WENT DOWN to the crime lab to retrieve her backpack. Nunez, her wedge-shaped, magenta-streaked hair canted forward to screen her face, sat on a stool hunched over a microscope. She glanced up at Lei's arrival, squinting through thick glasses Lei had never seen before. "What can I do for you, Sergeant?"

"Looking for my bag. You said it was drying out down here?"

Nunez slid off her stool, showing a length of shapely leg clad in fishnet stockings and a chain-covered pair of ankle boots beneath her lab coat. "Right this way."

Lei followed the tech as Nunez led her to a secondary storage room. Lei's familiar nylon backpack hung from a wall hook. Her personal items, including weapon, cuffs, radio, cell phone, a sealed bag of Kiet's favorite snack, Goldfish, one of Rosie's binkies, her wallet, a lipstick and comb, and the sodden evidence bags, were all laid out with surgical precision on a snow-white towel. A whirring floor fan was pointed at the area. "I did the best I could."

"And your best is always better than most." Lei's eyes stung at the homely lineup of her possessions—it reminded her way too much of an array of evidence collected at a scene. *If she'd died . . .*

"But you didn't die. You're fine." She hadn't realized she

spoke aloud until a small warm hand touched Lei's arm, bringing her back to the present moment. Nunez smiled at Lei.

Lei smiled back, a painful effort. "You're right. It's just a little spooky, all laid out like that."

Nunez grabbed one end of the towel. She plucked Lei's service Glock out of the lineup of items, handing it to her, and then rolled the towel up like a burrito, handing the whole thing to Lei. "Take it home and sort it out later. Don't obsess. Kiss your babies, and count your blessings."

Lei laughed. "When did you get to be so wise? What are you, Becca? Twenty-two?"

"Twenty-four. But I grew up in the barrio in Los Angeles. I'd seen more bodies by the time I was a teenager than Maui sees in a decade." She took off her glasses, sliding them into the pocket of her lab coat. "We're always one breath away from dead. We just try to forget it for as long as we can."

BACK AT HER CUBICLE, Lei took out the scrap of paper the Captain had given her and drew the department's desk phone over. She punched in the number, and after a moment of refined chiming, she identified herself to Peterson's lawyer's receptionist, then waited to be connected to Frederick Samuelson, Esq.

The man made her wait long enough that she'd begun to unroll the wrapped towel, blotting any excess moisture she found as she sorted her personal items back into her bag. "Maui Police Department. This is an unusual call. May I get your name and badge number?" Samuelson had a voice like warm chocolate.

Lei recited the information. "I'm calling because your client, Patrick Peterson, is missing. His rented yacht, upon which he set out with his family, has sunk off the coast of Lana`i, and there were signs of foul play on board."

"Dear God!" Frederick's voice shot into an upper register. "You must be joking! Patrick and his family are drowned?"

"We don't know that. They are considered endangered missing, at this point." Lei flipped open the case file. "We got your number off of Dream Vacations Luxury Yachts' emergency contact form for the family. What can you tell me about Peterson? Was there anyone who might have wished him harm?"

"Slow down. Wait a minute. I'm having trouble taking this in." Samuelson sounded winded. She heard the squeak of springs as he sat heavily in his office chair. "I have some questions for you, first."

Lei fielded those, mostly the nuts and bolts of how the yacht had been discovered by the Coast Guard, and then the gist of her own discoveries of disturbance on board—though she did not mention the blood trace they'd found—before the craft had sunk. Intuition told her that more information up front would yield the best results with this man. "Do you have any leads on who might have done this?" Samuelson asked.

"You know I can't discuss an ongoing investigation. And in fact, why don't you answer that question for me? That's the one I started with," she prompted gently.

"I worry about violating attorney-client privilege," Samuelson said. "Confidentiality still holds, even in the case of death."

Lei bit her lip to keep from arguing, though her neck had begun to heat. *Freakin' lawyers. They always wanted something for nothing.* "How about a hypothetical situation? Your client may still be alive. May need us to find him and his family, rescue them if they've been . . . kidnapped." She dropped the word gently.

Samuelson blew out a noisy breath. "If they have been, no one has contacted me. But hypothetically speaking, they don't have any money to pay a ransom, anyway."

Lei blinked. "They must have been rich. Not everyone can charter a private yacht for their family vacation."

"That was all for appearances. To pump things up before the

public offering," Samuelson said. "I worry that . . . maybe Peterson did this himself?"

Lei grabbed a pen and scribbled on a tablet to get the ink flowing. "Tell me more."

"Pete—he goes by Pete—was in over his head with the IPO coming up for Enviro Enterprises. Hypothetically speaking, there were some problems with his partner, who'd changed his mind about the stock offering and wanted to break up their partnership and sell off their different parts of the business. Pete was adamantly opposed to this. But maybe he . . . did something and tried to make it look like murder, while he and his family disappeared."

"Hmm." *This guy really suspected his client of faking his own death?*

Her phone toned—a text from Stevens.

Need you at the morgue to meet Pono for the ID of Chaz Kaihale's body. We found him washed up in the Lahaina Harbor.

A distinctive sensation of sorrow and apprehension hollowed Lei's belly. She had to get off the phone.

"This is very interesting and helpful, Mr. Samuelson, but I've just had an emergency notification that may be related to the case. I'll call you back if we need anything more from you."

She hung up on the lawyer's protestations, and grabbed the keys to her truck.

Poor Pono . . . This was going to be bad.

CHAPTER ELEVEN

L<small>EI</small> S<small>TOOD</small> on the concrete sidewalk outside Maui Memorial Medical's morgue, a utilitarian bay designed for vehicles to offload bodies. The bay sloped down to a basement entry that led into an automatic door and a sally port, and then the morgue itself.

Her hand slid into her pocket, and she rubbed the bone hook she kept there, a talisman she had once given Stevens for a journey that had gone badly wrong. That talisman was returned to her in a box . . . and she'd worried that his body would come back to her that way, too. But Stevens had returned, and they had healed and rebuilt.

The bone hook remained a symbol of hope, a comforting object to touch and ground herself with.

She needed all the hope and comfort she could get for this particular moment.

She was still adjusting to the devastating news that Chaz's body had been discovered in Lahaina. Captain Omura had broken the news to Pono, and he'd demanded to see the body right away. Lei had been directed by the Captain to keep a rein on Pono as he headed for the morgue. Lei'd already tried to call her partner, but he wasn't picking up.

She sighed, rubbing the smooth, carved bit of bone as her gaze flickered over the ornamental Areca palms and Plumeria trees planted throughout the hospital's parking lot on little grassy islands. The facility actually had a great view set on a knoll. From where she stood, Lei could see down across the busy, utilitarian town of Kahului to the harbor, gleaming blue in the distance. A white palace of a cruise ship was at anchor; tourists likely roamed the mall nearby. Further out to sea, a squall draped a rainbow across the horizon.

It was good to gaze on these beautiful things in preparation for what she'd see when she went down into her friend Dr. G's basement domain. She'd never got used to the smells, sights and sounds of his gruesome little kingdom.

Lei shut her eyes. *Was it too much to hope that the body wasn't Chaz?* But Stevens had made the identification himself . . . Her husband was cautious and careful with that kind of thing, knowing how emotionally harrowing a mistake could be.

Chaz had become a family friend over the years, a frequent visitor at gatherings in their home. He'd helped work on their house when they rebuilt it after a fire. At first, he'd come with his wife. Lei had found Cheryl less likeable than Chaz; she was a bitter, complaining woman with no reason that Lei could see for her negativity. After the divorce, Chaz had become someone Lei worried about and reached out to, often inviting him over for a home-cooked meal when he was between captain gigs.

But as much as she cared about Chaz, he was much more to Pono—he'd been the equivalent of a brother to a man who only had sisters.

Pono was going to be out for blood, just when they needed to keep a clear head.

Fortunately, the Captain had already pulled him, given him time off, and reassigned Stevens and Mahoe to help Lei.

As if she'd conjured him, Pono arrived. He drove Stanley up to her, past her, and down the cement incline to the sally port entry.

He jumped out, slamming the truck's door, and turned to face Lei as she trotted down the incline.

Her partner's skin was ashy with stress, but he looked terrifying with his face set in a fierce scowl and his muscles pumped.

"That's not a parking spot, Pono. You have to move the truck. What if they get a delivery while we're in there?" Lei used her voice like a whip, hoping to slash through across the single-minded rage and pain she saw in Pono's dark eyes.

Pono's mouth tightened behind his bristling mustache, but he said nothing. He brushed past her like a storm on the move, hitting the pneumatic doors with his shoulder.

Lei hurried after him. "I'm not sure if they're set up for you to make the identification yet. I didn't get a text from Dr. G . . ."

"I have to see him." Pono strode on.

Lei threw up her hands in frustration behind his massive back. *Well, she'd tried.*

They reached the second set of interior doors, which could only be opened from the inside. A glass safety panel threaded with wire gave view into the main work area. The privacy curtain was open, and Lei could tell at a glance that Dr. Gregory was not yet ready for them. He was bent over the naked corpse of a brown-skinned male. Dr. G wore magnifiers and moved a spotlight slowly over the body as he dictated.

The medical examiner was searching for evidence on Chaz's body.

Under normal circumstances in an identification, the body was presented to the next of kin neatly draped on a gurney in the sally port, all gore hidden except for the face. If the family member seemed too distraught, they were kept in a locked area outside the morgue, and only allowed to view the victim's face via a video feed.

Pono reached the safety glass window and looked in.

"Chaz!" His bass voice was a howl of grief, and it boomed in the enclosed space, making Lei, and Dr. Gregory inside, jump.

Dr. G wore his famous yellow smiley face rubber apron, and thankfully, it wasn't yet streaked with blood and bodily fluids. His voice reverberated through an audio feed. "I'm not ready for you yet, Pono."

"Let me see my cousin." Pono rumbled, but his voice cracked on the last word. He hung his head suddenly. "I promise I won't touch the body or do anything crazy. But I need to see him."

Dr. Gregory lifted the magnifying lenses off of his glasses, edging them up to the sides. The circles of glass on curved metal attachments were like comical eyebrows, but Dr. G's face was dead serious as he walked toward them. "I need your word you won't disturb anything. I'm still doing evidence collection."

"I'll be good," Pono promised.

Dr. G hit the big, round entry button with his elbow, keeping his potentially contaminated gloved hands away from the button.

Pono seem to freeze as the doors opened. His head was still lowered like a bull considering charging . . . but then, a hand came up to cover his eyes. The rage propelling her partner seemed to evaporate, leaving him stranded and frozen. *He was going to have to acknowledge the reality of his cousin's death.*

Lei stepped up next to Pono, slipping a hand through his, pressing against his side and tugging him forward. "You're not alone. We'll do this together." She gave him a gentle nudge. "You got dis, bruddah."

Dr. Gregory returned to the body, standing protectively at Chaz's head, as they walked into the big, open room with its shiny wall of refrigerator doors, metal tables, and useful drain in the center of the floor.

Chaz lay uncovered on one of the wheeled metal tables. His large, stocky physique was as empty of life as a discarded husk. Exsanguination had bleached the color from his warm brown skin, leaving it a grayish yellow and mottled with dark patches of lividity.

Dr. Gregory had propped up the man's head on one of the

portable stanchions. At first, Chaz appeared unmarked as they approached—but as they got closer, the cause of death was abundantly clear.

A deep slash had laid open the layers of tissue in his neck all the way down to the bone. The edges of the wound had peeled back in a gruesome imitation of a grin.

Lei kept the hand that wasn't curled around Pono's tense arm in her pocket, rubbing the bone hook, as she scanned the body for any other clues.

Nothing else appeared to mark him. No bruises, ligature marks, scrapes or scratches. This was the body of a healthy male in his mid-thirties, brutally murdered, with no sign of defensive wounds.

Had someone he'd known snuck up on him?

"As you can see, cause of death is pretty obvious." Dr. Gregory's usually cheerful voice was somber. "And as this is a formal next of kin identification, Pono, I need you to state, for the record, the identity of this man."

"That's my cousin. Charles Kalani Fukuhara Kaihale. *Chaz*." Pono covered his eyes, turning away. "Did he suffer?"

"It was very quick," Dr. Gregory said softly.

Lei pressed Pono's arm tight with both of hers, leaning into him.

Of course, Pono as a cop knew the mechanics of death as it resulted from a slash wound like Chaz's, but Lei had seen and heard that question many a time from a family member confronted by murder. Loved ones of a victim wanted comfort, the hope that the victim hadn't suffered, even when death had obviously been violent.

There was simply no way to psychologically prepare for a moment like this, and witnesses, even in law enforcement, seemed to go through the same stages: shock, denial, confusion, wishful thinking, bargaining, anger, and eventually, some measure of acceptance. Of peace.

But sometimes, that peace never came. *They knew too much.*

It wasn't peace vibrating through Pono's big body as she held his arm. "No defensive wounds. Chaz didn't see it coming." Pono's voice was dry and harsh. "He called me, you know. I thought it was an April Fools' joke. But he told me pirates were on their way. How did the pirates get him without him seeing it coming?"

Dr. Gregory cleared his throat. "I have the answer to that. He was tased first. I can't show you without turning the body, but there are prong marks on his upper back. So, to answer your question, Pono—no, he didn't suffer."

Pono's body shivered although his voice was a growl. "He was slaughtered like an animal."

Lei's phone vibrated against her hip. She dug it out of her pocket, glancing at the caller ID. "Pono, it's Tiare on the line. Why don't you step into the sally port and talk to your wife?" She hit the door button and pushed Pono out physically, handing the man her phone as it squawked with Tiare's loud exclamations.

The door shut, closing and locking. Her partner stood just outside, his head bent, his big body curved inward, the phone to his ear. Lei couldn't hear the couple talking through the thick glass.

His wife could calm him, help him. Lei couldn't do anything more for her partner.

She pulled the heavy privacy curtain shut so he wouldn't see the body again, and turned back to Dr. Gregory.

The ME had returned to Chaz. "I'm so sorry for Pono and his family." He shook out a fresh drape and settled it over the corpse, tucking it gently around the man's body. Lei had always appreciated Dr. G's compassion for the dead—he treated them with care, dignity and respect.

"You were right to tell Pono what you did. Chaz didn't suffer. But I worry that the crew and the family who were also on that boat were drowned. Having recently almost experienced that means of death, I don't recommend it." Lei grimaced. "Salt water inhalation hurts like crazy and unconsciousness takes way too long."

"I know." Dr. Gregory smoothed Chaz's black hair away from his brow. "This kill seems professional to me, Lei. No fuss, no sentimentality. The killer zapped Chaz from behind. Chaz fell down face first—the lividity on the front of his body tells me that. The murderer walked up, lifted Chaz's head up by the hair, slit his throat, and dropped him to lie face down and bleed out. There's lividity on his nose, chin, forehead, and the front of his body that suggests he lay that way for some hours."

Lei flashed to the blood pool in the stateroom they'd found on board the *Sea Cloud*. She told Dr. Gregory about that discovery. "That spot was likely where Chaz was killed. We have a viable blood sample. I'll have that sent over to you to compare with Chaz, and we can make sure it's his." She glanced over at the pretty painted shoji screen that Dr. Gregory and Dr. Tanaka used to separate their personal work area from the larger room. "Maybe killing Chaz quickly ensured the rest of the passengers were compliant with whatever the attackers had planned."

"Maybe so. It was certainly fast and brutal. I'll watch for your sample from the office." Dr. Gregory inclined his head. "Now if you'll excuse me, I have a post to perform. I'll let you know if it tells us anything new."

CHAPTER TWELVE

Pᴏɴᴏ ʜᴀᴅ ᴅʀɪᴠᴇɴ off to meet his wife when Lei hopped into her silver Tacoma, rolling down the windows to let the heat out and enjoy a breath of fresh air after the morgue. She headed back to the station to meet with the Captain, Stevens and Mahoe about the recent discovery of Chaz's body. Thankfully, Tiare had left her shift at the hospital, taking emergency bereavement leave, and she and Pono were united and heading for home. The Kaihales had always set a great example for Lei and Stevens to aspire to with their teamwork and unconditional support of each other.

Lei's phone beeped. She glanced at it on the seat beside her, and spotted Sophie's private number. She put in her Bluetooth and picked up the call.

"I dug up a lot of interesting information for you." Sophie said. "Peterson was in financial trouble."

"I already got that from his lawyer," Lei said.

"Peterson has a partner, John Ramsey. Ramsey has been making trouble, trying to get a higher cut of the percentage of their company when the IP goes public. As a result, Ramsey's lawyer has tied up the public offering. Meanwhile, leading up to this, Peterson had expanded, trying to fluff up the company before the release. He's heavily in debt for all of his personal wealth, as well as company expansion."

"How did you get all this?" Lei navigated onto busy Hana Highway. "The lawyer would only talk in hypotheticals."

"Better you don't know," Sophie said. "I have my ways, and you wouldn't have called me if you wanted to know what they were."

Lei snorted a laugh. "True dat, seestah! What exactly does Enviro Enterprises do as a company?"

"If what Peterson and Ramsey have invented works, they've built a pretty fabulous process to address the problem of ocean plastic pollution." Sophie's voice warmed with excitement. "It begins with a harvesting device that can be hitched to the back of any boat. The boat tows the device through the water, and floating plastic litter is harvested into a receptacle. The device sieves the water out leaving the plastic waste behind."

Lei frowned, swinging her truck around a tourist rental vehicle so loaded with surfboards and sports gear that the portable strap racks were listing to the side. "That doesn't sound revolutionary. We are still faced with the problem of disposing of the recovered waste."

"I'm not finished yet! The plastics are then fed into an integrated crusher. The crusher has a heating element that melts the waste into a compressed cube. And then, and here is the really beautiful part, the cubes are fed into a fuel conversion chamber. That device can be attached to an existing boat motor, and the plastic cubes become the fuel source."

Lei's mind was immediately buzzing with questions. "Are you sure? This sounds. . . too good to be true. Bulky as well. How can plastic cubes become the equivalent of gasoline?"

"Don't ask me for all the engineering details, but the science to do this has existed for a while already. The design is surprisingly streamlined, maybe double the size of an extra fuel container such as a boat would already carry. The resulting plastics-based fuel is not as refined as automobile gasoline, but boats run on a cruder grade. Even so, the prototypes are showing promise in the lab, and maybe the design can be refined further to create auto-grade gasoline." Sophie blew out an excited breath. "Just think of it—every boat out there, especially in third world countries where fishermen are living a subsistence existence and plastic pollution in the water is rampant . . . every one of them would now be on the hunt for plastic garbage to fuel their boat, and they would be able to run them almost cost-free! Plastic debris in the water would decrease in no time."

Lei tapped her fingers on the steering wheel, setting off a sparkle from her narrow, channel set diamond wedding band. "What was the problem between Peterson and Ramsey?"

"Ramsey was the one who came up with the fuel converter, while Peterson came up with the catcher and crusher elements. According to my hack into their company records, they're receiving many offers to buy the separate pieces of technology that make up the system, versus releasing a single integrated device, as they originally designed. Ramsey is claiming that his portion, the fuel converter, has more commercial value. He and his lawyer argue that if they keep the system intact, and release it as is, it will not be worth as much as selling off elements of it to big corporations."

The tightening of Lei's gut signaled a new appreciation for the ramifications of this case, and possible motives for Peterson's murder. "Let me guess . . . Ramsey inherits Peterson's half of the partnership should Peterson be killed."

"Exactly, and vice versa. That was one of the conditions of their partnership. They could not leave their ownership share of the invention to their families."

"The Peterson's lawyer speculated that he might have pulled a disappearance himself," Lei said.

"That wouldn't make much sense, at least from a financial standpoint. All Peterson would be able to do is sell his catcher and crusher designs, at a fraction of what the IP would have brought in for him. He only had title to his portion of the invention and copies of those plans, not Ramsey's converter design. Peterson's lawyer is right—the plastic fuel converter has bigger implications for application."

"Now we have motive for murder," Lei said. "Maybe the plan was to imitate a robbery gone wrong, to obscure the real reason if Peterson was killed."

"That's what I was thinking."

Lei pulled into the Kahului Police Station and navigated to her assigned parking spot under a well-trimmed rainbow shower tree. The ornamental planting cast multihued petals all over her truck in late summer, a cleanup problem she enjoyed each year.

"We need a time of death from Chaz's autopsy, and to check on Ramsey's whereabouts at that time," Lei murmured.

"Chaz?" Sophie's voice sharpened. "You didn't say anything about finding a body."

Lei filled her in on the recent discovery. "Dr. G thinks the killer was a professional."

"That would make sense, given what you've told me about his execution. I know it's not standard operational procedure, but I thought ahead of Ramsey and his alibi, and snooped a bit into his whereabouts. Enviro Enterprises headquarters is located in Seattle, and Ramsey was logged into and out of the building's security system all week while the Petersons were in Hawaii."

"That kind of work attendance can be faked," Lei remembered one of her cases where an accountant had checked in with his receptionist, went into a locked office where he was supposedly working, and then exited out a back door.

"Indeed, yes. But in my opinion, Ramsey would not have dirtied his hands personally with this murder."

"Especially given that Peterson's wife and daughters were on board. He'd have known them socially," Lei said. The diary she'd retrieved from the wreck waited for her in the office like a ticking time bomb—*it was going to make Peterson's missing daughter even more real.* "Find out anything else?"

"Isn't that enough?" Sophie huffed in mock outrage. "I could tell you Peterson's toilet paper brand, but that might be considered creepy. For the record, it's Charmin."

Lei chuckled. "*You* are creepy. I need you in my back pocket on every case."

"Ha. I was up most of last night scouting this for you. Good thing I'm working pro bono." Sophie's keyboard rattled with activity. "I still have some keyword searches out doing their data collection—I'll call you if anything new turns up."

"Thanks, Sophie. You're an angel." Lei said goodbye, and slid her phone into her pocket.

BACK AT THE KAHULUI OFFICE, Stevens finished unpacking his crime scene backpack, replacing any used evidence bags, fingerprint powder or gel tape and writing up his notes from the body discovery, while Mahoe processed the photos from Chaz's body retrieval. They had a meeting with Lei and Captain Omura in an hour to map out next steps on the case.

His burner phone vibrated in its leather holster at his waist. Stevens kept the cheap minutes-only texting phone separate from the one he used for work and home. The number was reserved for those who should have as little information as possible about him or his family—*confidential informants.* In the years since he'd been a lieutenant on Maui, in charge of his own station at one time, he'd built up a network of eyes and ears throughout the islands.

He flipped the phone open and put it to his ear. "Hey, Freddie. Haven't heard from you in awhile."

"Yo, LT." Freddie was a military veteran, a semi-homeless day laborer who hung around Kahului Harbor and picked up odd jobs. "Got a tip for you."

Stevens held up a finger to Mahoe to ensure the younger man's silence, then put the call on speaker and set the phone on his desk. Mahoe set aside his laptop and rolled his office chair closer to Stevens's desk to listen in.

"What's up, Freddie?"

"Got some work setting up a Matson container for human cargo. What's that worth to you?" Freddie's voice had the rusty timbre of a smoker.

Human trafficking was an evil they kept coming across, and sometimes in the oddest places. "A c-note to start. More if you give me something that leads to the arrest of the traffickers." Stevens's heart beat faster. An interagency task force was working on a rumored trafficking ring that operated out of the Kahului docks, but that trail had gone cold in recent weeks.

"Good enough to start. PayPal me the hundred bucks," Freddie said.

"Modern times, man. Everyone wants their money, and wants it now. Gimme a minute. I still have you set up from last time," Stevens said.

Mahoe rolled his eyes, but Stevens ignored his partner. The young detective had a streak of morality a mile wide and, while appreciating the necessity of CIs, basically despised them as junkies and snitches.

Stevens used his phone to log into an email proxy connected to the station's petty cash PayPal, and with a few taps of his finger, transferred the funds. "Sent."

"Got it," Freddie said, a minute later. "Okay. So, me and my friend Kimo got a call from a guy who gives us work. You know, off the books."

"Yep." Stevens tipped his chair back and laced his fingers over his belly. "Get to the part I'm paying for."

"Well, the guy had something different than our usual offloading trucks or whatevahs. This time, we fixed up the inside of this Matson container. Had to line it with soundproofing and insulation. Cut a hole in the side for a portable air conditioner. Brought in a small kine generator, like for a recreational vehicle. We put in two bunk beds and a portable toilet, a water dispenser too. I asked who was goin' ride in this fancy hideout, and the guy, you know what he said?"

"I'm waiting to hear."

"He said, 'Mind your business, Freddie. Zip your lip and get back to work.' So I did, but was grumbling cuz he nevah like treat me with respeck. After he left, my buddy Kimo, he tol' me he heard this was for ship women overseas. Four blondes and a brunette. Three of the blondes was young, just girls, but 'ready for get broke in,' Kimo said."

Stevens's heart rate spiked, and he exchanged a glance with Mahoe. *These could be the missing women from the Sea Cloud!*

"What else do you know?" Stevens shot forward to lean on his desk, pulling his little spiral notebook with its tied-on stub of pencil out of his hip pocket.

"I know where the container stay, down in the storage yard by the docks—when we *pau* working, they moved it down there, but I track 'em. Kimo nevah know nottin' bout when it would be used, and the guy wasn't saying, so that's all I got for you."

Stevens stood, picking up his shoulder harness as he replied. "I'll meet you at the Cash N' Carry in twenty minutes, and you can show us."

"Oh hey, I no can go," Freddie whined. "The guy, he likes breaking thumbs. You evah get one broke thumb?"

"Two hundred bucks, but I won't give you that second hundred until you show me the container," Stevens said.

"Deal. See you in twenty." The burner phone shut off.

Stevens scooped the cheap phone up and slid it into its holster. "My car this time, Mahoe. Get on the horn and let the Captain know we won't be going to the meeting. I'll call Lei and leave her a message. We're going after five women who might have been taken from the *Sea Cloud*."

CHAPTER THIRTEEN

Stevens pulled his battered old Bronco into the Cash N' Carry parking lot. The run-down discount grocery store, tucked behind the industrial warehouses near the Kahului docks, provided the ideal place for the comings and goings of people who did not want to be observed.

Freddie was lurking near a dumpster. A wiry little man closing in on fifty, he still kept his hair military short, but that was the only remnant of his past as a soldier. Grimy secondhand clothes hung on his frame, and he reeked of sweat and alcohol as he opened the back door of Stevens's SUV. "Hey, bruddah."

"Hey yourself. Got started on the Primo beer early today, eh, Freddie?" Stevens swiveled in his seat to make eye contact with the CI as the man fussed with his seatbelt. "This better be a legit tip."

"Oh, it's legit. Drive to the barge dock." Freddie tugged a folded ball cap out of his pocket and drew it down on his head, lowering it to cover his eyes. "I no like get made."

Mahoe's cell rang and he picked up the call on Bluetooth as Stevens navigated out of the Cash N' Carry's parking lot. He frowned and held the phone out to Stevens. "Captain wants to speak to you."

"Tell her I'll call back." Stevens pulled onto the narrow, two-lane road leading to the dock area.

"She says pull over. She wants to talk."

Stevens grunted with annoyance. He navigated over to the dusty side of the road, his mouth tight. He put the Bronco in *Park* and took the phone from Mahoe, putting it to his ear as he got out of the vehicle—he couldn't have Freddie listening in.

Stevens walked a few feet away, glancing out at the wind-whipped ocean, waving ironwood trees, and dusty *naupaka* bushes that lined the frontage road. "Yes, Captain? I have my CI in the car. I was about to search for the container Mahoe told you about."

Captain Omura's voice was brusque. "I want you to assess if anyone's inside. If it's empty, we pull back and surveil. I want to catch whoever's orchestrating this thing. We've been hearing rumors for months about trafficking; this could be the break we need." Omura's tone softened. "I know you're hoping to rescue those women, but chances are, they're being stored somewhere else until right before the ship is loaded. I already called Thomas, the Coast Guard investigator who's been working with Lei, to alert him that there's a ship that will be carrying that container coming into harbor. Ideally, we'll seize the container as it's being loaded with human cargo, and then we can scoop up the perps on the ship too."

"That makes sense. Anything else?"

"Team meeting when you get back to the station. Lei has a little more info from Dr. Gregory to share."

"Copy that." Stevens ended the call and hopped back into the Bronco. A drift of rust sifted onto his black athletic hiking boots as he slammed the door. He really needed to upgrade this bucket of bolts, but it was one of the few things he'd been able to hang onto for so many years, and since they'd lost so much in two fires, he'd become weirdly attached to it. "Where from here, Freddie?"

"I'll show you. Just a few blocks ahead."

Freddie directed Stevens through a warren of streets to the wharf area. A chain-link fence topped with razor wire surrounded the container zone, but the main gate was open for the business day. Stevens drove in, circling around to an employee parking area. "I'll show my badge if anyone stops us."

"I don't want to be seen walking around with cops. I want to stay here." Freddie folded his arms and sat back, a mulish set to his mouth.

"There's no way we'll find this container without you showing us where it is." Stevens gestured with his head to the maze of stacked metal containers lining the storage area. He pointed to a rumpled pile of clothing on the back seat. "There's a hoodie and a hat back there, and you can borrow my extra sunglasses. No one will recognize you."

Grumbling, Freddie put on the makeshift disguise. The three men got out of the Bronco. Heat shimmered off the metal containers and the freshly tarred blacktop of the parking area, as Freddie led the way into the stacks of huge, rectangular boxes.

Even with a portable air conditioner and generator—what if the women ran out of fuel, or something went wrong with the air circulation? They'd overheat and suffocate within hours. Stevens had seen crime scene pictures from other trafficking cases—that kind of mishap wasn't an uncommon occurrence, and it could lead to mass murder.

His belly clenched and so did his fists as he stalked after Freddie's stooped form in the shapeless, oversized hoodie.

The pirates had likely killed the other two men after Chaz, and then they'd caged the women like animals to sell for profit. Whoever had taken down the *Sea Cloud* "needed to get got," as Pono would say.

Freddie peered around the corner of a stack of containers, seemingly getting his bearings. "It's off by itself. I think whoever set this up had it put there so they could sneak the women in by cutting the fence."

Mahoe swiped his forehead with a meaty forearm. "How did you get the job? Get paid?"

Freddie shrugged. "It'll cost ya."

Mahoe tossed up his hands in frustration, and Stevens kept a rein on his temper with difficulty as well. "Just show us the container, Freddie. When I know that this is a legit tip, we can discuss more."

Freddie squinted angrily over his shoulder. "It's legit. Follow me." The little man darted forward, and this time Stevens had to stretch his long legs to catch up as Mahoe jogged, bringing up the rear.

Freddie reached the end of an aisleway formed by the giant metal rectangles. "Straight ahead, there." He pointed.

Painted rust red and emblazoned with "Matson", the name of one of Hawaii's top shipping companies, the container was set near the chain-link fence, indistinguishable from the rest except for its isolation.

Freddie took off the cap and wiped his sweating brow on his shoulder, his head swiveling as he checked for anyone around. The area was empty but for heat shimmer, the sound of the wind in nearby coconut palms on the other side of the fence, and the occasional raucous call of a mynah bird.

"Nobody questioned you guys working on this thing here?" Mahoe asked. He was still trying to get more out of Freddie without paying for it.

"We didn't work on it here, like I said. We worked on it at . . . another location. It's gonna cost ya more for that."

"We'll see." Stevens grabbed Freddie's shoulder and squeezed it hard. "This better be for real, man. Show us the alterations you made."

Freddie twisted out from under Stevens's fist, leaving him holding a handful of loose shirt. "No need fo' get aggro, brah.

You'll see." He hurried out into the open. Stevens followed closely, ready for Freddie to run or try to pull something. *The guy was a weasel, through and through.*

Freddie reached the container first. He peered around the side positioned away from them, close against the fence, and gestured for Stevens to come closer. He pointed. "See? The white edge sticking out near the top of the container? That's the air conditioner."

The size and shape were right—a slightly protruding rectangle. *Freddie was telling the truth.*

Stevens turned to face the padlocked double doors locking the container shut. He wanted to pound on the hot metal surface and yell, "Anyone in there? Maui Police Department. We're here to help you!"

But if there was any security around, they'd come running and the Captain's surveillance idea would be blown . . .

"We need to check if anyone's inside. The opening between the container and the fence is narrow for me or Mahoe to get through. I want you to squeeze in there, Freddie, and see if the AC unit is on. If it is, we'll get this container opened. If it isn't, it's empty and we have no case until it's got someone inside. The way to tell is by checking that air conditioner. No one could last more than a few hours in this heat with no air circulation."

"It'll cost . . ." Freddie got no further before Stevens grabbed his hand, twisting it up behind the man's back as he bent Freddie's thumb backward.

"This is all part of our initial payment, you little piece of shit. There could be women and girls inside there, right now, *dying*. Get over there and check that AC unit." Stevens let go and stepped back.

Freddie stood up, rubbing his hand, but said nothing more. He turned sideways and sidled into the narrow opening. They watched as he reached the AC unit. He rose up on his tiptoes, straining to get near it. "It's off. Nobody home. There's a vent in the roof, too. If we could get up there, you could see inside . . ."

"No need. Let's go," Stevens said.

"But what about . . ."

"We'll talk in the truck," Mahoe snapped.

The three of them retraced their steps through the maze of containers.

Near the entrance, they passed a man driving a forklift with a big wooden box loaded on the carrier.

It'd be so easy to pack the women in some kind of transport box and drive them on a forklift right into the container . . .

Stevens rubbed gritty eyes as he walked back to the truck. If only he didn't know too much about this kind of thing. Human trafficking hadn't bothered him quite this way before he'd married and had children. Imagining Lei, Kiet or baby Rosie trapped in a hot metal box, sold to human predators, made his blood pressure soar.

He got in, fired up the engine, and cranked on the Bronco's aging AC. Its feeble breeze fanned his overheated cheeks.

Five women, trapped in a hot container.

They had to find them.

CHAPTER FOURTEEN

If only she had one of those microphone headsets, instead of the clunky old departmental phone. Lei's neck had begun to ache with tension from holding the plastic handset between her ear and shoulder when Peterson's partner John Ramsey finally came on the line. She gazed down at a printed copy of Ramsey's driver's license photo in the case file before her. Ramsey had a boyish grin bracketed by a strong jaw, dark hair brushed with silver at the temples, and a little swatch of hipster beard on his chin.

The guy looked friendly, but so far, the interview wasn't going well.

"You need to speak to my attorney," Ramsey said, for the second time.

Lei clenched her jaw. *Time for a little sweet-talking.* "Mr. Ramsey. You are quite the brilliant inventor. Please. I'm asking you simple questions that your attorney cannot answer. Such as, how did you and Peterson meet? When did you come up with the idea for your invention?"

A long pause from Ramsey. Finally, "I guess it won't hurt to tell you that."

Lei bit her tongue on a threat to arrest Ramsey for obstruction of justice—but the guy would just lawyer up harder and drag his feet, and that wouldn't be good for the case. "Oh, thank you so much for your time and help."

"Pete—he goes by Pete, short for his last name—Pete and I met in college. We were engineering students together at MIT. Both scholarship kids." Ramsey had a tenor voice that sounded younger than his forty-something years. This was familiar ground for him, and Lei could feel him relaxing.

"Ooh, MIT. Please go on," Lei gushed. "I can just see the two of you, cooking up inventions in the lab!"

"We were roommates. BFFs, I guess you ladies call it. We wanted to do something to help the world and the planet. Early on, Pete was obsessed with plastics in the ocean and what they were doing at the cellular level to fish and wildlife. I was more interested in alternative fuel sources, and how that could help the global environment as a whole."

"Wow. When did you two begin working on your invention?" Lei kept her voice warmly enthusiastic. "That's so great."

"We came up with the initial concepts early in our college years together. We began trying to angle all of our class projects into research and development of our joint idea, a small engine that could run on recycled plastic." Ramsey sighed. "We started our company after graduation. I did more of the business's administration because Pete got married and began a family right away. I got so focused on solving the problem of the fuel converter, I stopped paying attention to Pete's part of the project, but we finalized our segments around the same time. I solicited funders and backers. And that's when my part of the invention first got a big offer from a major auto corporation. They were less interested in the raw plastics harvester and fuel cube maker that Pete had completed."

"So that's what prompted you to call a halt to the public offering."

A pause. "My attorney suggested a cooling-off period while we worked toward a mutual agreement." Ramsey said.

"Let's switch gears. Did you and Pete spend time together socially?"

"Not much. Pete has three daughters, and I'm on my second marriage with no kids. We aren't college roomies anymore."

"Sounds like you grew apart."

"You could say that."

"Second marriage, huh? I bet that got expensive," Lei fished.

Ramsey did not reply.

She had to schmooze this guy, not that she'd ever been particularly good at it . . . "These things happen in life. I understand growing apart from a friend, and I've been through some tough marriage times myself. So, your lives were heading in different directions . . . Did that affect the business?"

"It did. I felt like Pete wasn't pulling his weight with the company." Old resentment colored Ramsey's tone with bitterness. "Always with a sick kid, or a soccer game or something, while I stayed at the office to work long hours."

"That's not fair."

"No, it wasn't." Ramsey's tone hardened. "I have to get to an appointment. I fail to see how this has anything to do with Pete's disappearance."

"Were you aware that his wife and daughters have also disappeared? And that we've found the body of captain of the boat they rented? Captain Kaihale was murdered in cold blood. Washed up in a harbor, miles from where the boat was found, with his throat slit."

"Oh my God!" Ramsey sounded genuinely shocked.

"Yes. And the more time that goes by without us finding any of them, the worse their chances look." Lei's voice had gone cold. She'd listened to Stevens's message about the possible trafficking. That fate was only marginally better than being murdered outright —the women might live a little longer, but death awaited them at the end of a long period of being raped and used. *If only she had Ramsey on video call so she could see his expression.*

"I . . . holy shit . . ." Ramsey's voice trailed off and then sounded muffled, as though he were speaking through his hands. "I had no idea. I guess I was thinking Pete took off, tried to bail on his debts, and take his designs or something."

"And isn't it true that you inherit Pete's designs and his half of the business if he dies?" Lei rapped out.

Ramsey said nothing for a long, tension-filled moment. "How did you find that out? That's private, privileged information."

"I asked you a question, Mr. Ramsey. Isn't it true that you inherit Peterson's designs and his half of the business upon his demise? How handy it would be if his family were gone too, and there was no claim on any of it."

A long beat of silence. "My attorney will speak with you in the future regarding these matters." Ramsey hung up.

"Shit!" Lei exclaimed. She banged down her receiver. "That slimeball did it somehow, and I'm going to nail him."

"Scoop me in, Sweets." Stevens's voice came from the door of the cubicle. "Who's got you so riled up?"

Lei swiveled her battered old office chair to face her husband.

Stevens's height filled the doorway. His sky-blue eyes, deep-set under dark brows, looked tired. His mouth was tight, bracketed by pain—*probably one of his headaches*. His brown hair was disordered by the perpetual Maui wind.

"Mahoe with you?" Lei asked.

"He stopped in at the head."

"Good." Lei sprang up off her chair and tugged Stevens into the cubicle by the wrist. She shut the door behind him. "I need a hug. And a kiss."

Those blue eyes brightened. His mouth curved in a smile. "I live to serve." *An old joke of theirs.*

Lei took Stevens's face in her hands, feeling the dusky stubble on his cheeks, and drew him down, hungry for the touch of his mouth. Their kiss was both familiar and wild as Stevens's hands roamed over her, trailing sparks in their wake, and she wrapped around him.

Being with him restored her. Leached out the frustration. Refilled her with strength—*and it did the same for him.* She could feel energy kindling between them as their bodies caught fire.

Finally, they came up for air. "You always keep me guessing," Stevens breathed into Lei's ear. "This never gets old. You. Us. This."

"Nope, not for me either." Lei detached herself gently, sliding her hands down his arms. "I just . . . needed that. This case . . ."

"It's awful and just getting worse," Stevens said.

A light rap on the cubicle's door. "LT? Lei? You guys in there?" Mahoe sounded uncertain.

Lei grinned at Stevens. "Perfect timing. Come on in. We were just catching up."

Mahoe opened the door but didn't enter. "Captain waylaid me on the way from the bathroom. She wants a sitrep with all of us in her office."

"You guys go on. I need a sec to organize my notes," Lei said.

Stevens trailed Mahoe out, pausing in the doorway to wink back at her. "We've got a date later," he whispered.

"I live to serve," Lei said. He grinned, and shut the door.

Lei sat down and quickly imported the recording she'd made of her talk with Ramsey into the electronic case file. She shunted the voice duplicate to their voice-to-text translator program, and hit PRINT on a transcript of it for the team to review. She stuffed all the papers she'd gathered into the main case jacket after saving everything to the digital one, and hurried out toward the Captain's office, steeling herself for all the bad news they had to review.

CHAPTER FIFTEEN

STEVENS SHIFTED in his seat in the Bronco as evening deepened into night. "One of us might as well get a few winks."

"You first, old man." Mahoe's teeth gleamed briefly in the dark of the unlit SUV. "You seem like you need a nap." He lifted the binoculars back up to his eyes. "Still nothing moving over there."

"Hey. I know when to grab a good thing when it's offered. No shame here." Stevens reclined his seat and threw an arm over his eyes.

The temporary high from the quick makeout session with Lei had worn off long ago in the face of the review team meeting and the Captain's orders for him and Mahoe to spend the night watching the container. Omura'd put in for more surveillance to begin the next day, but it appeared that sleep was going to be in short supply until this case was solved.

The Bronco was situated on the other side of the chain-link fence outside of the container storage area, wedged in among bushes and an overhanging ironwood tree in the vacant lot. Stevens had parked off to the side, hanging a towel over the window of the passenger side to provide cover and disguise. The funky old SUV just looked like a homeless person was trying to stay out of view and camp in his vehicle.

Freddie hadn't given up "the guy" who'd hired him, in spite of increased bribes and threats. He had, however, shared the warehouse location where they'd done the remodel on the container. Lei was going to work on that at home tonight, along with reading the Peterson daughter's diary that she'd retrieved from the wreck of the *Sea Cloud*.

Stevens slowed his breathing deliberately, trying to relax. Beside him, Mahoe shifted his weight and his seat creaked. Night wind soughed gently in the long, feathery needles of the ironwood tree, blowing in through the open window and touching Stevens's face like a caress.

In the Marines, right out of high school, Stevens had learned to sleep on demand. That skill had come in handy over the years, but he hadn't been able to access it since the disastrous stint he'd done overseas as a troop trainer in Honduras. Images from that time, almost three years ago now, still haunted him when he let his mind wander—along with the chronic headaches.

But at least he'd kicked the booze habit he'd had going.

He and Lei had made it through that dark time, adding their precious daughter to a growing family that included his mom Ellen, her father Wayne, his son Kiet from his first marriage, and now, her grandfather Soga.

What were they going to do about Soga? Lei's grandfather was still in the hospital, but the clock was ticking until his discharge. If they didn't find a step-down facility soon, he'd just be put out on the street to make his way home. *Living on another island really complicated things.*

Stevens must have fallen asleep, because the next thing he knew, Mahoe was plucking at his sleeve. "My turn for some shut-eye, LT."

"Any activity?" Stevens moved his seat back up and took the binoculars from Mahoe.

"Nope." Mahoe put his seat down and turned on his side, away from Stevens. Only moments later, gentle snores filled the cab of the truck—the young man had obviously needed some rest.

Stevens put the binoculars to his eyes. The rust-red shipping container, parked near one of the overhead security lights, was unremarkable except for the slight square protrusion of the air conditioner mounted in the side.

He poured some coffee from the departmental thermos into its metal lid, and sipped. Mahoe had also stocked up for the stakeout with some protein bars. Stevens peeled one of those and ate it.

They had to be moving the women to this container and shipping it out soon. Every day that the captives were kept somewhere else on the island was a day closer to their possible discovery. The traffickers would want that container gone, ASAP. *Maybe they'd get lucky, and tonight would be the night.*

CHAPTER SIXTEEN

LEI SAT on the leather sofa in the living room with Rosie cradled in one arm, drinking her last bottle of the day, and the other wrapped around Kiet as Lei read him a story. Kiet could read fluently but still loved their evening ritual on the couch.

The little boy held the book and turned the pages, following along as she read. Lei caressed his jet-black hair and rubbed his back, snuggling him closer against her side. To add to the togetherness, Conan had climbed up onto the other end of the couch, crowding against Kiet with his warm, hairy bulk.

Lei finished the story and kissed the top of Kiet's head. "All right, little man. Brush teeth and bed while I put Rosie down."

Kiet sighed in exaggerated disappointment, and slid off the couch. "Can Conan come to bed with me?"

Conan usually slept in the living room, but since Keiki's passing, the big Rottie had mounted a campaign to join his humans, and Kiet was clearly the weak link. "Okay. Just this once." *It would turn into more, but what was the harm?*

"Yay!" Kiet trotted down the hall with Conan at his heels, heading for the bathroom. Lei stood up carefully, trying not to disturb Rosie's sleeping as she set aside the empty bottle.

She'd come straight home after the case review meeting with plenty of work to do, but thankfully, Captain Omura understood that both of her detectives couldn't be away indefinitely with two young children at home, even with babysitting in the form of Wayne and Ellen available.

Rosie burped as Lei lifted her soft, hefty warmth to her shoulder. "Good one, baby girl." Lei headed down the hall and settled the baby in her crib across from Kiet's bed. She covered her with the quilt as Rosie blinked sleepily and plugged her mouth with a thumb.

Lei turned on the angel nightlight and cranked the baby's silent mobile. Glow-in-the-dark shells circled above her daughter's head as Kiet returned.

Lei tucked him in, too, kissing his forehead and pulling his blanket up under his chin. "Goodnight, little man." Conan, sheepish and clearly prepared to be ousted from the room, hopped up onto the boy's comforter, making puppy eyes at Lei. She patted his head in answer, and the Rottie's ears relaxed in happiness.

"Goodnight, kids," she whispered from the doorway.

"G'night, Mama," Kiet whispered back. Rosie was quiet, which was excellent. It had taken months of training to get the children to go down at the same time and not disrupt each other. Lei left the door open an inch or so for Conan to exit if he wished, and tiptoed down the hall to the office/guest room at the back of the house.

Lei powered up her computer, an upgrade from the one at work, but still nothing like what Sophie would have to do research on . . . *but no*. She couldn't keep bothering Sophie for everything. Her computer whiz friend had her own cases.

While the computer booted, Lei turned on the desk lamp and picked up the Peterson girl's diary, bracing herself internally. *She hadn't even wanted to open it enough to see which of the three girls had written it.* Reading it would bring the girls even closer emotionally—*but it had to be done.*

Lei jimmied the little lock that sealed the diary with a paperclip. She opened the bright cardboard cover.

"Adelia," she breathed as she traced the name written on the inside flap, along with the girl's birthdate—clearly the diary had been a gift. "You're fifteen years old." Older sister Joanie was seventeen, and the youngest, Sarah, was thirteen. Their mother, Emma, was only forty-five, and Priscilla Gutierrez, the cook/maid crew member, was thirty.

The teen girls, particularly, were prime ages to be the victims of a sex trafficker. *They had to find them before they were shipped overseas.* She was relieved that Stevens had a good lead in the Matson container; they'd be able to intercept the women at that shipping container before it got away.

Lei leaned back in her chair and focused on clear, round script written in sparkly gel pen looping across pale pink pages. *"Got this journal for my birthday, and saved it for the Hawaii vacation Dad's taking us on. A real yacht! I hope it's fun. I am going to miss Zoe and Bella; but maybe there's Wi-Fi out on the ocean!"*

Lei pulled out her notepad, still stuffed in the back pocket of her jeans, and made a note of Adelia's friends' names, just in case she needed more background.

"Day one: OMG! We hadn't even got out of the harbor on O`ahu when we saw dolphins! I wanted to lie on the bowsprit so I could be as close to them as possible, but Captain Kaihale told me it wasn't safe. He's nice, really funny and likes to tell Hawaiian legends and stories. I especially liked the one about how the trickster demigod Maui hooked the Hawaiian Islands up from the sea . . ."

Lei began to skim, flipping pages. She was forming an impression of a cheerful, compliant middle child, always peacemaking between sensitive, tearful Sarah and strong-willed Joanie. *"Mom gave us all a time-out since Joanie was complaining that the cruise was boring and Sarah was whining about missing her friends; I didn't bother pointing out that I hadn't said anything one way or the other. I just wanted to be alone, to write in this journal and read my book and listen to my iPod without anyone bugging me.*

I also think Mom wanted a chance to be alone with Dad; they went into their cabin and locked the door, right in the middle of the day! Ew. I don't even want to imagine what they were doing in there; but on the other hand, I've been worried that they haven't been getting along, and I'd hate for them to divorce like Dad's partner John did, or Bella's parents.

That totally sucked for Bella. Her mom went from being well-off to scrounging for a job and living in this crappy apartment, and Bella had to choose which parent she went to stay with. She likes her mom better, but her dad had the house and could give her a car, so she stayed with him.

I'd never want to have to make a choice like that.

Yeah, I like that we are all together in one place, forced to be together, really, and it's helping our family get closer even if there are some bumps. It's sad how we never spend time with each other, with school and activities and friends, and Dad's never home because he's always working on that invention. As it gets closer to the product launch and the IP sale, I feel really proud of him. He and John are really going to do a good thing for the world! And we get to be a part of it."

That was the last entry, dated before the day of the attack.

Lei shut the diary and set it aside. She had a few more names to run down; she had confirmation of the purpose of the trip; she had a little fuller picture of the family and their dynamics. Now, more than ever, she wanted to find a fifteen-year-old girl named Adelia.

Lei opened up her browser, logged into the MPD website, and pulled up the search database that listed Maui's current owners and renters by address. She plugged in the location of the warehouse where Stevens's CI had done the work on the container the women were going to be housed in. She cut and pasted the name and business address into the case file's notes area.

She ran a search on the import company and found a website

with a catalog of home furnishings imported from other countries: carved wooden end tables, lamp bases and nesting stools from Bali, and Asian-style vases and statues from Taiwan. There were also coconut fiber products like woven floor mats and decorative pounded fabrics from Guam, and textiles from India and Sri Lanka, custom printed with hand-stamped designs. "Could be a front," she murmured. "For drugs or other trafficking."

What if they shipped women, kidnapped in the US, to those locations, then filled the containers with these imports and brought them back to supply to retailers here in Hawaii? "Not a bad turn-around," she murmured, turning the bone hook in her fingers as she scrolled through public records. "No sign of anything going over to those countries in their containers."

She glanced at the clock on the corner of the desk—glowing red letters showed one a.m. already. *Poor Michael. He was going to be up all night watching that container.*

Lei was just taking out her phone to send him a text when the phone buzzed with an incoming call. She frowned when she saw the name and number. "Aina? Hey. Why are you calling so late?"

"We're sending a team to answer another distress call at sea—same MO as the first one. Another yacht's been attacked."

CHAPTER SEVENTEEN

LEI TUGGED her MPD ball cap low and tight on her forehead, threading her curly ponytail through the gap in the back. The early morning breeze was chilly, so she also pulled a windbreaker hood up over the hat and tightened the elastic cord under her chin. She zipped the jacket up, and turned toward Aina Thomas, sensibly dressed in Coast Guard heavy weather gear. The *Defender* peeled away from the dock, making her stagger and grab the handrail. "Thanks for waiting for us to get to the docks."

Thomas shrugged. "We had to wait until dawn, anyway. Like I told you on the phone, we're just going over to Moloka`i as part of the search. We haven't found the *Golden Fleece* yet."

"Gotcha." The wind in Lei's face was as cold as if she were on the mainland, and she huddled in the lee of the boat's cabin as the rigid inflatable bounced at full throttle across dawn-lit, pewter-gray waves. Wetness chilled her further as spray flew back from the bow. She leaned forward to shout into Thomas's ear. "Can we go inside the cabin?"

"Not this time. My commanding officer's inside, doing a sitrep with the rest of the search team from Moloka`i," Thomas shouted back. "We've pinpointed where the call came from, near the

Kaunakakai Harbor, so Commander Decker thought it might save time to bring you two along. Good thing you were able to get your crime scene tech to come." Thomas indicated Becca Nunez with his chin.

Lei turned to glance at her colleague. Nunez was more sensibly dressed than Lei, swathed in a bright yellow slicker and boots. She looked distinctly green, however, as she gripped the boat's safety rail. "Nunez doesn't like boats, but she's never one to back down from a challenge."

"That's good." Was there an assessing light in Thomas's eyes? Nunez was cute, even buried in foul weather gear, and the handsome Coast Guardsman was still single three years after their brief flirtation.

"Yeah, Becca's a real badass. Runs triathlons when she's not in the lab processing evidence." Thomas just grunted, so Lei moved on. "So, what does your commanding officer think about what's going on?"

"With this second attack, we're considering that there might be pirates operating in the area. Commander Decker is asking for extra patrols to Maui and the small surrounding islands, to search for a place where perps might be hiding. Like I told you the first time we talked about this, we don't get many pirates in Hawaii because we're usually able to keep them from finding places to hide. Kind of like how the state highway patrols monitor freeways and keep them safe."

They hit a particularly vicious chop, and Lei slammed into Thomas. She hung onto the bench with both hands as the inflatable came out of the wind shadow cast by Lana'i, and was slammed by crosscurrents and even more wind.

Nunez lost her battle with seasickness and upchucked over the side. Thomas shook his head and turned away. *So much for setting those two up.*

It was a long hour of rough seas across another channel to Moloka'i, and even though Lei spotted flying fish and a pod of dolphins off to one side, she felt nothing but relief when she saw the arid, golden-topped island looming close.

The fifth smallest island in the main Hawaiian chain, Moloka`i was a long wedge, with one larger, elevated side rimmed by cliffs facing the west coast of Maui, and the far end sloping down to a windswept beach facing far-off Tahiti, the next bit of land on the globe. Moloka`i's main town, Kaunakakai, was built near a harbor and small airport at the center of the island, where supplies arrived that were the island's lifeblood.

Instead of entering the harbor, the *Defender* inflatable slowed down. Lei stared curiously as several uniformed sailors came out of the cabin and went to the stern, deploying some sort of metal mechanism using a winch.

"That's our sonar search gear," Thomas pointed away from them to another inflatable similar to theirs off their starboard bow. "See that other vessel? We're running a search pattern grid and taking pictures of the bottom."

"Cool." Lei checked her phone—she had a few bars now that they were closer to civilization. "Ok to call my husband and check in? He's been added to the case."

"Sure."

Stevens answered right away. "Hey, Sweets." She heard the crack of his jaw as he yawned. "Great of you to set up a ride to school for Kiet with your dad, and Mom already has Rosie over at the cottage. I needed a little more shut-eye."

"I thought you would. Like I told you in my message, the Coast Guard hasn't found the boat yet, but they wanted someone from MPD as well as a scene tech on hand in case they did find it."

"Keep me posted." Lei could hear, by the rustling of the bedclothes, that he was getting up. "No activity at the container last night, which is a bummer. The captain sent over a couple of plainclothes officers to keep watch today. We're committed to surveilling it until there's some movement. Did you find anything out about the warehouse where they did the work on the container?"

"I did." Lei filled him in. "I didn't find much, though, and it's likely a shell corporation pretending to be an import/export company, with only imports on the books." Nunez came up, and Lei nodded to her. "I have to go. I'll call you as soon as I know anything real. Love you." She ended the call and addressed Nunez. "Feeling better?"

"Not really, but Petty Officer Thomas gave me some Dramamine, so hopefully I'm done puking." The CSI pushed her hood back. Her purple-streaked hair was a mess, her eyes ringed with dark circles. "I'm not sure this is the best use of our time. Maybe we should have waited until they found the wreck to liaise with the Guard."

Lei nodded. "Ugh. I think you might be right."

The women soon grew tired of standing as the boats criss-crossed in their search pattern, and sat on the bench. As if on cue, the other search vessel gave a klaxon blast. Their boat hove about and headed over toward it. Lei moved to the bow, Nunez close behind her.

They were headed for a dark object floating in the water.

The Coast Guard boats side-tied to each other, a quick and effi-cient process. Lei and Nunez, along with Thomas and Commander Decker, a short, thickset, but well-groomed officer, went aboard the other vessel.

The floating object was hauled up on deck by the crew. Lei's belly tightened at the sight of a male victim, approximately six foot, two hundred pounds or so, stiff with rigor. The cause of death was a single deep slash to the neck, similar to the one Lei had seen on Chaz Kaihale.

Decker took charge of the body and ordered it transferred over to his boat, the *Defender*. This challenging maneuver was executed with a boom and a winch, and soon the body rested at Lei's feet.

The corpse oozed water onto the tarp used to transport it.

Nunez, already gloved up, moved in to investigate, her camera clicking, dictating into a headset recorder. "Mid-thirties male victim of undetermined mixed race. Height, build and coloring match the captain of the *Golden Fleece*, though no positive identification available at this time. Appears to be same MO as the *Sea Cloud* victim we retrieved—severed jugular leading to exsanguination. Body appears to have been immersed in water for a number of hours, though still in rigor." Nunez glanced up to meet Lei's eyes. "See the rope around his waist? Seems like it wore through on something." She held up a frayed end. "Maybe there are more bodies down there."

"No telling where he floated from." Lei bent for a closer look.

"Actually, we can pinpoint a likely radius," Commander Decker said. "Based on the time of the distress call and the area we located for its origin, the speed and direction of the currents last night, and the condition of the body—I think we can keep working the grid we already set up to search for the yacht, as well as more victims."

Lei frowned, gazing down at the pale face of the corpse. "What if they didn't sink the yacht this time? After all, the pirates' stealth plan is blown; we're looking for them, and they know it. Maybe this time, they offed the captain and whoever they think might have been a problem, then they took the yacht. Didn't sink it. Towed it somewhere to sell, and dumped this body here as a red herring."

Decker had deep-set blue eyes framed by fans of sun-squint crinkles, and they flicked over Lei, dismissing her. "No time for all of that."

"I think it's odd that you haven't found the yacht yet, with all that sonar equipment," Lei persisted. "What if, after their attempt last time to sink the ship didn't work, they changed things up?" She stared down at the body. "We haven't had time to work up a background on the *Golden Fleece*, but from what we've already found out about the *Sea Cloud* and the family who chartered it, there was a lot more going on than initially met the eye." Lei had everyone's attention, and she pressed on. "There were powerful motives to kill Peterson, and apparently, now there's a plan to sell his wife and daughters. If this is the same perp, maybe this murder isn't random either."

Nunez continued to work her way around the body, searching it carefully and murmuring notes into her phone, but Thomas and Decker stepped closer to Lei. "Tell me what you're thinking," Thomas said.

"Perhaps there's a reason that the *Golden Fleece* was targeted, and part of that may be the two teen girls and their friends who were on board, traveling with their billionaire father. If you assume the MO is the same as last time, then the pirates knew exactly who they were going after. Only, instead of attempting to scuttle the ship, this time they set up a false location for the Coast Guard, knowing that the response time would be good as everyone is on high alert." Lei glanced around, making eye contact with Decker, Thomas and Nunez. "Not sure how they did it exactly. Maybe they sent out a small tender craft to make a fake distress call near the Kaunakakai Harbor, a well-trafficked area, and they dumped the body so that we'd continue to search in the wrong location. Meanwhile, they're long gone in some other direction, with the girls and the yacht as prizes."

Decker snorted. "What evidence do you have that this is true? Your own crime tech just showed you a rope around the body's waist that seems like it could have worn through on the rocks."

"I don't have any evidence. I just know we're going to find out there was a reason this ship was targeted, just like there was a reason they went after the *Sea Cloud*. I don't believe these attacks were random."

"We got the distress call at oh one hundred hours." Thomas tapped a dent on the front of his chin thoughtfully, as he gazed at the other Coast Guard boat, already resuming its search pattern.

"We had a response craft to the source of the call within an hour, isn't that right, Commander Decker?"

"That's right."

"But they found no sign of the craft, nor anything anywhere near where the call came from."

"We assumed they sank the *Golden Fleece*, like they tried to do with the *Sea Cloud*. We dropped a buoy in the area, and sent out the call for more craft to search as soon as day broke."

"And have you found anything to indicate that the *Golden Fleece* was sunk here? Floating debris, life vests, etcetera?" Lei asked. "Besides the body, of course."

Decker's jaw tightened. "No."

"I was wondering . . . how long would it take to sink a ship the size of the *Golden Fleece*?"

"Depending on the size of the hole in the stern . . ."

"I looked at the specs. The craft was a hundred and twenty feet long and had a ballast compartment and sealed interior rooms. They'd have had to basically dynamite that hull to get a hole big enough to sink it in an hour," Thomas said. "I'm starting to wonder, too. Maybe the call and the body were a delaying tactic, to give the pirates time to get away and hide or disguise the stolen craft."

"If so, where the hell is it?" Decker growled. "We know that the *Golden Fleece* left O`ahu two days ago. We know it made a distress call off the coast of Moloka`i, supposedly. Now we know that one of its crew has been murdered. That's all we know."

"I think you need to go back to what is known about where the yacht was going," Lei said. "Did they file a navigation plan for where they were headed?"

"Boats don't have to file a plan, though it's considered best practice," Thomas said. "Charter companies, like Dream Vacations Luxury Yachts who owned the *Sea Cloud*, do that as part of their insurance policy requirements. But the *Golden Fleece* was privately owned. According to what I could dig up, the owner,

Willem Janssen, was an experienced sailor with his own crew. All we know about the craft was that they had sailed all the way here from Tahiti, that the boat is registered in Norway, and that Janssen filed a general application to tour the Hawaiian Islands. Very different scenario than the first crime as far as target. One of the crew had his throat cut, and that's the only real similarity to the other case."

"I disagree. It's too much of a coincidence not to be related," Lei said. "But I think that this perp, or gang, since it is likely a group, is perfecting its technique. Learning along the way. And they might have multiple goals."

Decker, his hands on his hips, swept the empty ocean around them with a glance. "What would you have us do?"

"Go on the offensive, sir. Yes, leave a boat here searching this grid—but get some more patrols in the water from O`ahu, and begin to comb Maui, Lana`i, Moloka`i and Kaho`olawe for the *Fleece*. Once you find that yacht, you'll find the pirates. Meanwhile, we've got eyes on the container and the warehouse that they may be using to hold the women. Maybe we'll catch them that way."

Decker took a step back and eyed Lei with increased respect. "I'd like to know more about Janssen, his family and his crew. Maybe you and your team can work on that. I'll make the call for reinforcements, and we'll run you, Nunez and this body back to Maui."

"We'd appreciate that. I think we can be of more use to you once we have a crime scene to investigate," Lei said.

"I've already called the Maui ME, Dr. Gregory," Nunez chimed in from behind. "Maybe there's more this body can tell us, too."

Decker turned to Thomas. "We'll leave our sister craft here to continue the search. I'll talk to O`ahu about a sweep to search for the yacht in Maui's outer islands."

"Yes, sir." Thomas gave a crisp salute.

"Thank you, Captain." Lei stepped aside so that he and Thomas could go back into the cabin. The powerful engines throbbed into life, and the inflatable spun and headed back toward the much larger island of Maui.

Lei watched the low-lying, golden shoreline of Moloka`i recede in the distance. *Hopefully she hadn't just steered the whole investigation in the wrong direction.*

CHAPTER EIGHTEEN

STEVENS GOT out of the shower, relatively invigorated by a heavy drumming with cold water. *Thank God for Wayne and Ellen helping with the kids!* They were already at school and nursery care.

Stevens dressed in his usual work clothes, a pair of jeans and a polo shirt with athletic style hiking boots. He strapped on his shoulder holster and ran his belt through the loops, making sure the pouches for cell phones and a knife were properly placed. His phone, resting on the dresser, buzzed with an incoming call from Omura, and he picked up. "Good morning, Captain."

"Get over to that container with Mahoe. Surveilling officers report activity. I am sending two additional units for backup," Omura rapped out.

"On my way!" Stevens slid the phone into its holder, grabbed his Glock out of the mini-safe where he and Lei stored weapons, and sped through the house, grabbing a can of cold coffee and a granola bar. He checked that Conan had been fed, and the Rottweiler barked with excitement, chasing him as he ran out to the Bronco. He peeled down the driveway, barely waiting for the gate to open before him.

Stevens glanced back in his rearview mirror as the gate rumbled shut on Conan's vigilant stance, legs braced and head up, standing guard over their place. That dog was all heart and protection, just as Keiki had been. He deserved more than a cup of dry kibble tossed in his bowl, and a pat on the head.

When would he be home next?

This case was going nuts. Stevens hadn't even laid eyes on his children in more than twenty-four hours.

And what was going on with finding a step-down facility for Soga? Neither he nor Lei had any time to work on that pressing problem.

Stevens sped through the narrow, winding back roads of Haiku, overgrown ferns and palm trees brushing the sides of the Bronco, his light on the dash to clear the way as he encountered residents on the road. He swerved around a truck loaded with coconuts, and another with decorative yard waste, beating them to the one-lane bridge at the bottom of Maliko Gulch. Cranking up the hairpin turns on the other side, headed for the larger highway, he called Mahoe and made sure his young partner was on the way to the shipping container storage area.

"Don't approach the container without me," he instructed. "We don't want this thing turning into a standoff."

STEVENS ARRIVED TOO late to prevent disaster.

He pulled the Bronco up into the ironwood trees where they had been observing the container, only to see that the two units the Captain had sent over had boxed in a white cargo van, presumably used to transport the women, in front of the container. The patrol cars faced the Matson shipping crate, the officers using their doors as cover. They were pointing their weapons at the slightly open front door of the modified container.

"Shit!" Stevens grabbed his radio off the dash. "Units twenty-seven and thirty-four, be advised. This is Lieutenant Stevens. What the hell are you doing?"

"Sorry, Lieutenant, we thought we'd grab them before you got here, but the perps escaped into the container," one of the uniforms said sheepishly. "We're holding 'em for you."

"Thanks for nothing!" Stevens gave his disordered hair a yank in frustration. "How many are in there?"

"Two, with the women. There were four of those."

"Did it occur to you that approaching might not be a good idea? Now we've got a hostage situation!"

Mahoe pulled up next to Stevens's vehicle and approached, his weapon drawn. "What's our play, LT?"

"We have to establish contact with the kidnappers." Stevens swore a few more times, leaving the radio open so the uniforms could appreciate how badly they'd screwed up. "They're going to feel like there's no way out."

"There won't be a landline into that container. I don't know how you're going to establish contact," Mahoe said.

Stevens thought rapidly, and clicked on the radio. "Unit twenty-seven. One of you guys give up your cell phone. Raise your hands, walk forward, and set it on the ground. Then both units, back the hell up. Pull all the way out of visual range, back until you're outside the gate. We also need to clear any nonessential personnel from the container area. Do you think you can do that?"

"You got it, Lieutenant." Clearly eager to rectify their mistake, the patrol officers put their vehicles in gear. One of the officers walked forward with his hands up. He set his phone down on the asphalt near the door of the container. No shots were fired from the container. They then backed their vehicles away and disappeared.

Stevens sat down in the Bronco. Mahoe got in next to him. A moment later, the officer whose phone had been surrendered texted him the number with a message: *This is my private burner phone. Good luck, LT.*

Stevens wasn't the only cop with a private burner phone.

He took a pair of binoculars out of the side pocket of his seat and applied his eyes to the lenses. He scanned around the container. "They've barely got the door open. Wonder if that AC unit is hooked up—if it isn't, they won't want to be in there long as hot it is today. Can you run that white van's plates, Mahoe? We should see who that's registered to."

"On it." Mahoe pulled the Toughbook laptop out of the glove box and booted up.

Movement in the container's doorway. A man with a hat pulled low, wearing a light gray zip-front work coverall, stuck his head out, peering around. "Think he's seen us, LT?" Mahoe asked. "We're hidden behind the bushes . . ."

"Oh, I'm sure they're aware of us." Indeed, the man was looking right at Stevens. "Yep, he's casing us right now. He knows we wouldn't leave without eyes on them."

The man kept his gaze on Stevens. Even with the binoculars, Stevens couldn't make out his features behind sunglasses and the shadowed brim of his hat. Slowly, the kidnapper raised his hands— and then sidled out through the door, darted over and picked up the phone. In a moment, he was back inside the container and the door shut. "He's taken the phone. I'll call him now."

"The van's registered to the same company that owns the warehouse where they did the alterations to the container," Mahoe said. "Interesting."

"A shell company, Lei said." Stevens took out his own burner and manually entered the number of the officer's cell. He put the device on speaker and rang through.

"Yeah?" The kidnapper's voice was gravelly when he answered —*he was trying to disguise it.*

"This is Lieutenant Michael Stevens of the Maui Police Department. I'm sure you're aware that we've got you surrounded. Is that air conditioner on?"

"Screw you." The man was breathing heavily.

"You can call me Mike, and I take that as a no. What's your name?"

"We're not going to be on a first-name basis, cop. We will kill one woman every half hour that we're in here. So get your people the hell away from the entrance, and get us a helicopter."

The hairs rose involuntarily on Stevens's arms, and he exchanged a glance with Mahoe, whose eyes had gone wide. Stevens signaled his partner to call the captain for SWAT. Mahoe eased outside the cab, his phone in his hand.

Stevens kept his voice low and even. "Hey now. Whoa. No call for any violence. You saw that I got those officers out of your hair as soon as I got here and saw that those knuckleheads had backed you into a corner." He blew out a sigh, as if weary of idiots—*here they were, stuck in the same boat.* "I don't want this situation any more than you do. I get that you're hot and uncomfortable, and this is a cramp in your plan. But right now, if you turn yourselves in, it's no big deal. Most you'd get is six months for accessory to kidnapping, and the Maui jail's a country club. I'll put in a good word . . ."

"Obviously you're not taking us seriously. Maybe I haven't made myself clear enough." The women began screaming—a simultaneously horrible experience. Cries came through the phone, while echoing off the metal walls of the container directly in front of them. Mahoe had returned, and his eyes met Stevens's in shock.

The crack of a gunshot inside reverberated with the metal sides of the container.

Stevens recoiled. His hand was shaking so bad he almost dropped the phone. "What did you do, man? What did you do?"

"You know what I did. Now get me that chopper, or I'll do another one in a half hour!"

The phone went dead in Stevens's hand.

"Auwe," Mahoe breathed. "Holy shit."

Ahead of them, the door of the container creaked open. A woman's body rolled out, arms flopping like a rag doll as she landed on the ground. A booted leg appeared, briefly, kicking her through the opening and out of the way of the door. Then a broom appeared, shoving the body aside, moving it so that the door could close once more.

The woman lay unmoving, her back to them, just to the side of the container's entrance.

"Holy crap, LT! What do we do now?"

Stevens speed-dialed Captain Omura on her cell. She answered immediately, her voice crisp. "I'm on my way. I have called for our FBI backup liaison, who in this case is your wife. SWAT is also on their way."

"The kidnapper shot a hostage. Rolled her outside the container and closed the door again." Stevens gulped down the horror and made it disappear into that place where he kept such things. "She has short brown hair. I think it's Priscilla Gutierrez."

"Damn it! We're at a whole new level then. Don't escalate the situation. If he calls back, tell him his chopper is on the way."

Overhead, Stevens could hear the sound of the helicopter approaching.

"What about the woman? She might still be alive."

"Is she moving?"

Stevens squinted. "No."

"We can't approach the container until we have reinforcements in place. Any movement on our part could escalate the kidnappers, and now that they showed they're capable of deadly force, we have to operate on a cost-benefit analysis as far as saving lives." He could hear Omura's fast breathing. *She was running.*

"I didn't think he'd go this far." Stevens pushed the words out through frozen vocal cords. "I thought these guys at the container would have been lower echelon soldiers, moving the human merchandise. But this kidnapper . . . he seemed to take it personally."

"You did all the right things: moved the officers who got this confrontation started out of play, established a line of contact with the kidnapper, and set us up to come in and support you. You had no idea how prepared he was to act—most people in this kidnapper's position would have given us more time, negotiated more." He heard the beep of the captain unlocking her vehicle. "Stop second-guessing yourself. That can be deadly." Omura ended the call.

Stevens cursed, long and fluently, his gaze on Gutierrez's unmoving form.

"What did she say, LT?" Mahoe's voice was wobbly with stress.

Stevens recapped the plan Omura had laid out. "I'm sure the FBI will be deployed from O'ahu, but it's going to take them time to get here. Lei is their representative for the moment, per her contract with them." Stevens picked up the binoculars and trained them on the woman.

They would probably kill Mrs. Peterson next, saving the young girls, most valuable as hostages, for last.

Gutierrez faced away from him, lying on her side. He couldn't see where she had been shot, but her hair was darkening with blood, and a pool of it was forming on the asphalt under her upper body.

And then she moved.

Just a little, at first, one of her arms reaching forward, then she flopped onto her belly. She reached the other arm forward, with excruciating slowness, and dug her fingers into the asphalt. She drew up a leg, digging her foot, clad in a white tennis shoe, into the pavement, and pushed herself forward.

She was crawling away from the door area.

"Gutierrez is alive. She's moving!" *He had to help her!* Stevens handed the binoculars and his phone to Mahoe. "Call for an ambulance. Monitor the kidnappers' phone for a call from them, and report in to the captain if anything else happens. I'm going to get her."

CHAPTER NINETEEN

"WHAT THE HELL are you doing, LT?" Mahoe's voice had gone squeaky with alarm. Stevens ignored his partner. He jumped out of the Bronco, ran around to the back of the truck, opened the hatch, and scrambled frantically around in his toolbox. He grabbed a pair of bolt cutters and a beach towel, and headed for the fence.

The kidnappers would not be able to see him immediately, if he approached from further down than the opening at the front of the container. He just had to hope that they wouldn't hear the sound of him cutting into the chain links. He moved to the left of the entrance and approached the fence, staying low and keeping the bushes as cover.

Using the towel to muffle the sound, Stevens clamped the bolt cutters over the heavy gauge steel. The *crack* of the heavy steel wire separating, even with the towel over it, sounded as loud as a gunshot to his ears. No help for it—he was committed. He grabbed the next link in the bolt cutter's teeth, covered the area with the towel, and cranked down on the handles.

He glanced over at Gutierrez. That tough lady was continuing to drag herself in his direction, inch by agonized inch, along the narrow opening between the container and the fence in no more than eighteen inches of space. The gap was so narrow he hadn't originally thought he could fit into it. *He had to, now.*

Their eyes met. "Hang on. I'm coming for you," he whispered, mouthing the words in an exaggerated way so she could understand. She shut her eyes for a moment, clearly getting the message.

These were the moments when Stevens felt most alive. His blood was pumping, his vision had focused to laserlike detail. Colors were brighter, sounds sharper. *Nothing existed now but this moment of life or death, for himself or another.*

No movement from the front of the container as he glanced at it, making his next cut.

He could feel Mahoe's gaze on his back.

Hopefully he'd called for an ambulance already. *And wouldn't it be great if Mahoe remembered to have them keep their sirens off . . .* but likely Omura would have called for one. She seemed confident in her protocol.

His thoughts floated by, each one as separate and distinct as if it were in its own little bubble.

Finally Stevens had cut enough of the heavy, stiff wire to peel it back, making a triangular opening. He bent the chain link aside and crawled through the opening, then stood up and turned sideways, sliding along the fence, avoiding touching the container in case he made any sound or vibration.

Gutierrez had only made it a couple of feet in his direction, but that was enough for her to be out of visible range of the front of the container, unless the perps intentionally stuck their heads around the corner to take a look.

A heavy blood trail marked her agonizing progress. *Hopefully they'd just assume she'd crawled a little way and died . . .*

There was no time for niceties as he squatted beside her. "Stay quiet. This is going to hurt." Stevens grasped Gutierrez's wrists, dragging her forcefully along the gap in the fence as he backed as fast as he could toward the opening he'd made. Gutierrez whimpered, biting her lips, tears streaming from her eyes, her tan bleached to a sickly yellow—but they'd reached the hole in the fence.

Stevens backed through the triangular cut and bent to whisper in her ear. "Just a few more minutes, and you'll be safe. I'm sorry I have to hurt you." She gave a tiny gasp, and fainted as he wrestled her through the tight opening in the fence.

Once on the other side, he scooped her up into his arms. Unconsciousness had made her completely limp, and he broke into a run, crashing through the bushes, passing the Bronco, and jogging down the rough dirt track to the small frontage road beyond.

Sure enough, an ambulance was waiting for them, the doors open, a gurney ready, the EMTs standing by. Relief swamped Stevens as he laid Gutierrez on the padded transport bed.

He stared down at her, getting his first real look at the woman he'd rescued.

Priscilla Gutierrez's round, pleasant face was ashen, her lips bleeding where she'd bitten them, likely to keep from crying out when he dragged her. She had been shot in the upper right chest. The team swarmed around her, covering her face with an oxygen mask, punching an IV into her arm, taking a pulse and blood pressure, speaking to each other in codes.

He stood back as they strapped her down, lifted the gurney into the ambulance, and roared off, lights going but no siren.

With any luck at all, she'd make it.

A touch on his arm. Captain Omura gazed up at him, her dark eyes wide, her jaw set. "I told you to stay put, Michael, and wait for orders from me."

He shook his head. "I had to try to save her. I just hope I wasn't too late."

"Well, you pulled it off, so I hope so, too."

SWAT arrived in their black van. Omura strode off to meet their commander.

A silver Tacoma truck drove up from the other direction, dirt and gravel flying from its tires as his wife braked beside Stevens. Lei leaped out of the driver's seat, leaving the door ajar. She grabbed his arms, her eyes wild. "Are you shot?" She cried. "I'll kill you if you're shot."

Stevens glanced down.

The entire front of his pale blue shirt was soaked with blood. "Not mine. The victim's. Priscilla Gutierrez. Kidnapper shot her and threw her outside the container. She was alive, so I went and got her." He met Lei's eyes. "I have to get back to my phone in case he calls."

He turned, and sprinted for the Bronco.

CHAPTER TWENTY

LEI RAN after her husband as he headed for his SUV. Technically, she should wait to collaborate with the captain and the SWAT team, as she was not only a team member on the case, but the liaison for the FBI on Maui.

But she couldn't stand to let her blood-soaked spouse out of her sight. No telling what he would do next, and he was right—*he had to get back to that phone.* He was the familiar voice that had already established contact with the kidnappers.

The Bronco was parked in a nest of beach heliotrope and naupaka bushes, hardy shrubs that thrived in sandy, arid areas near the ocean. The vehicle was shaded by an overhanging ironwood tree. Dead ahead, behind a tall chain-link fence with a triangular hole cut in it, brilliant sun blazed down on a rust red metal container with *Matson* boldly emblazoned on the side.

Stevens jumped into the front seat of the Bronco. Lei yanked open the back door behind him, just as Mahoe, in the passenger seat, handed her husband the ringing phone.

The young man's face was pale and shiny, and he smelled of stress and sweat. "You got here just in time, LT. The phone started ringing—I didn't know what to do."

Stevens took the phone and answered it on speaker. "This is Stevens."

"You're running out of time before I blow away the next hostage. Where's the chopper?"

"On its way. Listen, man, I'm doing my best. It takes time to get things approved. No one wants to mess up in a situation like this, and I can tell you mean business. Just give me a chance to talk to my captain . . ."

"I gave you a chance. Fifteen whole minutes. You wasted those minutes!" The kidnapper was yelling now. Lei heard the bone-chilling sound of screams in the background—both coming from the phone, and muffled on the inside of the container. "I've got another one here. This one's worth more—the Peterson wife. Think people will be happy that you let her die?"

"NO, please, no. No!" Stevens bellowed, his voice echoing with old pain. His eyes were wide and blank, the hand holding the phone trembling—*he wasn't even here right now.*

Stevens was back in a hotel room with his ex-wife, she was dying before his eyes, and he couldn't save her. Lei recognized the stuff of his nightmares—she'd witnessed them too many times.

Lei reached over and grabbed the phone out of his hand. "This is Special Agent Lei Texeira of the FBI. We are taking over this case."

She turned off the speakerphone feature as she shoved the Bronco's back door open, ignoring Stevens's howl of rage as she slammed it. She pressed the phone against her ear and ran through the screening bushes until she stood in front of the container in an open area, clearly visible from the slit of the container's open doorway.

Lei had donned her navy blue FBI ball cap when she got the call from Omura about the standoff. The hat's bold white letters made a perfect target of her head as she stood in the line of fire. Her heart pounded and her breath strained against the tight constriction of her protective vest, but she kept her voice strong and commanding. "I'm authorized to negotiate with you."

"Screw you! I didn't ask for the FBI!"

More screams. Emma Peterson appeared in the door of the container.

The kidnapper, barely visible in the opening, held the woman by a handful of blonde hair, a gun trained on her temple. Mrs. Peterson's hands were at her scalp, trying to keep the strain off, but she lowered them and pushed the door of the container wider with a screech, writhing and weeping in the man's brutal grip.

"Calm down, sir. We're all going to get what we want." Lei breathed deeply and deliberately, tapping into a core of calm within herself that she'd worked years to build. "What do I call you? I've told you my name."

"You can call me your worst nightmare, bitch!" the kidnapper yelled. He was clearly losing it. "Where's my goddamn chopper?"

"The bird is on its way." Lei was thankful that the *whump-whump-whump* of helicopter blades overhead backed up her words —but the truth was, she had no idea what was going on with SWAT. She hadn't taken the time to get wired up with a mic or gather with the team for a plan. *She was going to hear about this later, no matter the outcome.* "I can tell that you mean business, sir —we are taking you very seriously. Your first victim has got our full attention. No need to add another. In fact, why don't you give us a sign of good faith, and let this one go?"

"Why don't you fuck off?" Without warning, the man fired out the door of the container in her direction. Lei instinctively threw herself to the ground, but too late—she felt a burn at her shoulder. "The next one's going in this woman!"

Lei glanced at her shoulder. The fabric of her shirt was frayed by a black crease mark. *He'd almost hit her!*

She stayed down on her belly, shutting out anything but the man's voice on the line as she clutched the phone to her ear. "You've made your point, sir. You are in charge of everything that's happening." She slid her ball cap off. *No sense giving him a bigger target.* "The chopper you asked for is approaching."

In fact, a chopper *was* directly overhead—but instead of the commercial Bell Jet she'd anticipated, this bird was a heavy military model in green camo. A line snaked out from its belly and two black-clad SWAT members were already rappelling down.

Lei's throat went suddenly dry. *There was an entry point on the roof of the container!* Lei had been briefed on the modifications to the container by Stevens. *SWAT must be planning to go in through that opening.*

Lei had to keep the kidnappers distracted. She thought fast. "The chopper is here, sir, but the pilot's telling me there's not a safe area for him to land. What do you want us to do?"

"There's room! Have them put it down in that open area in front of the container!"

"I'm sorry, but the pilot is telling me he's afraid he's going to hit the containers nearby. He has to move to the parking lot. You can take a hostage and meet him there."

"Bullshit! Maybe you need more proof of how serious I am!" The Peterson woman was shoved forward abruptly. She turned in Lei's direction, her eyes huge and pleading, her mouth open on a scream—and the pistol moved. The kidnapper put it against the back of her arm and pulled the trigger.

As he did so, two of the SWAT team dropped silently onto the roof of the container, the sound of their landing obscured by the shot.

More screams echoed from inside the container at the sound of the shot. Mrs. Peterson's eyes rolled back, her knees crumpled, and her hair tore loose from her captor's grip as she fell to the ground, wedging the door of the container further open with her body. The helicopter lifted up, the black ribbon of line retracting as the SWAT members squatted in the middle of the container—likely trying to get the roof hatch open.

"You don't need to convince me you're serious, sir," Lei

yelled. "The chopper is moving into position as you directed. Don't shoot her again, please, don't shoot! If you open the door a little further, you can see for yourself that the helicopter is landing straight ahead!"

The chopper was, indeed, settling down—but as it did so, it disgorged two more SWAT members who ran to take up positions covering the opening of the container. The two who'd landed on the roof had removed the covering over the ventilation opening and crouched there, weapons at the ready.

Out of the side of Lei's eye, she saw another two SWAT officers moving through the bushes, entering the opening Stevens had cut in the fence. *That made six highly trained professionals ready to breach, waiting for the right moment.*

This was all going to be over, one way or another, in a matter of minutes.

CHAPTER TWENTY-ONE

STEVENS HUNCHED in the lee of the Bronco, his Glock resting on the metal doorframe, trained on the opening of the container. He clenched and unclenched his hands on the grip, trying to discharge tension. Across from him, on the other side of the vehicle, Mahoe had taken up a similar defensive posture.

Between the Bronco and the container, Lei was flat on her belly on the sandy ground. She held the phone to her ear, but thankfully she'd taken off that damn FBI hat that made her head a target. All around the edges of the standoff, SWAT officers were getting into position to make their move.

Lei had just grabbed his phone and taken over. They were definitely going to have words about that . . . She was clearly trying to keep the kidnapper distracted, yelling into the phone—*but she was losing him.* Any minute, the kidnapper would notice his first victim was gone, or he'd hear the odd sounds that must be coming from the roof as the SWAT members opened the ventilation hatch. *And he'd for sure see that the chopper on the ground was no civilian transport craft.*

The kidnapper must have realized he was hampered by his lack of visibility, because the man pushed the container door wider, stepping over the fallen body of Mrs. Peterson and peering around toward the chopper.

Stevens had a clear shot.

Here was a chance to end things. There was still one kidnapper left inside, but with the more aggressive perp out of the way and SWAT on the move, hopefully the other one would be neutralized without further bloodshed.

Stevens sighted down the barrel, his weapon steady on the frame of the door, and took the shot.

He'd gone for the man's head, but he hit the kidnapper in the throat. Still, the wound was enough to drop the guy.

Enough to cause him to fall, clutching his neck, spewing blood all over fallen Mrs. Peterson.

Enough to give SWAT the distraction they needed to rip the roof cap open and fire inside, hopefully disabling the remaining kidnapper, as the two SWAT who'd come through the fence stormed the front, kicking the downed man aside and penetrating the interior.

Screams.

Shots.

Silence.

"All clear!" the SWAT leader yelled from inside the container. "We have the hostages!"

Stevens slumped back into the Bronco, dropping his weapon into his lap from suddenly nerveless fingers. The relief made him dizzy.

Omura, who'd been standing back among the trees, approached. "Good shooting, Lieutenant."

Stevens shrugged. His gaze had gone to his wife.

Lei hadn't got up, even though the all clear had sounded. *Had she been hit when that perp took a shot at her?*

Stevens bolted out of the Bronco, knocking Omura to the side.

He had no idea how he got there but seconds later, he was

hauling Lei up from the ground and into his arms, inspecting her. "Are you okay?"

"Michael! Stop it, let go! I'm fine." Lei wriggled and fought, slapping at him in fury. "This is freakin' embarrassing."

Stevens let go, but spotted a frayed line of char on her sleeve. He grabbed her arm and pointed to it. "You almost weren't fine."

"Don't you dare lecture me after you went and dragged that woman through the fence and met me covered with blood." Lei's brown eyes seemed to blaze, wide and hot, and she poked him in the chest with a stiff forefinger. "I don't ever want to be that scared again. Ever."

"And don't *you* ever grab my phone and take over from me in the middle of an op. Who do you think you are? I outrank you!"

"You weren't thinking straight. Your PTSD and your emotions had control!" Lei stepped back from him, hands falling to her hips. "*I'm* the FBI rep on Maui, the closest thing they have to an agent over here, and it was *my job* to take over. You were about to get another victim shot."

"And you almost got shot, yourself!" Stevens yelled. "You'd leave our kids without a mother, just so you could do *your job*?"

"And what about you, cutting a hole in the fence and hauling that woman out, just about giving me a heart attack, and then taking an unauthorized kill shot at the kidnapper?" Lei was spitting with fury. "How dare you endanger yourself like that, you flaming hypocrite!"

"Boys and girls." Omura had approached without them even noticing. She stepped between them, holding up her hands. "I hate to break up this display of happy matrimony, but you're *both* in deep shit as far as I'm concerned. We'll deal with who did what wrong later, and believe me, there's plenty of that to go around. Now get back to work. You need to help secure the scene and get the victims' statements."

Stevens ignored Omura, still staring at Lei. *She needed to break first.*

But Lei wouldn't back down. She vibrated with fury, her brows drawn together in a fierce frown. A nimbus of curls framed her face, escaping a careless ponytail. A smear of dirt on her cheek set off the scattering of freckles across her nose, pointing like an arrow to her mouth, set in a mulish expression.

Stevens's anger evaporated. *He was just scared shitless at the idea of losing her.* He loved her more than his own life.

Stevens shook his head ruefully. "You win, stubborn woman."

"There are no winners or losers, you arrogant ass. Only survivors, and I want you to be one of them." Lei spun on her heel and stomped over to the fence, slipping through the hole he'd made. SWAT members trained in first aid were already attending to the fallen outside the container. Lei wove around them to go inside. His gaze followed her as she disappeared.

"Earth to Stevens." Omura was pissed—her jaw was tight and her eyes narrowed. For the second time that day, he endured a female finger poking at his chest. "Lieutenant Stevens, this is why I generally don't allow spouses to work the same case. I'm going to have to take your weapon and recuse you from the case until we've gone over the shooting of the kidnapper."

Stevens pulled his handgun, holding it out to her by the grip. Omura held open an evidence bag, and he dropped it inside. "For now, until I can get some more help on the case, I want you to go with Mahoe and follow the wounded to the hospital. Mahoe can get their statements there. Lei can work with the Peterson girls and interview them; she's good with kids. We'll sort the rest of this out down at the station. Now get moving, soldier."

CHAPTER TWENTY-TWO

LEI STEPPED around a cluster of SWAT attending to the fallen kidnapper as she entered the container—he did not seem like he'd be around to interview later, from the amount of blood pouring from his throat. Mrs. Peterson had come back around and was sitting up, also getting first aid.

Lei paused for a moment just inside the shadowy opening of the container, assessing. The remaining kidnapper had what appeared to be a minor shoulder wound and was secured on the ground. The three Peterson girls were clustered together on the bed at the back of the room. One of the SWAT members had been trying to talk to them, but he glanced up in relief at her approach and came toward her. "They seem to be in shock, Sergeant."

"Thanks. I'll take it from here." Lei liked that that guy didn't question her, simply pulling back with the rest of his team. Such a refreshing change after her tangle with Michael—*that brave, crazy Neanderthal!* She was still pissed at him, not only for his hypocrisy, but also for embarrassing her in front of the rest of the team.

She'd deal with him later.

Lei refocused on the task at hand, approaching the girls and moving slowly as if approaching a feral cat. "Hey, ladies. My name is Lei, and we're so glad to see you. We've been searching for you so hard."

Sirens sounded in the background—more ambulances arriving.

Loud voices.

Crackling radios.

The chopper taking off again.

Lei shut all of that out, focusing on the girls with their bodies wrapped around each other in a tangle of arms and legs. Three tousled blonde heads were pressed close together. The sound of soft sobbing rose from one of them; another seemed totally silent. But one of them responded.

The girl lifted her face from the knot of traumatized humanity she'd formed with her sisters, and gazed at Lei through a screen of tangled, ash-blonde hair. "Is our mom alive?"

Lei nodded. "She is. She was shot in the arm and she fainted. They're giving her first aid now and taking her straight to the hospital." Lei sat gently on the bed. "We've called for an ambulance for you, too, so you can each get checked out."

Fresh sobs met this. One of the girls was crying hard, the oldest one sitting in the middle wasn't making a sound. The one who'd spoken to Lei seemed to be a spokesperson. "We won't be separated. We're staying together."

"Totally fine, and I understand that. We won't do anything you aren't comfortable with. Again, my name is Lei. What's yours?"

"Adelia. This is Joanie, in the middle, and Sarah, on the end." *The sobbing one was thirteen-year-old Sarah. The silent one was seventeen-year-old Joanie. Fifteen-year-old Adelia was the one who'd written the diary.*

"Good to meet you." Lei smiled warmly. "Now I know what to call you."

The captain of the SWAT team stepped up. "An ambulance transport is here. We need to triage the victims."

Lei held up a hand, halting him. "Let me check with them."

She turned back. "Adelia, what do you think? Are any of you injured?"

Adelia pushed her hair out of her face. Her eyes were the dusky blue of approaching twilight. "Joanie's hurt. They raped her." Adelia's lips trembled. "And Mom, and the other lady too."

Fresh sobs from Sarah. Joanie seemed to hunch even smaller in the shelter of her sisters' arms.

"I'm so sorry that happened. I'll stay with you girls every step of the way and we'll try to make this as painless as possible." She turned back to the SWAT officer. "Captain Hiro? Tell the first responders at the hospital we need rape kit preps for three victims, and I only want female medical personnel attending these girls."

"I'll do my best." Captain Hiro left and Lei turned back to the girls. They were slowly unknotting from each other, preparing to move. Adelia was their glue, stroking their arms, whispering in their ears. *A classic middle child, holding the center, keeping them together.* Her heart gave a little squeeze as they sorted themselves out—*it would have been great to have a sibling.* "Would it be okay if I rode with you in the ambulance? They will probably want to do a basic assessment on each of you, to see if you're hurt."

"We're staying together," Adelia reiterated. "But that would be okay."

The SWAT captain reappeared. "The ambulance personnel say there's not room for four people in the back."

"Then we will figure something else out, right, girls?" Lei held her ground—establishing trust with the girls now would pay off later. "Would it be okay if a female EMT came in to check you out? If you're safe to be transported in a regular vehicle, I'll drive you to the hospital myself."

"That would be good," Adelia said.

Lei turned to Hiro. He nodded, spoke into his radio, and soon a female uniformed EMT appeared. She was short, plump, and had a warm manner as she smiled, moving over to the girls. "Hi. I just want to do a little screening, so we can see if any of you need immediate first aid, and so that the hospital can get ready for you. My name's Sarah."

"Her name's Sarah, too," Adelia squeezed her little sister's shoulders. The youngest Peterson girl nodded, blinking tear-filled eyes.

Lei stepped back. "Girls, I'm going to let Sarah here do her thing, and I'm going to call a friend of mine to meet us at the hospital. Is that okay?"

"Who is it?" Adelia asked.

"Her name is Dr. Wilson, and she's a psychologist. She used to be my therapist—yeah, I know, I don't seem that crazy." Lei crossed her eyes and stuck her tongue out, startling a snort of amusement out of Sarah. "Dr. Wilson helped me a lot when I needed it, and I think she might help you too."

"Okay," Adelia said. "But don't leave us alone here."

"No way. Not for a minute," Lei said.

She slipped through the doorway and thumbed to Dr. Caprice Wilson's number in her phone's favorites.

The petite blonde psychologist had been a friend and more to her and Stevens over the years, and she couldn't think of anyone better to do a trauma debrief with these girls. "Hey, Dr. Wilson. Any chance you're able to hop a flight to Maui? Like, now?"

CHAPTER TWENTY-THREE

THE HOSPITAL HAD DONE as Lei asked: when she drove up to the emergency room area in her silver Tacoma with the Peterson girls in the extended cab and front seat, a female doctor and nurse met them in the covered turnaround.

"You got this," Lei encouraged the girls. "Everyone here cares about you. I'll be with you every step of the way."

Adelia got out first, unwinding long coltish legs as she stepped out of the front seat. She opened the rear door and coaxed Joanie and Sarah. "Come on, you guys. We've already been through the worst." The other two, clinging to each other, got out to follow Adelia after the nurse, with Lei bringing up their rear.

The three teens were put into a private exam room and checked over, one after the other, by Dr. Kelly Asuki, a petite woman with a gentle, professional manner.

Finally, it was time for Joanie to disrobe for the rape collection kit and Lei to photograph her injuries for the case. Joanie still had not spoken a word the entire time, but Adelia interpreted for her. "Joanie understands you need to examine her and collect DNA and samples for the case, but she wants us together," Adelia said. "I know that's not the usual way you do it, but she won't take off her clothes unless we're here too."

"I'm not sure you should be exposed to this, especially your little sister Sarah," Dr. Asuki said.

"We were there. We were forced to watch it happen," Adelia said harshly. "We've been plenty exposed." Sarah hunched up and covered her face as Joanie stared straight ahead, blank-faced.

"All right. I understand you wanting to be together," Dr. Asuki said. "You all can stay."

Joanie stood up and stripped off her clothing with trembling hands. Once naked, she stood silent against the white wall, the medical exam light throwing her youthful, tanned body into high relief as she held one hand over her pubic area, the other over her breasts.

Bruises dappled Joanie's face, ribs, arms and legs—*she'd put up a struggle*. Bite marks, scrape marks, and deep purple bruising told the story of her defeat. Lei swallowed down bile as she photographed the girl, zooming in on the cruel damage done by a rapist.

These wounds would heal—but the marks on Joanie's soul, and on her sisters, traumatized by watching their sister's and mother's rape, would take much longer.

Still, the girls were alive, and that was better than the alternative. They all had to remember that.

"Please put your hands at your sides. I need to document everything. I'm sorry it's so invasive," Lei said.

Joanie hung her head and dropped her hands. The camera flashed and clicked.

"You gave him hell, Joanie," Adelia said. "You made him work for it. I'm fuckin' proud of you."

Lei glanced over at Joanie's younger sister. Adelia's lips had drawn back from her teeth in a snarl—Lei doubted the girl even knew she wore such a fierce expression. "Joanie bit his neck so hard she drew blood. It was awesome."

"I'm going to record us talking, okay?" Lei held up her phone. "Hopefully that way, we don't have to keep asking you the same questions."

"That's fine," Adelia agreed for all of them.

Next came the physical exam and swabbing of private areas. Dr. Asuki was as gentle as possible.

Right after her call to Dr. Wilson, Lei had been able to put a call in to Elizabeth Black, her favorite social worker, someone she'd worked with on several cases. She trusted Elizabeth to find a crisis shelter where the girls could go to be supported and cared for as well as possible until their mother or another relative was available to take them.

At last the ordeal was over. The nurse had brought a change of clothing for each girl. "These are donated to the hospital and we keep them on hand for anyone who might need them." A huge shirt declaring, *"Life's a Beach"* swallowed Joanie, and she shimmied into fresh undies and yoga pants. The other girls dressed similarly in oversized cast-offs.

"Can we stay in this room to do the interview?" Lei asked Dr. Asuki. "I'd like to minimize transitions for the girls. I've called a social worker from Child Services who's on her way."

Dr. Asuki nodded. "Keep the room as long as you like. The nurse here will bring you some food and drink." The doctor left.

"I didn't say we'd go with a social worker," Adelia flared at Lei. "We're staying right here and waiting for Mom."

Lei shrugged. "For sure, that's the ideal scenario. Hopefully, she's able to take charge of you. This is just in case she has to stay in the hospital." A light touch worked best with belligerent teenagers.

While the nurse told the girls about the hospital's cafeteria lunch offerings and took their orders, Lei texted Dr. Wilson. The psychologist had dropped what she was doing on the Big Island and was en route; she hoped to meet them in another hour.

What a relief. Now the girls would have some emotional first aid to accompany the physical. Dr. Wilson was a talented psychologist who never seemed to run out of patience or innovative ways to help; she'd worked with Lei herself as a young patrol officer in need of counseling. Sometimes Lei forgot how long she'd known the psychologist, and how far she'd come from the damaged young woman she'd been.

The room cleared but for the four of them. There wasn't much seating: a doctor's rolling stool that Lei perched on, the padded exam table with its roll of crinkling white paper, and a couple of stacked plastic chairs.

"Is everyone comfortable, girls? We have one more thing to get through—your official statement of what happened."

Adelia and Sarah got up on the exam table to cuddle with Joanie. The air conditioning was overly chilly, so Lei opened cabinet doors under the table to uncover a stack of blue cotton drape cloths. "Here's another layer to wrap up in."

The girls settled close together on the padded table, wrapped up as best they could. Lei rolled near to them on her stool and turned on the record feature on her phone. "Let's begin. When did you first know that the *Sea Cloud* was being attacked?"

CAPTAIN OMURA and SWAT were finishing up at the crime scene: taking statements, photographs, and otherwise dealing with the aftermath of the crisis, as Stevens and Mahoe followed the kidnappers and Mrs. Peterson to the hospital.

The short trip through Kahului was just long enough for Stevens to feel bone-weariness set in, and the onset of one of his headaches to take up throbbing residence at the back of his skull. "You seem wiped out, LT," Mahoe commented. "You should have let me drive."

"I'm fine."

Mahoe snorted. He dug around in the back seat, producing a

bottle of water. He opened the glove box and shook two extra strength Tylenol into his hand. "Take these. And drink all of the water."

"Yes, mother." One hand on the steering wheel, Stevens tossed the painkillers into his mouth and washed them down with the water, chugging the bottle. He tossed the empty into the back seat. "Happy now?"

"I'd be happy if you were, LT. It was a righteous shoot. You ended the standoff." Mahoe folded his muscular arms. "Don't know why *you're* bummed. You were a hero today. I was just your rookie sidekick, too freaked out to do anything."

Stevens slanted his partner a glance. "You don't know the shit I'm in for those supposedly heroic actions. I'm in trouble at home, and with Omura."

Mahoe shrugged. "It'll be fine. It's me who has to live with knowing I froze when the pressure was on."

"Hey. Don't be hard on yourself." Stevens plucked his shirt, stiffening with blood, away from his chest. "I got used to combat when I joined the Marines right out of high school and we saw action overseas. You haven't had much exposure to intense situations like that, because they don't come up often on Maui—and thank God for that."

"Still."

"You did everything you were supposed to do, Brandon. You watch and see—I'll get written up for saving that woman and taking that shot. And if the kidnapper dies, I'll be put on leave pending the investigation. I'm sure the whole thing won't be fun."

"I know what I know about how things went down. I had a clear shot at the kidnapper, too, but I didn't take it. Maybe I'm not cut out for this job." Mahoe stared out the window, his jaw tight and arms tighter.

"That's bullshit. You're making my headache worse." Stevens had no patience left to deal with his partner's existential crisis. He pulled into the hospital parking lot. "The Captain said you need to go in and take statements by yourself."

Mahoe turned to him with wide eyes.

"Yeah, man, you heard me right. I was involved in a shooting and I'm officially off the case, so I'm dropping you off alone to handle this, and I know you'll do a good job. In fact, I'm so sure of it that I'm going find a clean shirt, and then I'm taking a little nap." Stevens radioed the EMTs, asking about the kidnapper's status. Stevens turned to Mahoe. "Good. The kidnapper's still alive. Maybe you can get an ID and his statement. Text me when you're ready for pickup."

Moments later Stevens pulled away. He glanced in his rearview mirror, and smiled at the sight of his young partner heading into the hospital with a spring in his step. *Sometimes, you just needed to get out of the way and let the young people step up.* Handling the interviews would bolster Mahoe's confidence, and Stevens would be there for backup.

CHAPTER TWENTY-FOUR

NONE of the Peterson girls said anything in response to Lei's question about what had happened aboard the *Sea Cloud*. They sat cuddled together on top of the exam table, wound in each other's arms. The sharp scent of fear, trauma, and unwashed bodies filled the room.

Lei sat on the doctor's rolling stool, holding her little notebook with the stub of pencil tied to it, waiting patiently. Her gaze moved from one girl's face to the next. "Take your time. But you need to tell me what happened, or I'll have to turn you over to another cop for the interview. Keeping quiet about what happened isn't one of your choices."

Adelia straightened up between her sisters, still in spokeswoman role. "We had just got done with dinner and were doing the dishes in the galley. The three of us were in there, horsing around, listening to music. Even though we had Ms. Gutierrez there to do the cooking and cleaning, Mom and Dad always made us do chores. They didn't want us to get spoiled or stuck-up."

"Chores are stupid," Sarah piped up for the first time. "I don't need chores to remind me how it is to be poor. I'm the youngest, but I still remember before Dad's invention got us money."

Adelia snorted. "Are you kidding? You're the spoiledest of all of us."

Sarah elbowed her, and Adelia met Lei's eye. "Yeah, we were playing around. Only Joanie was snapping us with a wet dish towel, and it *hurt*." She elbowed Joanie.

Joanie's curtain of bedraggled blonde hair still hid her face. She didn't respond.

Adelia went on. "Anyway. The boat was under sail, so you couldn't hear anything but the sound of the water on the hull, but then suddenly we heard this super loud engine noise, like really roaring, and it was outside the hull. And then we heard Captain Kaihale yelling on the intercom, "Pirates! We're being boarded! Take cover inside your cabins and lock the doors!" I totally thought Captain was joking, that this was some kind of prank, like —part of the fun of the cruise." Her voice wobbled and her eyes filled. Her hand came up to cover her mouth. "It wasn't an April Fools' joke like we thought."

"Go on." Lei nodded encouragingly as Sarah snuggled close, clinging to her sister's arm. Joanie leaned on Adelia's other side.

Adelia cleared her throat. "So, we didn't take it seriously. Instead of doing what Captain Kaihale said, the three of us ran to the nearest porthole and peeked out. We couldn't see anything, so we ran up the stairs onto the top deck to see the pirates. I was thinking of how this was a great April Fools' and it would be like a modern *Pirates of the Caribbean*." She pleated the paper covering the exam table. She seemed to have run out of steam.

"Tell her," Sarah whispered. "Tell her what happened to Dad."

"Yeah, okay." Adelia looked down. The paper ripped between her fingers. "We went up to see the pirates, not thinking it was real or serious . . . and there were these guys in two Zodiacs that had come along on each side of the boat. They threw grappling hooks onto the stern." She sucked a trembling breath. "Dad screamed 'Get below!' the minute he saw us. He and Mom had been up on the front deck watching the sunset." Adelia met Lei's eyes.

"There's a front deck and a back deck. The pirates had come up really fast on the back deck. Mom and Dad tried to lift their grappling hooks off the railing, but they were big metal hooks and they were too heavy with the weight of the boats. I still thought it was all part of the cruise because the pirates wore costumes. But then, one of them climbed up onto the deck." Adelia spoke as if expelling the words by force. "Dad hit him with one of the oars from the rescue craft. The guy fell to one knee, but then he pulled out a gun and shot Dad—just shot him. *Bam!* Right in the chest."

"What did the costumes look like? Hats? Bandannas?" Lei prompted gently.

"No. They were wearing Hawaiian costumes."

Lei's scalp prickled. "What do you mean?"

"I was thinking they'd be like the Pirates of the Caribbean, you know—peg legs, eye patches—but they weren't. They were like— old time Hawaiian warriors. They wore these gourd helmets on their heads, and tapa cloth robes tied at the shoulder. That's another reason I thought it was fake, until the guy pulled a gun—because they were in costume."

"Are you sure? Sometimes the mind plays tricks when . . ."

"She's telling the truth!" Sarah yelled fiercely. "The guys were dressed up like ancient Hawaiian warriors! The only modern things they had were real guns and real knives!" She burst into tears. The other two girls folded her in, moving her into the middle, sandwiching her between them.

Lei's free hand crept into her pocket. She rubbed the bone hook as she took a couple of steadying breaths. *This was bad.* This was not going to be well-received by anyone—*pirates dressed as Hawaiian warriors?* The Hawaiian community would be outraged and defensive. What possible reason could these killers have had for such a ploy? "I believe you. Just keep going. Tell me what happened next."

"I grabbed Sarah and ran for the steps. Joanie ran to help Mom and Dad." Adelia stopped again, covering her face with a hand.

"They did have other modern things. They wore bike shorts under their robes, and rubber sandals with Velcro—you know the kind that you wear for wet-dry hiking? I remember thinking how funny that was."

"And then?"

"Sarah and I ran below and went into Mom and Dad's state-room, which was the closest. We locked the door and hid under the bed." Adelia said. "At first, all we heard from above was a bunch of yelling and thumping around. Sarah and I were wedged together under there, and it was really tight. Then I heard Mom screaming, so I covered Sarah's ears. And then we heard someone pounding on the door. "Open up, girls, it's Captain Kaihale!" So I crawled out and let the Captain in . . . But he wasn't alone. That guy, that guy that had shot Dad, he had Captain Kaihale by the hair with a knife to his throat." Abruptly, Adelia covered her mouth with a hand. "I'm going to be sick."

Lei scrambled for the waste can. Adelia heaved into it as Sarah cried and Joanie silently rubbed her back. "Okay now?" Lei asked.

"Yeah."

Lei took the can outside. The lunch tray had been left on a chair outside the door, and Lei carried it in, setting it on the counter as Adelia went to the sink and rinsed her mouth thoroughly. Lei filled a paper cup with water and handed it to her. "Glad I didn't eat lunch yet," Adelia said.

"Maybe you should finish telling the story before eating," Lei agreed.

"Yeah. I just want to get it over with." Adelia hopped back onto the exam table and into her sisters' arms. "Anyway, Captain Kaihale tried to pull away—he lunged forward, yelling, 'Run!' and he fell across the bed when one of them zapped him with a Taser on the back of the neck. He jerked around on the bed and then went limp. We tried to get around the guy who zapped him, but two more men were behind him in the doorway, and they grabbed us. Then the guy who shot Dad walked in, and he grabbed Captain

Kaihale by the hair and slashed his neck right in front of us."
Adelia shivered.

"It was super, super gross and sad," Sarah said. "Poor Captain.
He was so nice and fun." Tears dripped off her chin.

"I'm so sorry you had to see and experience that. Captain
Kaihale was a good friend of mine, so it's extra hard for me to hear
this, too. We will always miss him," Lei said. They all sat quietly
for a moment.

Adelia rallied. "After that, they tied our hands behind our
backs with those plastic zip ties and forced us to go up on deck.
We searched around but we didn't see Dad. Sarah started
screaming, "Dad, Dad! Where are you Dad?" The mean guy, the
main guy who shot Dad and killed Captain—he slapped her face.
Told her to shut up, that Dad was feeding the sharks, and if she
wasn't quiet, she was going to join him. Mom and Joanie were
sitting on the deck, tied up with Ms. Gutierrez." Adelia trembled
but forced herself to go on. "I was so worried that they'd throw
us overboard with our hands tied, or we'd fall in accidentally,
because the ocean was really rough. The Zodiacs were swinging
around and banging into the deck of the *Sea Cloud*. And it was
super scary when they basically threw us into the Zodiacs and
left us there while they stole stuff and made a hole in the ship's
hull."

Lei could picture the terrifying scene. "Where did they take
you when you left the *Sea Cloud*? Where's their hideout?"

Adelia shook her head. "I don't know. One of the guys came
back onto the Zodiac and tied strips of sheets over our eyes. Sarah
was crying so loud that he gagged her. He told us he'd gag all of us
if he needed to, so no making noise. Mom was lying between me
and Joanie; she whispered to us that we didn't want to be gagged
or hurt any more, so try to cooperate and wait to be rescued. She
said it was a good sign that they blindfolded us because it meant
they weren't going to kill us. They didn't want us to see their faces
or where they were taking us, and that meant they planned to keep

us alive." She coughed, and Lei handed her another paper cup of water.

Adelia drank it and went on. "I was so glad that she said that, because I was starting to lose it. I couldn't stop seeing the blood shooting out of Captain Kaihale's throat. I didn't know blood could do that. Like, it was shooting out every time his heart beat."

"So gross and sad," Sarah said. "I wanted to put my hands over the cut in his neck, but I knew it wouldn't help."

"If it's any comfort, that form of death is very quick. Captain Kaihale didn't suffer for long," Lei said.

"Neither did Dad," Adelia said flatly. "I think he died the minute that guy shot him."

A long pause as they all sat with that. Finally Lei said, "Would you girls like to take a break?"

"No," Sarah and Adelia said at the same time. Joanie had hardly moved from her slumped position.

"Go on, then."

"The Zodiacs were slamming through the wind and waves for a long time. It was kind of hard to tell how long with our blindfolds on, but I started counting to keep myself calm and keep track. And then we came into somewhere quieter, a sheltered bay or something. Then we entered an enclosed space. I thought it must be a cave, because I could hear water slapping on the walls and the Zodiacs slowed way down. Maybe it was a big boathouse. I don't know."

"About how long was it from when you left the wreck to when you got to the cave or whatever it was?" Lei's mind was churning —depending on where the attack had actually occurred, the pirate hideout had to be either on Lana`i or Moloka`i. She wasn't aware of any ocean caves on either island.

"I think it was more than an hour. They had to put gas in the Zodiacs. I know it's hard to believe, but I got kind of sleepy and dozed off."

"Me, too," Sarah said.

"It's not hard to believe. After our bodies are flooded with adrenaline, they crash. You can feel super tired even if you're still in danger, as long as the danger isn't imminent." Lei had experienced that herself. "What happened next?"

"They tied up the Zodiacs. There was some kind of rocky bank, they got us out onto it, but it was slippery and hard to get up on with our blindfolds on and our hands tied. Mom fell and got hurt; she cried out that she had wrenched her ankle. But they didn't care. They hauled us up the rocks, and then inside some kind of metal room. Mom said it was probably a shipping container. They just threw us in and left us there at first."

Sarah picked up the thread of the story. "We helped each other take off our blindfolds, but it was pitch-dark inside. We just huddled together and tried to rest. Finally, the main guy came back, and he acted nice this time. They had a battery lamp for light, and he had taken off the gourd war helmet and wore a bandanna tied over his face. He untied us and had one of the other guys check out Mom's ankle. She had sprained it and it was all puffy, but she was brave."

Adelia nodded. "They gave us a bucket to go to the bathroom in, and a gallon jug of water, and they left us there and locked us in. We had some blankets, so we just huddled together and slept." She covered her face with her hands. "But in the morning, the main guy and two of his sidekicks came back. And then, they raped Mom, Joanie and Ms. Gutierrez right in front of me and Sarah. Told us to watch and learn, because we'd be next when we got where we were going."

"This main guy. What did he look like?"

"He was darker than the usual Hawaiian, but he had Hawaiian tattoos. He also had an accent," Adelia said. "About six foot tall. Muscles. Not too old, but not young either."

Lei made notes as her scalp prickled again. "What made you think he wasn't actually Hawaiian?"

"The accent. The color of his skin. Some of the other guys

were, though." Adelia stared down at her feet. "It's hard to talk about it."

Tears slipped down Sarah's cheeks and she touched Lei's arm. "I want to see Mom. Is she okay?"

"She's going to be," Lei said. "We'll take a break now. I have enough for the moment." She turned off the recorder and fetched the lunch tray, setting it down in front of them on the exam table. "If you feel up to it, eat."

Adelia and Sarah nodded, and lifted the metal lids off of the food as Joanie watched. Delicious smells swirled up. Adelia handed Joanie a plate and silverware. All three girls dug in, the needs of their bodies, temporarily at least, overcoming mental and emotional trauma.

The girls weren't the only ones who needed a break.

Lei's knees were wobbly as she headed for the door. "I'm going to talk to the nurse, see if I can get word about your mom and how she's doing. Hopefully you can be together soon."

CHAPTER TWENTY-FIVE

AN HOUR OR SO LATER, Lei stood in the doorway of Emma Peterson's room as the three girls ran in to see their mother. Sarah was the only one to fling herself on Mrs. Peterson, embracing her mother through the bedding and bandages that swathed her. The other two grabbed chairs and pulled them close, one on either side —but all four of them were crying, noisy sobs that made Lei glad that the patient bed beside Mrs. Peterson was currently empty.

The same nurse who'd helped with the girls' exams touched Lei's shoulder. "I met with Mrs. Peterson's medical team and got briefed so I can tell you what's going on with her. She has to stay overnight—she has a couple of cracked ribs, probably from beatings, and a sprained ankle. That gunshot wound, while in the arm, was pretty close to a major vein—so the doc wants her kept overnight for rest and observation."

"Okay. That means I have to have the girls go to a crisis foster home tonight. Is Mrs. Peterson able to be interviewed?"

"Yes. She already gave a statement to Detective Brandon Mahoe when she first arrived."

"Good. I don't have to retraumatize everyone with more questions right now," Lei said. "Has a next of kin or other emergency contact been notified?"

"Yes. I don't know who that was, but the team assured me measures were being taken for when she's discharged."

"Sounds like things are well in hand." Lei met the nurse's eyes. "Tell Dr. Asuki that her gentle approach minimized the trauma for the girls, and that made it easier for them to tell me about their experiences, which will assist with the case. You were a big help, too."

"Just doing our jobs," the young woman said, but she ducked her head and her eyes brightened. "I'll pass it on to Dr. Asuki." She walked off on squeaky ergonomic shoes.

Lei took another minute to text Elizabeth Black to meet them at Mrs. Peterson's room. The social worker replied that she had the crisis home in place and was just pulling up to the hospital. *Perfect.* The girls could go with her, shower, rest and relax. Something would be in place for the four of them by the time Mrs. Peterson was discharged—Lei would make sure of it.

She approached the bed. "Mrs. Peterson. Hi. I'm Sergeant Lei Texeira with the Maui Police Department. How are you feeling?"

Emma Peterson smiled. Her good arm was around Joanie, Sarah embraced her waist, and Adelia had snuggled up against her bandaged arm and was brushing her mother's hair. "I'm much, much better now that my girls are with me."

"I can see that. They are incredibly brave, strong, resilient young women." She pulled up a third plastic chair and scooted close. "I hear you gave your statement to Detective Mahoe. That's great; we don't have to go through that again right now. I just heard they are keeping you overnight, so I've arranged for a safe, supportive place for the girls to stay at temporarily."

"No!" Sarah wailed, snuggling her face into her mother's abdomen. "I want to stay with Mom. I can sleep on the floor."

"Us too," Adelia said. Joanie said nothing, but pressed in closer. "We all want to stay with Mom."

"Of course you want to be with your mom." A new voice from the door. "What a beautiful sight."

Lei glanced up, relieved to see Elizabeth. The Native American social worker wore jeans, boots, and a snap front denim cowboy shirt with a squash blossom turquoise necklace visible in the neck of her shirt. Her long black hair, ribboned with white, hung in braids over her shoulders, and her strong-featured face was wreathed in a big smile. "Hello, ladies. I'm Elizabeth, and I'm so glad to meet you. What amazing heroines you are."

Lei moved her chair back and sighed with relief as Elizabeth worked her magic.

The social worker approached each of them, individually shaking their hands and getting their names, beginning with Emma Peterson. Her charisma and warmth were like a soothing perfume, relaxing the traumatized women into trust.

"Say goodbye to Sergeant Texeira. She's in charge of your case, so I'm sure you can call her anytime with whatever's on your mind," Elizabeth said. "But I bet she has a lot to do right now to work on catching the evil men that started this whole thing."

"Elizabeth's right, I do. In fact, I'm supposed to be at a team meeting right now," Lei said, ostentatiously glancing at her phone. "Let me leave my number with you, Emma." She wrote it on the pad by the hospital phone. "Call me anytime, and I'll pick up, no matter what."

She didn't make that promise lightly. "Thanks, Lei," Adelia said.

"Yes, thank you," Emma Peterson said. "For all you've done. I saw you out there—standing in the open, talking to the kidnapper who had me by the hair. You saved my life. I know he only shot me in the arm because of you."

Lei left with her heart a little lighter than it had been when she arrived.

CHAPTER TWENTY-SIX

STEVENS WOKE DISORIENTED to the beeping of his phone. Stretched out in the Bronco's driver's seat parked in the shade of one of the hospital's Plumeria trees, Stevens picked up the call. "Yeah?"

"Very professional, Lieutenant Stevens." Omura's voice was frosty. "I'm assured by your partner that you are mere moments from picking him up. Do that, please. We need to meet at the station. The press has got hold of the case, and we need to get out in front of it."

"On it, sir." Stevens ran a hand into his hair, trying to reorder it. *At least he was wearing a clean shirt, now.* He'd been able to call a friend to bring him one out in the parking lot.

"Fifteen minutes, in the conference room. The head of SWAT will be there to lead the discussion on how events went down. Oh, and the kidnapper you shot is dead. Be prepared to surrender your badge until the investigation is complete." Omura ended the call with a click that echoed in his aching head.

He'd been out way too long. Sure enough, Mahoe had been texting him for pickup for the last half hour.

"Shit!" Stevens groaned aloud. "How did I oversleep so bad?" Maybe he really was losing it.

On my way. Meet me in front, he texted his partner, and fired up the Bronco.

STEVENS AND MAHOE walked into the team meeting in Kahului Station's conference room only five minutes late, which was how long they'd needed for Stevens to pick Mahoe up and get a brief update on the interviews his partner had conducted with Gutierrez and Mrs. Peterson in the hospital; the remaining kidnapper was being treated, so was unable to be interviewed right away.

The station's battered Formica table was headed by an immaculately groomed Omura. To her right sat Lei, and to her left, SWAT captain Hiro, his black hair still sweat-slicked to his head in the shape of his helmet, though he'd stripped off his body armor. Also seated were Coast Guardsman Aina Thomas and Becca Nunez from the crime lab.

Omura had pulled down a projection screen on the wall behind her. The *Maui Now News* latest tidbit, narrated by Lei's old nemesis reporter, Wendy Watanabe, was playing on silent in the background: an action shot of the SWAT team rappelling down onto the roof of the container, and then a jerky clip of the rest of the takedown, including Stevens's fatal shooting of the kidnapper.

Stevens jerked involuntarily at the sight of the man clutching his throat and falling on top of the hapless Mrs. Peterson. "Who the hell was filming that?"

Omura's short red nails continued to tap on her laptop's keyboard as if he hadn't spoken. Captain Hiro from SWAT finally replied. "We think it was one of the workers in the storage area. The angle is high up from the corner, where there's a utility pole. You asked the uniforms who got the whole confrontation started to clear the area—but I guess we know how well that went."

"It's unfortunate that the video got out, but it's too late to do anything about that. Though gruesome, it ultimately shows that we freed the hostages. The video doesn't end until the girls get out of the container and go with Lei to her truck. Unfortunately, the clip that keeps playing is the one containing the fatal shooting." Omura still didn't look up.

Stevens took a seat beside his wife, but she, too, avoided eye contact.

Omura went on. "They don't have much information, just that some women were being held hostage in the shipping container area, and police action was required to rescue them." She paused a moment, letting that sink in. "I've called for a press conference as soon as we finish this meeting, to brief the public enough to mitigate some of the outrage being expressed in social media at what appears to be overly aggressive police action." Omura finally met each team member's eyes. "Let's check in and get on the same page. I'll plan some talking points with what we come up with."

"I'll go first," Hiro said. "As you know, Captain, my team and I arrived when the situation had already gone sideways. We didn't have time to coordinate, or plan our approach, before the lieutenant here took off and intercepted a call from the kidnappers. Things escalated from there as I worked trying to get our team into position for a takedown."

"I took over the phone from Stevens when the kidnapper appeared to be escalating." Lei lifted her chin defensively —*Stevens knew that stubborn look.* "Yes, it's too bad that we didn't have time to form a clear plan and establish communication with each other. But considering that, we were able to bring the standoff to an acceptable conclusion."

"How nice that you think so, Sergeant, but I didn't ask for your opinion. Just the facts," Omura said.

"Let me rephrase, then. I overheard Stevens on the speakerphone and could tell it wasn't going well. In my estimation, the kidnapper was winding up to shoot his next victim. I decided to buy some time by taking over the communication in my role as

FBI liaison. I hoped to scare the kidnapper into slowing down, thus giving SWAT more time to move into position."

"And did you achieve that, in your 'estimation'?" Omura's brows rose in skeptical arches.

"I'm not sure that I did. I hope I did. In any case, instead of killing Peterson, the kidnapper shot her in the arm."

Hiro spoke next. "We were able to get names from the perp who remains alive. His name is Keone Nisake, and he claims he and his partner, Greg Steele, who Stevens shot, were not involved with the pirates. Their job was to move and ship the women. He only told me a little in the first moments of the takedown—just his name and that they weren't involved with 'the pirates' who attacked the ship."

Omura cocked a finger at Lei. "Follow up with backgrounds and everything you can find on these guys. I want to know if they are connected with the rumors of human trafficking out of Kahului Harbor, or if this is an operation associated with the pirates. Interview Nisake ASAP."

"Of course, Captain." Lei was scribbling notes in her spiral notebook, and Stevens's heart gave a little thump at the sight of her bent curly head. *Would she always affect him this way?* He sure as hell hoped so, even if it meant she kept winning their fights.

Mahoe broke in. "I interviewed Mrs. Peterson in the hospital. She claims she didn't really faint after she was shot. Instead, she took the opportunity to escape the kidnapper's grip on her hair by dropping to the ground, while forcing the door open further to make way for SWAT. She had noticed that Priscilla Gutierrez's body was missing and she spotted the SWAT team approaching alongside the container. She concluded that the standoff was going to be ending in minutes, so she tried to create a diversion while reducing herself as a target."

"That did work," Stevens said. He'd had time to think about his wife's actions and to see their utility. "Lei kept the kidnapper on the phone, also potentially reducing harm to Mrs. Peterson. I was sure he was going to kill her when I was talking to him. He clearly believed he had already killed Gutierrez. In my opinion, the escalation to FBI intervention represented by Lei made him reconsider immediate deadly force. Mrs. Peterson's quick action of falling to the ground probably saved her life." His throat had gone hoarse, so he grabbed one of the glasses set in the middle of the table with a carafe of water. He filled a glass, drank, then continued. "Mahoe and I were observing and covering the container's entrance from our position in the trees. After Mrs. Peterson dropped, the kidnapper identified as Greg Steele stepped over her and tried to see around the door to check on the helicopter. I had an opportunity for a shot, and I took it, figuring that would give SWAT a chance to overwhelm Nisake, still inside the container with the hostages."

Hiro nodded. "The distraction provided by Sergeant Texeira allowed SWAT to get into position. When the kidnapper was shot, we knew it was our chance. No peaceful resolution was going to come from this particular situation. Steele was too aggressive."

Omura tapped her nails together like tiny castanets. "Be that as it may, Captain Hiro. Were you able to verify the kidnappers' supposed identities?"

"They had no ID on them, so currently Nisake's word is all we have. He has a substantial gunshot wound to his shoulder, and has been in surgery all day."

Omura glanced around the table. "Lieutenant Stevens will have to be recused from the case until the investigation into his shooting of Steele is completed. I need some more detectives on this now that we're down both Stevens and Pono Kaihale. I put out a call to Gerry Bunuelos and Abe Torufu, but they're out on one of their cases now. Captain Hiro, you can go. Thanks for your role in the takedown."

Hiro glanced at his watch. "Thanks, Captain, I do need to debrief my men and make sure the crime scene area is secure and our gear is dealt with."

Everyone said goodbye. When he'd exited, Omura turned to Lei. "Texeira, you'll have to bring Abe and Bunuelos up to speed when they get in. Report on your interview with the girls."

Lei shut her eyes, opened them again. She was pale, and that smudge of dirt that had so disarmed Stevens was still on her cheek. "They're doing okay, all things considered. I was able to see them through medical examinations, Joanie's rape kit procedure, and a preliminary statement." She sketched out what Adelia Peterson, with support from her sister Sarah and Joanie as a silent witness, had reported. "I left them with their mother, Elizabeth Black, and Dr. Wilson doing a family debrief."

"This 'main guy' that Adelia described—was he the same guy I shot?" Stevens asked. "Because that guy sounds as aggressive as Greg Steele."

"No. She said they spent the first couple of nights in a metal container in an unknown location that she described as a sea cave or maybe a large boathouse, but they were blindfolded through the transition. Joanie, Mrs. Peterson, and Mrs. Gutierrez were raped by the 'main guy and two sidekicks,' who kept their faces covered whenever they interacted with the women. Adelia said, and Sarah confirmed, that they'd never seen the two kidnappers we shot before."

Mahoe nodded. "Mrs. Peterson confirmed the men who moved them were not the same as the pirates, even though all kept masks on. She said their builds and voices were different."

Stevens rubbed the scruff of unshaven beard on his chin, making a rasping sound. "Seems like there could be two crews operating: the pirates, and the human traffickers. If the pirates raped the older women and said what they did to the younger ones, they were likely going to be sold overseas as sex slaves. Perhaps the younger girls were spared because virginity made them more valuable."

Omura cocked a brow. "That's obvious, Lieutenant!" *She was still pissed at him.* She turned to the Coast Guard investigator. "What do you know about the attack on the *Golden Fleece*?"

Aina Thomas, who until then had been quietly working on his tablet, glanced up. "As you know, Captain, we retrieved a body with a similar MO to the killing of Captain Kaihale—but as Sergeant Texeira put forth, we don't think the *Fleece* was actually sunk off of Kaunakakai's harbor as they set us up to believe by dumping the body there. The Coast Guard has mounted an all vessels, all surrounding areas search for wherever the pirates are hiding out. They have some kind of place in or around Maui County waters where they are hiding the Zodiacs as well as the women and goods from their raids. While the team was reviewing, I was sending all the information we've gathered to Commander Decker, my superior." He set the tablet down. "We now know we're searching for two high-velocity, good-sized Zodiacs that they use to approach their targets and overwhelm them. We just put out a warning to boaters, a 'Be On the Lookout' for that type of craft approaching. Hopefully someone will spot them and call it in." He gazed around the table. "We have all available craft on their way from O'ahu to search for the perps' base in a sea cave or a large boathouse. We will check every harbor and inch of coastline until we find it."

"Excellent. I hope you do, sooner rather than later," Omura said. "Nunez, do you have anything to report?"

"Just confirmation that the blood sample retrieved from the carpet in the *Sea Cloud*'s stateroom matches that of Chaz Kaihale," Nunez said. "And an ID on the second male we retrieved with a cut throat—Perry Castanela, the captain of the *Fleece*. In my professional opinion, the perp who killed both captains, from the angle and depth of the cuts, was likely the same doer."

"We need to get these pirates before they strike again," Omura said, shaking her head. "Dismissed."

CHAPTER TWENTY-SEVEN

Lᴇɪ ᴍᴇᴛ Stevens in the shower at their house forty-five minutes after the meeting. The walk-in tiled shower room was one of Lei's favorite things about their place.

She was relieved to be home, even if it was just for a break. She felt sticky, and filthy, but that was nothing compared to the brownish stain on Stevens's chest—he'd been wearing a clean shirt at the meeting, but Gutierrez's blood had soaked through and dried on his skin.

Blood was like that—it always wanted to stick.

Thank God he'd rescued that poor woman. Lei wetted herself under the extra-large, rain-style showerhead as Stevens soaped up.

"Are you still mad at me?" Stevens asked.

"Not after what you said in the meeting. Here, let me get your back." She squirted gel into a loofah. He turned and braced his arms on the wall. She stroked the rough organic sponge over his long back and tense glutes, enjoying the deep sigh of pleasure he gave. "How about you? Still mad?"

"No. My manhood was bruised, but as you can see, it's made a recovery." He turned to face her, grinning wickedly. "My turn." He took the loofah from her hand

Lei smiled and shut her eyes, enjoying the slippery-rough feeling of the soapy scrubber moving over her skin, around her curves. "My. Aren't you thorough in making sure I'm clean."

He dropped the loofah, drew her close, and slid his hands up and down her slick body. "I'm one of the best there is at getting into every nook and cranny."

She laughed, smacked him. "Oh, that's just terrible."

"But you love it."

"I definitely do. Thank God the Captain gave me time to go home and rest. I think we can sneak in an extra half hour alone. But I absolutely need a real nap before I go back into town to meet with Gerry and Abe about the case."

"I can make a half hour work," he replied. "Get to the bedroom, woman."

CHAPTER TWENTY-EIGHT

ROSIE WHACKED Stevens with a stuffed animal. "Hey, Baby Girl. Show your dad a little mercy."

Rosie giggled and hit him again, then crawled away across the king-size bed, trying to get him to chase her.

After leaving Lei napping peacefully in their office at the back of the house, the only adult sanctuary with a functioning lock on the door where they could always be sure of privacy, Stevens had gone and fetched Rosie from Ellen and Wayne's. Stevens had given his daughter her bottle, and they'd both fallen asleep on the big bed that took up most of the master bedroom.

He glanced at the clock—hours had passed. Kiet would be home from school on the bus soon. Lei must be in Kahului already, bringing Gerry and Abe, her new partners on the case, up to speed.

Rosie sat back on her padded bottom and slapped her plump thighs. "Dada!" She was getting impatient. "Chase!" It was her favorite game.

"Rowr," Stevens growled, rising up slowly, pawing the bedclothes as he rose to all fours. "I'm a big hungry lion, and what do I see? A tasty, yummy little girl."

Rosie shrieked with delighted mock terror. She turned to slide off the mattress, toddling full speed out of the bedroom.

Stevens roared theatrically, and groaned a little too, as he pursued his daughter down the hall. His muscles were stiff from the exertion of earlier in the day, and he was still fighting a headache. Chasing Rosie down the hallway, he was guiltily relieved he didn't have to go back to work until he was cleared for duty again. *Was he burning out?*

Best to just enjoy this moment.

His daughter would only be a baby for a little while. He'd been through enough to know that these days would never come again, and each one should be savored.

Conan, familiar with this game, got up from his dog bed in the living room and stood, blocking the front door and adding excited barks to Rosie's high-pitched giggles. Stevens chased the tot around the couch, finally catching her by a leg, then swinging her up into his arms to blow a kiss on her round little belly as she wriggled and squealed. "Phew, Baby Girl, I think someone needs a diaper change."

"No!" Rosie yelled authoritatively. "No diaper!" *No* was her new favorite word.

"You're supposed to be two years old before you start saying 'no' all the time," Stevens said, tucking her, arms and legs kicking, under his arm. "You can have a gummy bear if you lie still and let me change you."

"Bear!" Rosie yelled. "No diaper!"

"That's not how it works, babe. Good girl diaper change, THEN gummy bear."

The next fifteen minutes were a blur of shrieks, wiggles, and wrestling, until finally the fresh diaper was on. Rosie wailed and cried, throwing a tantrum, and he put her in her crib with a frozen washcloth to chew on, and shut the door on her angry shrieks.

"And just that fast, the sweet goes sour," Stevens told Conan. The dog gazed at him with a worried wrinkle on his broad forehead. "I think we need a book on raising a strong-willed child. Kiet never threw a fit like that in his life. And for what, I ask you? Getting her diaper changed, like we've done ten times a day since she was born?"

Conan whined and lay down, his eyes darting from side to side, clearly stressed by the conflict.

"I feel ya, man." Stevens walked past the Rottie. The familiar urge for a drink, an urge he had beaten every day since he got back from that ill-fated trip to Honduras, tugged at his guts. He walked to the fridge, got out a non-alcoholic beer, popped the top, and sipped. "At least it tastes like the real thing."

His phone, plugged in on the sideboard, buzzed. Stevens picked it up, frowning at the sight of *Queens Hospital* in the display window. "Lieutenant Stevens here."

"Lieutenant, hello. This is Dr. Rappaport, Soga Matsumoto's surgeon."

"Yes, Doctor. Hello." Stevens's mind scrambled—*where were they on finding Soga's care facility?* Had Lei been working on something, or had this urgent bit of family business fallen through the cracks?

"Your wife's number went to voicemail, so I called yours," Dr. Rappaport said. "Soga is doing well, post-op, but we're running out of time here at the hospital. Has your family lined anything up for him? We are planning his discharge tomorrow."

Stevens's heart rate jumped—*this was a disaster!* Poor Soga. Not only had none of them been able to fly to Oʻahu and see him through his rehab, they hadn't finalized plans for his care. He and Lei had been caught up in the pirate case to the exclusion of everything else. "I'm sorry to tell you, Doctor, that though we've tried, we haven't been able to line anything up. There's a dearth of those kinds of facilities on Maui. Do you have a social worker or someone who can help us?"

"Arranging aftercare is not a part of our responsibilities, Lieutenant. Family is the first line of support for elders. Yes, we have a social worker, and she's been apprised of his situation. Soga's lucid, but mobility is an issue. He could fall and reinjure himself if left alone, and he'll have follow up appointments to get to."

"I understand that. What time is the discharge planned?"

"Let me get his chart." Dr. Rappaport rustled pages in the background.

Maybe being off the case was perfect timing after all. Stevens walked down the hall to the kids' room and opened the door. Rosie lay on her back in her crib, sucking on the frozen washcloth peacefully, watching her mobile. She sat up as soon as the door opened, and held up her arms. "Dada!"

"Good. No more tantrum," Stevens murmured, and scooped her up, the phone plastered to his ear. "You're learning to calm yourself down. Great job, Rosie." She offered him the mangled washcloth, pressing it against his lips for him to suck on too. "No thanks, sweetie."

"Soga Matsumoto will be discharged tomorrow at eleven a.m.," Dr. Rappaport said. "We'll call him a cab at the curb to take him home if no one is there to accompany him."

"Someone will be there," Stevens said. "Thanks, Doctor. We take our responsibilities seriously regarding Mr. Matsumoto. He's my wife's grandfather, and he has no one else. We know we need to come up with something. There are just a lot of demands on my wife and I."

"Preaching to the choir," Dr. Rappaport said, and hung up.

Stevens set Rosie on his hip and slid the phone into his pocket. "We need help, little girl. Time to call for reinforcements."

Rosie batted long, damp lashes at him, and rested her cheek on his shoulder. Stevens smiled and kissed her forehead. "Yeah, you're a handful all right. But you're my handful. And so is your great-grandfather, Soga."

STEVENS TURNED on the sprinklers after Kiet got home from school, and put both kids in their bathing suits. Kiet hauled his sister in a red wagon back and forth through the water as Conan chased them, while Stevens trimmed some of the overlong hibiscus bushes around Wayne and Ellen's cottage.

Wayne had returned from work an hour or so before and immediately gone in for a shower and a nap in front of the TV, his late afternoon ritual after cooking at his restaurant for two shifts. Eventually he emerged, coming out on the little porch, carrying two old-fashioned Cokes in bottles.

Wayne had a face with high cheekbones, seamed lines, and the same brown eyes Stevens recognized on his wife, only deep-set. Curling hair, now more salt than pepper, skimmed his shoulders, and he wore a faded Aerosmith tee and jeans with holes in the knees. Wayne Texeira looked a lot like Carlos Santana.

"Why aren't you at work?" his father-in-law asked, handing Stevens one of the frosty bottles.

Stevens took it, and drank. "Thanks for this." He turned to keep an eye on the kids as they played. "I'm on leave until they clear me from a fatal shooting on our latest case."

"Oh, that pirate thing? Nasty business. Saw it on the news. Don't like the way they edited that video to seem like the guy got shot for no reason." Wayne shook his head and seated himself on the top step of his porch. "I never believe what I see on the news."

"Well, thanks for that, but the basics shown in the video are true. I did shoot the guy." Stevens sat beside Wayne on the step. "It's actually a good thing I've got some time off. There's a situation I need to talk to you about."

CHAPTER TWENTY-NINE

LEI SETTLED herself in one of the hard plastic chairs beside Keone Nisake's hospital bed. The kidnapper's shoulder was heavily wrapped and a handcuff circled his good arm, holding him to the bed. He wasn't going anywhere—though his sweating face and darting eyes told her he wished he could.

"My name is Sergeant Leilani Texeira, and this is my partner, Detective Abe Torufu." Lei gestured to Torufu, looming in the doorway, cleaning his nails with a combat knife roughly the size of a machete. "We're here to do your official interview of the events of yesterday."

"I asked for a lawyer," Nisake said. "You can't talk to me without him here."

"Well, there you're mistaken." Lei smiled. She'd been told her smile was not always friendly when aimed at a perp. "We can question you at any time, and it's your right to remain silent. But, to respect your request, we've called for a public defender. That said, it'll be worth your while to help our investigation, and your cooperation will go a long way in deciding what charges we bring."

"I want my lawyer present," Nisake insisted, plucking the

coverlet nervously.

Torufu put away his knife and advanced to perch on one of the chairs beside Nisake's bed. "We have an offer for you. An offer that will expire when the lawyer gets here."

A pause as Nisake considered. Sweat beaded on his upper lip. "What's that?"

"Reduced charges in return for telling us who you work for," Lei said.

"What am I being charged with?"

Lei made a show of consulting notes on her phone. "Hmm, let's see. Conspiracy to commit murder, murder in the second degree, kidnapping, rape, piracy, resisting arrest, attempted murder of law enforcement officers, and human trafficking. You won't see the sun for a very long time, my friend." Lei met Nisake's eyes, and smiled again.

Nisake cringed. "I didn't do any of that!" His voice raised in fright. "I mean, okay, yeah, I helped move the women, but nothing else. I had nothing to do with anything else, I swear!"

"You'll have your day in court to prove that," Torufu rumbled. The knife was out again. Now he was trimming his cuticles with it. Evidently, the blade was very sharp.

"I want the deal. I want the reduced charges!"

"We can go as low as conspiracy to commit kidnapping and human trafficking," Lei said. "If you cooperate. Tell us all you know."

"Okay, okay. Do I have to sign something?" Nisake swiped the sweat off his face with the back of his arm. "I want to be sure I'm covered."

"We'll draw something up after we find out how valuable your intel is," Torufu said.

Just then a knock came from the door. A pretty young woman in a short skirt and perilous-looking heels stood there, frowning. "Hello. I'm Ms. Fogarty, court-appointed representative for Mr. Nisake. An interview is in progress that has not been cleared with me. Mr. Nisake, not another word." Fogarty minced forward and glanced around for a chair. "Where do I sit?"

"I don't believe you do," Lei said.

"They offered me a deal and I want to take it," Nisake exclaimed. "Reduced charges in return for my testimony."

"Detectives, clear the room please. I'd like to speak to my client privately," Fogarty said. "And any agreements we come to must be presented in writing or we won't consider them. I'll call you when we're ready for your interview."

Lei eyed the man on the bed with contempt. "Your lack of cooperation is duly noted, Mr. Nisake."

"Yeah. You'll be sorry you hid behind this lady's skirt. What there is of it," Torufu added.

Fogarty held her ground, staring at Nisake and clearly willing him to shut up, and he did. "I want to speak to my lawyer alone."

Lei and Torufu withdrew to the hall and shut the door. "Just when we were getting somewhere," Torufu said.

Lei shrugged. "He wants to talk. Better we don't give them any grounds for appeal in future, anyway." She rubbed her stomach. "I don't know about you, but I'm starving. Let's go to the cafeteria and see what they've got down there."

She and Torufu went downstairs to the Maui Memorial dining hall. Lei glanced at the clock overhead as she got in line with doctors, nurses, and crumpled-looking hospital visitors.

Six hours had passed since she left home after sneaking a peek at Stevens and Rosie, asleep in their big bed: the baby on her tummy, padded butt in the air, thumb in her mouth, tucked up against Stevens's side as he slept in his usual position—one arm bent with a hand beneath the pillow, the other arm down, encircling the baby.

She'd taken a phone picture so she could enjoy that precious sight again if needed, and had sneaked out past Conan and gone straight to the station. She'd met with Gerry and Abe, gone over the case file, and then sicced Gerry on catching up with the Coast

Guard's search progress for the *Golden Fleece*, while she and Torufu went to interview Nisake.

Lei reached the ordering area, smiling at the server behind the glass shield. "I'm hungry! I'll have Big Local Special." The attendant filled a sectioned cardboard tray with two scoops of white rice, a pile of scrambled eggs, a mound of sliced, fried Portuguese sausage, and a half a papaya with lime. Lei took the mounded plate. "*Mahalo.*" She slid it onto her tray and moved to the cashier. "Looks so ono," she said, handing over payment.

"Bumbye, you finish all that, get plenny energy for work," the cashier said, grinning.

"Fo' sure." Lei carried her tray back to a corner. Torufu joined her with an even bigger platter of breakfast, and they dug in.

She took her refreshment where she could get it, and this breakfast was likely to be the last meal she'd have for a while.

STEVENS CALLED Lei on his way to the airport, using his Bluetooth because of Maui's cell phone ban, but his wife didn't pick up. "Hey, Sweets. I know this is the worst possible time for this, but isn't it always? Your grandpa is being discharged and can't go home alone. I know you don't have time to deal with it, so I roped your dad and my mom into taking care of the kids and Conan for the moment. I'm on my way to O`ahu to arrange for a caregiver and bring him home from the hospital at eleven a.m." Stevens wove around a tourist rental car as he passed Ho`okipa. A windsurfer board was listing dangerously off to one side, held onto the bright red Ford Focus's roof with temporary straps. He honked and gestured to the driver to pull over. "Anyway, sorry for that noise, some lame tourist is about to lose his board and cause an accident. I asked Wayne if he could be the one to go to O`ahu, etcetera, but he said he knew Soga would prefer me. Soga's bound to be feeling vulnerable." He downshifted behind a pineapple truck, enjoying the rich smell of the ripe fruit through the Bronco's open window. "I hope you don't mind that I'm taking initiative here. I know you'd rather be doing this yourself, but someone has to deal with it right now, and the case needs *you* right now. Call me back when you can and I'll update you." He ended the call.

Maui's airport was being expanded—a huge new parking garage was being built along with an extended runway, so it was a confusing welter of crisscrossing roads for Stevens to find parking, and then getting his boarding pass and ticket for Hawaiian Airlines. Sitting in the waiting area at last, Stevens called Soga's hospital room.

"Soga, this is Michael, Lei's husband," he said, when the older man's tremulous voice answered the phone.

"I know who you are," Soga said. "Coming to help me get out of here?"

"That's exactly what I'm doing." Stevens had been prepared for resistance to his help, and smiled involuntarily. "Any excuse to ditch my dad duties for a couple of days and come visit you."

"You don't have to lie," Soga said with asperity. "I know this is hard for you. It is also hard for me. But we must make the best of things, so I thank you."

Sobered, Stevens pushed a hand through his hair. "I'm happy to come, Grandfather—that is all I meant to say. Wayne and Ellen are caring for the children. Lei would want to come, but she is tied up with a serious case that's eaten up her time. I'll meet you at the hospital at discharge, which your doctor told me is eleven tomorrow morning. I am working on finding someone to come in to help you at home."

"We can talk later." Soga hung up.

Clearly, he didn't like that part of the plan.

After the quick half hour flight, Stevens took a ride-share to Soga's house near Punchbowl as evening began to drain the heat from the day, replacing it with the sherbet-colored sky of a Honolulu sunset. The peaceful neighborhood of older homes tucked into a little cul-de-sac calmed his heart rate after the busy drive through Honolulu and Waikiki.

He walked up Soga's driveway in front of the closed garage door. Soga had a car inside, a sensible older Toyota Corolla that he'd driven until the fall that had put him in the hospital, and Stevens knew where the house keys and a spare door key were stashed.

He found the keys under a certain rock in the zen garden Soga had created beside the entry to the front door, a carefully raked plot the size of a dining room table, with three elegant black stones holding down one end of it. The middle stone hid the keys, and Stevens squatted outside of the area's carefully raked lines, reached in, tipped the stone and removed the keys.

He unlocked the front door, immediately frowning at the smell of something ripe and rotting, and several large, lazy buzzing flies. "Phew." He walked through the sparely furnished front room, done in classic Japanese tradition, and opened the window over the kitchen sink to bring in some fresh air.

Guilt tugged at him—neither he nor Lei had been able to find the time to fly over and deal with the house. Soga had fallen in his backyard workshop and called a friend, who got an ambulance to take the elderly man to the hospital.

Finally, he found the source of the smell—the trash under the sink had taken on a pungent odor, and flies had discovered it.

Airing out the house, cleaning spoiled food out of the refrigerator, changing the bed linens, and making a list of food and supplies, Stevens was grateful he'd come over now, and not on the morning of Soga's discharge as he'd considered doing.

And he still needed help.

Fortunately, Lei had a friend who might be able to help him find the needed caregiver. He took the ripe trash out, hauled the big can to the curb, and then scrolled to a number on his phone. "Hello? Marcella? It's Stevens. I'm in Honolulu, and I need a favor."

CHAPTER THIRTY

FOGARTY OPENED Nisake's hospital room door to Lei and Torufu. "We want to see your offer in writing."

"Good. Because the reason we took a while getting back here is that we swung by the DA's office and got it written up." Lei handed the agreement over to Fogarty. As the lawyer skimmed over the paperwork attached to a clipboard, Lei approached Nisake's bed and resumed her seat on the plastic chair beside him. Torufu took up a less-threatening position behind her on a rollaway chair. "How are you feeling, Mr. Nisake?"

"A little better, now that I've had some legal counsel." The man's color and composure had improved.

"That's good. Do you mind if I record this interview? Saves going over things again later." Lei took out her phone and set it on the edge of the bed.

Fogarty handed the contract and a pen to Nisake. "It seems aboveboard to me, but please read through and ask us any questions you might have."

Moments later, the interview got underway after Lei had stated the place, time, and people present for the recording. "Tell us about the man who hired you."

Nisake glanced at Fogarty, who answered for him. "My client wants to go into Witness Protection."

Lei threw up her hands and turned to address Torufu. "Can you believe this guy? Who does he work for, anyway? One of the Changs?" The notorious crime family seemed to have fingers in every pie.

Torufu lifted his brows and chin. Lei turned back to Nisake, who was smoothing the sheet in his fingers and nodding. "I can't say anything or they'll kill me."

If she had a dollar for every witness who thought their testimony was that valuable . . . "I can call the Marshals Service for you, but it's going to slow everything down. They will want to interview you, assess the situation, and make their own decision based on how prosecutable the information is. It could take up to a week, and you'll have to talk to them first, anyway. Tell them what you're going to end up telling us." Lei tried to keep her impatience in check. She couldn't afford to spook the guy—if they found out who was behind the rumored human trafficking activity out of Kahului Harbor, it would be a major bonus.

Fogarty tapped the contract. "I think you're okay to share some of the information you told me, Mr. Nisake. We can save specifics for the Marshals and see what they say."

"I don't think you're going to get Witness Protection, Nisake. You're just a grunt," Torufu rumbled from his position. "You won't know anything good enough to merit that level of security. I guarantee it."

"I do know something! I know the first name of the man who rents the warehouse where they stashed the girls!" Nisake exclaimed.

Torufu yawned. "We have that information from a computer search. Along with his last name, too, by the way. Tell us something we don't know."

"Detective Torufu is right. We are your best bet for protection right now unless you have evidence and names of people in a high level of involvement with the human trafficking operation." Lei leaned forward, modulating her voice to make it soft and appealing. It wasn't often that she was in the position to play "good cop," but Torufu had her beat as far as muscle and menace. "If you tell us what you know and we think it will put you in danger, we'll take steps to keep you safe. You'll go to an isolation unit at the jail, for instance."

"I have to agree with the detectives in this instance," Fogarty told her client. "I've tried to have my clients placed in Witness Protection before, and it's not an easy process."

Nisake sighed and his shoulders slumped. "Okay, then. I work for a dude named Felipe Chang. He's in charge of the containers and shipping of the people that come through this harbor."

Lei's pulse picked up as he described how young women and some teen boys, usually runaways who congregated on the streets of Lahaina for panhandling and partying, were lured with a promise of shelter and meals by a recruiter they had, a charismatic young man from the Big Island. "A guy named Keo talks the kids up. I never got his last name. Gives them free *pakalolo*, tells them there's a party they're going to love. They get in his car—he has a red Viper." Nisake's mouth tightened a little in an expression of either disgust or regret. "Stupid kids. He drives them to one of the containers. We keep them in there, take care of them until the container's full. Then we ship it out."

"Wow. This sounds like quite the operation. How did you get involved, and what's your role exactly?" Lei hoped her tone sounded admiring.

"Me and Greg Steele were a team. It was like you guys." Nisake gestured with his chin. "Good cop, bad cop. I was the good cop. People needed anything, I got it. I'd calm them down. We had a line that they were going to go be cruise ship waiters and waitresses, that we needed them to stay hidden since they were underage. You'd be surprised how many of them believed it all the way until the container was put on the ship, still locked. But by then, whether or not they believed it didn't matter." Nisake stared down at his hands. "I'm glad to be out of it, to tell the truth. I couldn't find a way to get out."

Torufu snorted. "We're supposed to feel sorry for you."

Lei touched Torufu's arm. "Abe. Please. Can't you see how Mr. Nisake got caught in the life?"

"And I'm still trapped!" Nisake's eyes had gone wide, ringed with white. "I tried to quit, but Steele came after me. Roughed me up. Said once you work for the Changs, you always work for the Changs. Some partner he was!"

"Nice guy, Greg Steele," Torufu said. "Glad he's on a slab right now."

"Me too," Nisake said fervently. "He really enjoyed his job. Not in a good way, if you get my meaning."

Fogarty scrunched her over-plucked brows. "As you can see, my client is taking a considerable risk in cooperating with you."

"And we thank you for it." Lei addressed Nisake. "But right now, we need to know more about the pirates and the women that ended up causing your capture. Tell us about that."

"I don't know much about that. Just that my partner got a call to go pick the women up in our company van from where they'd been brought into a bay on the West Side."

"Where was this?"

"One a.m. down at the pier at Mala Wharf. No one's ever around down there at that time of night. My partner and I brought the van down. We met a beefed-up Zodiac with the five women in it at the wharf. They were tied up and wearing blindfolds. Seemed pretty upset." Nisake had begun plucking at the coverlet again. "We moved them into the van. Took them to our overnight warehouse. The next day, we brought them to the container for shipping. Well, you know how that went."

"Yes, we do." Lei got eye contact with the young man. "We were surprised at how ready and willing Steele was to be aggressive and take lives. Can you tell us more about that?"

"He's a Chang. Not by name, but by marriage." Nisake described the convoluted relationship linking Greg Steele to the Chang crime family. "He told me right off once we realized that cops were onto us that he didn't care if he had to kill all of the women. We were either escaping or going out feetfirst."

"And you knew you were in danger at that point," Lei said.

"Totally. The women knew it too; they were crying. It was awful. I tried to talk him down, but . . ." Nisake shook his head. "Turns out, he was right. He went out feetfirst."

"Back to the men in the Zodiac. Did you know any of them?"

"No. Steele said they were new customers, but that they'd offered Felipe a great percentage of the sale on the women. You have to understand." Nisake sought eye contact with Lei. "The women were really valuable. The younger and prettier the better, and especially if they were virgins. Dudes overseas pay a lot for that." He named a figure that made Lei's eyebrows rise. "That kind of money does things to people."

"In more ways than one. Are you sure there's nothing more you can tell us about the pirates? They've attacked another ship and taken more people prisoner."

Nisake shook his head. "I guess you're right. I'm just a foot soldier, like you said. I don't know anything but what I've told you."

CHAPTER THIRTY-ONE

STEVENS PUSHED Soga's wheelchair out of the hospital at eleven a.m. the next day. The older man seemed unbelievably light to Stevens as he navigated the sidewalk—it was like pushing a basket of laundry, nothing more. He rolled the chair over to where he'd parked Soga's Corolla at the drop-off zone outside of the hospital.

"I told you I can walk," Soga muttered grumpily.

"I know you can, Soga. It's part of the discharge requirements for your operation. But it's also hospital regulations that everyone being discharged has to ride in one of these chariots—so just enjoy, okay?" Stevens made his voice as humorous as possible, but the truth was, he was alarmed at how tiny and frail his octogenarian grandfather-in-law seemed.

Stevens helped Soga from the chair into the front seat, and then ran the chair back into the lee of the building. He jogged back and got into the Corolla, glancing at Soga as he lowered the windows. "Thought you might want some fresh air after being shut up in that building."

"Thank you." Soga turned his lined face toward the sun and shut his eyes, clearly savoring the warm breeze, as they left the area of the hospital and wended their way through downtown. His crepey skin was almost translucent.

Stevens had been able to get a housecleaner to go over the house before Soga's arrival. He'd restocked the groceries, and met with Marcus Kamuela's young niece. Sabrina Kamuela, a nursing student, was bright and sweet. She seemed motivated and outgoing, so Stevens had hired her and shown her around the place, guessing at Soga's needs.

He'd gone early to the hospital with some downloaded forms, and prior to Soga's discharge, Soga had signed Power of Attorney papers naming Stevens and Lei as his health care representatives. He'd also added Stevens to his bank account, allowing Stevens to pay for the various items needed, as well as a signing bonus for Sabrina. Soga had dealt with the hospital bill himself.

They got underway, and all of these details were still fresh and worrisome on Stevens's mind. "You sure you're okay for money, Soga?"

"I live frugally. Always have." Soga's eyes were still closed and he rested his head against the seat back, apparently enjoying the bright sunshine and breeze coming through the window. "I had good investments from my work." Soga had retired as a county employee, a planner for the city of Honolulu, many years before. "I will not be a burden to you and Lei—at least, not in that way." His mouth closed, a tight seam of pain.

Stevens patted Soga's shoulder. "Don't worry about that. Just think about healing up. But while we're talking about all of this, I want to bring up something Lei and I have talked about. We searched long and hard for a facility for you on Maui, and couldn't find anything we thought was appropriate—but we don't like having you so far away." He glanced over at the older man, but Soga remained turned away. "We'd like you to consider moving to Maui and living with us. We have a big property with plenty of room, and we've checked out the regulations. If you sell your house, you'd have plenty of money for us to buy or build you a 'tiny house' on our property."

Still no response from Soga.

Stevens frowned, focusing on the road. "Maybe I should have waited until Lei was here to talk with you about this, but I'm concerned about leaving you, even with the caregiver situation I set up. I know you're involved with your work for the Shinnyo Temple, making those beautiful floating lanterns . . . but I have a workshop at our place, too. I'd be happy to share it with you. I already contacted the Temple and asked if the work could be done long distance; they assured me of how much they value you, and that they'd make any accommodations needed, like setting up and paying for shipping."

Soga finally turned. His dark eyes, set in pleated folds of wrinkles, were unreadable—but emotion was revealed in the soft tremble of his mouth.

"I would be honored to spend my last years with my family," he said. "Now get me home and into bed, please."

"Yes, sir," Stevens said. "You got it." He pressed down harder on the gas.

CHAPTER THIRTY-TWO

LEI'S BROW knit as she listened to Stevens's message. Maui Memorial Hospital had notoriously poor reception, and his voicemail had been left hours before. *Stevens was already on O`ahu, dealing with her grandfather and his situation.*

A rush of love and gratitude brought warmth to Lei's cheeks. *This guy.* He just stepped in and did whatever needed doing, and so did her dad and Ellen, helping out with the kids!

Lei's finger was moving to call Stevens back, when her phone rang. She frowned—Aina Thomas's number had appeared in the little window. *Something new on the case?* "Texeira here."

"Lei, we've got a lead on the pirate location. Several Coast Guard craft are going to raid it. We're leaving from Ma`alaea Harbor in half an hour. Can you get here with your team?"

LEI, Gerry Bunuelos, and Abe Torufu hurried up the short, narrow gangplank onto the *Defender* craft still tied at Ma`alaea Harbor, brisk wind tugging at their hair and clothing. Thomas met them, along with Decker, his commanding officer.

"This is a Coast Guard operation, so you are not to get involved," Decker said. "You can stay up on deck, especially if you have any seasick issues, until we approach the back side of Kaho`olawe, where we've identified a possible sea cave matching your witnesses' description."

"Kaho`olawe!" Bunuelos exclaimed. "That bombed-out rock?"

The atoll of Kaho`olawe, off the southwestern shore of Maui, had first been used by US armed forces in World War II, and later by the Navy, for target practice. The federal government had cleaned up the debris and ordnance littering the little island and returned it to the Hawaiian people in 2003, and now only cultural and restoration practices were allowed on the island.

"A lot has changed on Kaho`olawe since it was returned to the *Kanaka Maoli*," Torufu rumbled. "The people have been bringing back the native plants and recreating dwellings. It's coming back alive."

"Be that as it may," Commander Decker said. "We didn't think Kaho`olawe had many geologic features that could provide shelter for this kind of operation, but one of our smaller boats did a careful pass along the southernmost coast, the side furthest from the main island of Maui. The terrain there is at a high point of the atoll, with a sheer cliff on one side. Well, it turns out that cliff hides a good-sized sea cave. An outcrop hides the opening. Our boat got in far enough to verify that there were other craft at anchor inside. None of our other searches have yielded anything that substantial." Decker tugged down his crisp uniform jacket. "We have reason to believe this may be the pirate hideout."

As the captain was speaking, the crew had been bustling about. The *Defender* cast off. Lei grabbed onto the rail, but didn't have time to warn Abe and Gerry, who ended up crashing into each other as the rigid-hulled inflatable spun away from the dock.

Decker and Thomas left to enter the boat's cabin, and Lei guided her partners to a familiar padded bench, where the three sat down.

Lei turned her face into the wind, invigorated by the speed and the spray. Sunlight sparkled off of the cobalt-blue waves, and she fastened her gaze on the purple-brown smudge of Kaho'olawe off in the distance. *They were going to take these pirates down!*

Thomas reappeared, carrying three heavily padded vests. He shouted into the wind and engine noise as he handed them each one. "These are bulletproof life preservers. The commander wants you below when we see action, but just in case . . ."

Lei nodded. "I appreciate that, Aina. Last thing we want to do is be a liability to your crew during a sensitive operation."

Thomas's eyes warmed as they held hers. "Appreciate your cooperation with our regulations, Lei."

They blasted across the waves toward Kaho'olawe at top speed, and nothing but the roar of the engines and the slap of the craft against the waves could be heard. As they approached the island, its muted shades changed from mauve and brown to a rich reddish cinnamon. Lei shielded her phone from the spray, doing a quick search about the island.

Kaho'olawe was the smallest of the official main Hawaiian island chain—crescent moon-shaped Molokini atoll, which they were nearing, was not included in that count. Located in the wind-shadow of Maui's dry western shore, the eleven-mile island had been scarcely populated due to a lack of fresh water since the late nineteenth century, when warring Hawaiian chiefs had burned and laid waste to its forests. Subsequent incarnations as a penal colony and cattle ranch had further scoured away topsoil, and its use for Naval target practice had finalized its barren state.

Lei stared at the rising bulk of land as they approached it. After so much harsh punishment, it was good to read that the replanting efforts were helping to restore the battered little island.

Pre-raid jitters sped up Lei's heart rate. She could still remember each of the times she'd been a part of an armed confrontation. They seemed emblazoned on her psyche, tattooed there by the intensity of the experience—but only as a series of snapshots. "Adrenaline and cortisol are involved in any highly emotionally charged or dangerous encounter," Dr. Wilson had told her once. "Those chemicals prepare the body for fight or flight—but they have a downside. Memories may just be impressions when a person is highly stressed."

Thank God Dr. Wilson had been available to meet with the Peterson girls and their mother . . . hopefully, their work with the psychologist would help with the highly charged, traumatic memories they carried from all they'd endured.

The *Defender* flew by the cliffs and sheltered bay that made up the crumbling volcanic cone of Molokini, continuing past it along a deep, rough channel of surging waters to Kaho`olawe.

Lei had never been to the island so recently regifted to the Hawaiian people. She scanned its forbidding, arid form, dark red with iron-rich soil, etched with canyons formed by runoff that led to black volcanic rock beaches, pounded by the restless sea. Only a few bushes were visible and added patches of green, and no clouds hovered above the fourteen hundred foot elevation at its highest point.

The *Defender* throttled back, moving into the shadow of a huge boulder just off the coast. "Kaho`olawe's a work in progress." Bunuelos was holding up binoculars and surveying the island. "My kids have gone on school trips to plant more trees and bushes. They're focusing on regrowing only native Hawaiian plants on the island."

"It makes sense to try to restore it to what Hawaii was like before all the invasive species took over," Lei agreed, her eyes scanning the cliffs. "Where is this cave? I sure can't see anything."

The *Defender* joined two other Coast Guard craft in the lee of the offshore boulder outcrop: one a large, sleek cutter, the other a rigid inflatable like theirs.

Aina Thomas rejoined them. He stood next to Lei and pointed past her shoulder. "See that formation? It just appears to be a rock ledge coming out from the cliff."

Lei adjusted the bill of her hat and her sunglasses, trying to see what he was pointing at. "I think I see it."

Bunuelos aimed his glasses at the outcrop. "There's a shadow next to it!"

"Yeah, that's how well hidden it is. That ledge comes out maybe fifty feet from the main face of the cliffs, but behind it is the entrance to the sea cave."

"What's the plan?" Torufu put his hands on his hips. "Seriously, we can help."

"I'm sorry. You can't. All three of you need to go inside the cabin during the operation. I'll keep you abreast with one of these." Thomas handed Lei a high-powered walkie-talkie, and tapped the partner to it that he'd slid into a pocket in his vest. "There's only one way in or out, and we're hoping they don't know of our approach. We're sending some divers to swim into the cave underwater and do a recon." He gestured to the cutter. "They're already on their way. They launched fifteen minutes ago. They're using a submersible device to get there faster, so we should know soon what the status is inside the cave. Once we have an idea what we're getting into, the Zodiacs will go in. The cutter will wait outside the cave for backup."

"Thanks for the rundown," Torufu said.

Thomas tapped the Bluetooth in his ear as he received an order. "We're moving out. Head into the cabin, guys."

The three detectives went inside the crowded cabin as the *Defender* got underway. Lei sat between her two partners on a bench against the wall as the Coast Guard personnel went about their tasks efficiently.

Tension filled the room as the *Defender* and her sister craft, trailed by the cutter, approached the opening of the cave. The Guardsmen had taken up defensive positions around the railing, their weapons at the ready.

Lei could see out the cabin's window how the ledge protected and hid a large opening. "This is amazing. Never would have known it was here!"

Waves surged in and out of the entrance, amplified in the space, and so was the low throb of the boats' motors. Shadow snuffed out visibility as they made the turn and headed inside.

Sweat burst out on Lei's body underneath the heavy vest, and along her hairline. She focused on breathing deeply and slowly through her nose, keeping her body calm, as the *Defender* passed under the lip of the cave's opening, and darkness surrounded them.

CHAPTER THIRTY-THREE

THE *DEFENDER* and her twin inflatable glided into position, parallel with each other, and switched on high-mounted strobe lights at the same time.

The illumination was a powerful blow on Lei's eyes, and the bullhorn amplifying Commander Decker's voice hurt her ears, too, bouncing off the harsh rock walls surrounding them. "This is the Coast Guard. We have you surrounded. Put down any weapons. Come out with your hands up, and you won't be harmed."

Lei's pulse pounded as she crowded close to the *Defender*'s window with Torufu and Bunuelos, trying to see what was going on, still partially blinded. Her breath fogged the glass, and she swiped the mist away with her arm.

The sea cave's interior was lined with smooth, treacherous-looking black rocks, and moisture dripped from the ceiling, falling as gentle rain. The area was surprisingly large, and the boats' powerful lights shone onto a crude floating dock mounted on plastic barrels, and several prefabricated plastic sheds positioned around the landing area.

"Nothing moving out there," Bunuelos said. "I don't see any other watercraft, either, just that broken-down Jet Ski." He pointed to an obviously wrecked craft lying on its side on the rocks next to the dock. "They got out ahead of us."

Torufu swore in Tongan, a long guttural chain of words Lei was glad she didn't understand.

The *Defender* bumped up against the dock. The Guardsmen left the craft, running down the dock, boots echoing hollowly against the water and cave walls, weapons in ready position.

"I hope they're checking for booby traps!" Lei frowned. She'd never forget a raid she'd been on that had been rigged to blow. She and her team had barely been able to identify the trip wires in time.

"Looks like they're checking with flashlights," Bunuelos said. They watched as the Guardsmen spread out, inspecting the sheds before cutting the padlocks on the doors.

"It sucks to sit here watching," Lei muttered. "I sure as hell hope the women from the *Golden Fleece* are in one of those sheds."

As if on cue, Lei's walkie-talkie crackled. "MPD staff, come to our position in the third shed on the right. We have captives here."

"Roger that!" Lei and her partners hurried out of the cabin, clambering clumsily onto the dock and running toward the shed. Lei thumbed to the video feature on her phone as she hurried forward, turning the camera on and aiming it around the scene as she approached the shed. "This is Sergeant Lei Texeira of Maui Police Department," she said loudly, to alert the team. "Camera recording now." She stated the time and location as she approached the shed door.

A Guardsman flanked either side of the opening, and she videoed as she stepped inside.

Aina Thomas shielded his eyes with a hand as she entered the large plastic shed, holding a flashlight beneath the video recorder. The beam from her flashlight played over two women and two girls, huddled in the corner.

Their hair was matted, their clothing ripped, and all four of them had haunted, wild eyes.

"Aw, dammit," Lei whispered to Thomas. "These women appear to have been assaulted, too. Stay back. Let me approach them. Gerry, you run the camera." She thrust the phone into Bunuelos's hands, along with the light.

She moved forward to approach the women, holding her hands low, palms facing outward. "Hey there. We're here to help. I'm Sergeant Lei Texeira from Maui Police Department, and these other two are Detectives Gerry Bunuelos and Abe Torufu. You're safe now."

The women slowly let go of each other. "Water," the one in the middle croaked. "Water, please."

"On it. I'll bring blankets too." Aina Thomas hurried back out.

Lei squatted next to the cluster of women. "Are you injured? We have a medic aboard."

"We can walk, if that's what you're asking," the woman in the middle said. She had a European accent.

"What are your names?"

"I am Siggi Janssen. These are my daughters, Nanci and Erica. And this is their nanny companion, Betta Schorz."

"Thank you for introducing yourselves," Lei said warmly, making eye contact with each of the women in turn. "As I told you, my name is Lei, and these are my partners, along with the Coast Guard, who located this cave. I hope it's okay that we are videoing this. It helps us not to have to keep asking you difficult questions. Are you okay with that?"

Siggi nodded, so Lei went on. "We're so glad we found you! We've been searching for you and the *Golden Fleece* since we got your distress call. Is there anything you can tell us about the whereabouts of whoever took you?"

"No," Siggi said. "We were captured. They—assaulted Betta and I. I am thankful they left my girls alone, though they made them watch . . ." She lowered her head, visibly gathering herself, tightening her arms around her daughters. "They put us in this shed and locked us in here. At first, we thought they'd be back any minute . . . but time went by. They didn't leave us any food or water. We thought we were going to die here."

Thomas and a fellow Guardsman returned. They handed the women each a liter of water and a silver thermal blanket. "Don't drink it too fast, or you'll just make yourself sick," Thomas warned. "We've got some emergency food rations on the boat for later."

As the women sipped the water, Lei shook out the crinkly blankets and draped them around each of them. "You're safe now," she murmured. "You're going to be okay."

Lei could hear coded conversation outside the shed as the Guardsmen continued to search for signs of where the pirates had gone. "I'd like to take your statements, please. This will save time and further interviews in the future. We'll close the door for privacy. Would that be all right?"

The women nodded.

Lei sent her fellow detectives outside the shed. Thomas remained, holding a bright electric light, to represent the Coast Guard. "I know this is hard, but to aid in the investigation and stop the pirates, we need to know what happened. Who would like to go first?"

CHAPTER THIRTY-FOUR

LEI SAT HUDDLED on the bench as the *Defender* headed back toward Ma`alaea late in the evening. Lei was exhausted by the harrowing tale of what the women had been through. The Janssen women and Betta Schorz had been transferred to the larger Coast Guard cutter, and were being taken to Tripler Hospital on O`ahu to be treated, since they were foreign nationals and Siggi had asked for family to be contacted to meet them there.

Aina Thomas squeezed in beside her, pushing Bunuelos and Torufu further down on the bench. "That was rough."

"No kidding. I'm glad they're going to O`ahu —Dr. Wilson is already fully booked working with our other victims." Lei tugged her ball cap lower, screening out the penetrating rays of sunset reflecting off the waves as the craft sped back toward the Maui main island. "Siggi Janssen said the main guy just executed all the men and pitched them overboard . . . We've got to capture these pirates."

"You were so busy with the victims that I didn't want to interrupt, but the pirates left us a message. Rather public one, in fact." Thomas took out his phone and gestured for Lei, Torufu and

Bunuelos to look on. "Commander Decker found this message already loaded and playing on a computer set up in what they'd been using as a workroom." He pressed *PLAY*. Lei and the MPD detectives crowded close to watch.

A white sheet and a strobe light threw a man facing the camera into stark relief. Lei instinctively assessed him: muscular build, tribal tats on one arm, wearing a *kihei* robe made of tapa cloth, a large, carved gourd helmet hiding his face. His voice echoed as he spoke, resonant and deep, with a hint of vibrato emphasized by the helmet.

"I am the Pirate King. I represent an oppressed people—the *Kanaka Maoli*, the native Hawaiians. We are not going to allow the illegal stealing and using of our lands and oceans any longer. We are going to own our native waters and make the wealthy who take, and give nothing back, regret they ever came here." Dark eyes glittered in the shadow of the mask's holes. "We will kill the men who travel these seas in their obscene boats. We will use and enslave their women, as our women were used and enslaved. And as we do so, we will take back what was stolen from us. We've had enough of watered-down politics that get us nowhere—so I'm declaring myself king. The Pirate King. You will fear my name."

The video ended. Lei wanted to laugh, to mock it—but she found her throat unexpectedly dry, and she shivered.

"The Pirate King, eh. Pretty frickin' cheesy." Torufu folded his big arms. "How dare that mo'fo' claim to represent anybody." He spat impressively, making it over the boat's railing.

Bunuelos squinted at the YouTube counter. "Half a million views. Yikes."

"Turns out 'pirate' is a popular video search category," Thomas said. "And this one's gone viral."

"It's pure theater." Lei sat back on the bench and rubbed her eyes. "This is . . . wow. He's justifying himself for the horror he's inflicting on his victims."

"It's a PR stunt," Thomas said. "Check out the comments. People are egging him on, coming out in support."

"It reminds me of the anarchy movement that the Smiley Bandit provoked," Lei said, remembering her first FBI case. "Evil dressed up with a political label. Only this is much worse."

CHAPTER THIRTY-FIVE

BACK AT THE STATION, Lei and her partners dropped the evidence samples they'd collected at the lab, updated Captain Omura on the turn the case had taken, and went separate ways to follow up on elements from the case: Torufu working on who might be leaking the names and identities of rich yacht owners to the pirates, Bunuelos following up on loading fingerprints gathered at the scene into AFIS, and Lei following the connection she'd uncovered through the kidnapper Nisake that pointed to the Changs.

She knew one Chang she could call: *Terence Chang.* The young computer whiz businessman was heir apparent to notorious Healani Chang. He'd once been an enemy, and had become a sometime ally.

She hung a *Do Not Disturb* sign and shut the door of her cubicle. Sitting down, she took a moment to gather herself, then called him on the burner phone she used for confidential informants.

As she'd expected, Terence didn't pick up, but she left a message identifying herself. A few minutes later, he called back. "Lei Texeira. Hoped I'd never have to talk to you again."

"Well, never is a long time, especially in Hawaii. I'm calling about a human trafficking operation out of Kahului that we've

197

uncovered. I'm hoping you're still working on steering the family business in healthier directions."

"I am always working toward that goal, yes," Terence agreed cautiously. "Tell me what's happening over there on Maui."

"I'm hoping you know." Lei described the situation with the pirate attacks and the victims being sold through a Chang warehouse on Maui, as well as the separate runaway recruitment ring. "Our witness has a powerful incentive to tell the truth about this. Can you tell me anything about a trafficking operation on Maui?"

"Things have changed a lot in how we operate. I am basically in charge of the family operations, and as you've heard through the 'coconut wireless', I am moving us toward legitimate enterprises. That said, not all of the family went along with my new direction. Some of my cousins continue to operate independently, running women, drugs, meth labs and the like. We at Terence Chang Enterprises Incorporated have nothing to do with them."

Lei rolled her eyes. "That's too easy, Terence. I need more. A name. An address. I don't want women and kids being kidnapped and shipped like cattle off of my island."

"I'm hearing a lot about what you want, and not a lot about what will make it worth my while to betray a family member. Quid pro quo, Lei. What've you got that I want?"

Lei sat back in her creaky old office chair. "I'll owe you a favor, Terence. You can cash it in anytime, when you need it . . . and even though you're trying to go legit, there are a lot of Changs still out there that are bombs waiting to blow a hole in your plans. If we take out the cousin who's doing business over here, it could make room for you to expand a legitimate operation out of Kahului Harbor."

"I like the idea of a straight cop owing me a favor," Terence said. "All right. I'll play along. My cousin Harold Chang has a warehouse and shipping operation on Maui. It's supposed to be an import/export business—koa wood furniture."

"Perfect," Lei said. "I owe you, now. Call me when you need to, at this number." Lei hung up.

She stood up. Did a few jumping jacks in the narrow confines of her office. Hung her head upside down to get circulation going, then took out her regular phone and called Stevens.

Her husband's voice sounded crisp, like he was right in the next room. "Hey, Sweets. Was wondering when you'd find time to call."

"Sorry, honey, it's been nuts. I'll tell you more in a minute—but how's my grandpa?"

"Holding up pretty well. We just got him home and settled, and Sabrina came over." She could hear Stevens walking. "I'm going in the guest bedroom so I can speak to you privately."

"Thanks. Who's Sabrina?"

"She's one of Marcus Kamuela's nieces. She's a nursing student and was hunting for a job in the field. Worked out perfect."

"Oh, that's great." Lei sat back down in the chair and it gave a protesting squeak. "I'm so glad it worked out that you were off and could handle all of that."

"And don't forget, it still wouldn't work if Ellen and Wayne hadn't stepped up to handle the kids," Stevens reminded her. "We owe them. Big-time."

"I know we do."

"So, I talked to Soga about coming over to Maui. Told him we wanted to be closer to him, but we understood he had a commitment to the lantern making and the Shinnyo Temple. The Temple is happy to have him work long-distance, so he agreed to come. When we got to the house, he wanted to show me all his personal papers: his will, his accounts, etcetera. He's not hurting for money, and if he sells his house, he will have plenty to purchase a tiny house and put it on our land with more to invest in long-term care if he needs it."

"A tiny house! I love it." With the high cost of living and building in Hawaii, small prefabricated houses mounted on wheeled trailers were becoming a viable alternative for seniors and others seeking to build a low-cost home without a lot of infrastructure and permitting costs. "How long are you going to be over there?"

"Now that Sabrina's set up and coming in to be with him daily, I think I could leave tomorrow. I don't want to push him, but I might be able to get a realtor in to assess the house and get the ball rolling for his transition soon."

"That would be awesome. I could come over on weekends and bring Kiet; we could help him pack and clean out." Lei smiled. "I can't wait to have Grandfather Soga closer. Thanks so much for stepping up to handle that situation!"

"That's what family is for."

"I love you."

"I know. Now catch me up on the case!"

Lei filled him in on recent developments and yawned hugely. "I have to get home, pick up the kids and get some rest. Today was endless."

"Keep me posted," Stevens said. "I should get home tomorrow. Stay safe, Sweets."

"I'll try."

He snorted. "You always do, and it doesn't always work."

She had no answer for that.

CHAPTER THIRTY-SIX

Bunuelos knocked on the doorframe of Lei's cubicle the next morning, his wiry body vibrating with excitement. "I got a hit on a fingerprint from the cave! Captain says we need to go by the last known address of this perp and grab up anyone that's there."

Soon they were out the door, taking Lei's Tacoma, and fifteen minutes later, they pulled up at the address.

"Do you really think anyone who lives here has anything to do with the Pirate King?" Lei asked as they parked, facing a tidy fifties-era plantation house built on the edge of Happy Valley, a small community that struggled with drugs and poverty in the shadow of Wailuku, Maui's capital.

"I just follow the evidence, and that evidence is a fingerprint belonging to a guy who has a record for B&E, whose last known address was this house," Bunuelos said.

Lei glanced at the house again. Dark green paint, white trim, a cute little porch with pots of orchids, flowered curtains in the windows. "Let me see his record."

Gerry handed over his computer tablet. Lei touched the photo of the guy whose fingerprint they'd found, opening it to details.

"Name: Keo Avila. Ancestry: Filipino/Hawaiian. Age: twenty-six." She expanded the photo: a handsome young mixed-race man with dimples. "He looks like a charmer . . . I'm betting this is his parents' house." She frowned thoughtfully. "Didn't our witness Nisake mention someone of that name?"

"I don't know, I wasn't at that interview," Gerry said.

Lei dug her spiral notebook out of her pocket, thumbed to the page. "Yes! I videotaped the interview, but I jotted down any names he mentioned. I just haven't had time to run them down. According to Nisake, someone named Keo is the one who lures runaways into the containers, then Nisake and Steele imprison them. This is a Chang operation, by the way—Felipe Chang is in charge of the actual trafficking operation and was Nisake's boss, but a Harold Chang owns the warehouse and containers. Behind a corporation front, of course."

"No shit." Bunuelos scowled. "As a father of five, I particularly hate people like this Keo guy."

An older woman dressed in an aloha print shirt and capri pants came out onto the porch holding an old-fashioned aluminum watering can. She wore a pair of cordless headphones, and was bopping along to a song as she watered the plants.

"I think we're about to ruin her day," Lei said. "I bet that's Keo's mama."

"Ah, crap. I bet you're right."

They got out of the vehicle at the same time. Lei hung back, letting Bunuelos approach the woman first as they both held up their cred wallets. "Hello there. Can we have a moment of your time?"

The woman slid her headphones back so they encircled her neck, and Lei could faintly hear *"Stayin' Alive"* by the Bee Gees as she smiled down at them. Dimples showed in her cheeks. "Sure. What can I do for you?"

"I'm Detective Bunuelos, and this is Sergeant Texeira of the

Maui Police Department. We're looking for someone named Keo Avila."

The woman's face fell and her smile disappeared. "Just a moment." She fumbled in her pocket and turned off the music player. "Keo is my son. Why don't you come up and sit for a moment, and tell me what this is about?"

Lei and Bunuelos ascended the steps. They took seats on a worn rattan loveseat as the woman sat down across from them in an equally weathered rocker.

"What's your name, ma'am?" Lei asked. She wished she knew the woman well enough to call her "auntie" as was done as a title of respect in Hawaii, but this wasn't a time for such informality.

"I'm Pohaku Wasabe. Keo is my son from my first marriage." She seemed to steel herself, straightening up and squaring her shoulders. "What's he done now?"

"We don't know that he's done anything." Lei smiled with as much warmth as she could put into it. "We just want to ask him some questions about a case we're working on, and this address was on his driver's license."

"Oh." Wasabe visibly relaxed, almost sagging in her chair. "I was so afraid . . ."

"What were you afraid of, Ms. Wasabe?" Bunuelos smiled too. "I'm a father of five, so I know how these kids can get up to no good, no matter who their parents are."

"That's Keo. He was raised to be a good boy, but he was always getting into trouble." Wasabe set aside the watering can she was still holding, clearly eager to unburden herself. "I don't understand what went wrong, but he's always been . . . not like other kids. He could smile as sweet as the sun coming over Haleakala, but still lie and steal without ever being sorry for it."

"I'm sorry you've had all that *pilikia* with your boy. If it helps, we just want to talk with him about a very important case. We think he might have some information that could help a lot of people," Lei said.

"Yeah," Bunuelos said. "I take it he's not actually living with you. Do you know where we might be able to find him? Just to talk?"

🌴

Lᴇɪ ᴀɴᴅ Bᴜɴᴜᴇʟᴏs got on the road toward Lahaina, and the address Mrs. Wasabe had given them as a "hangout" where her son could be found.

"I don't think Keo's going to be there," Lei said as they drove past the courthouse onto Highway 30, leading out of Wailuku. She always enjoyed driving down this picturesque avenue, bracketed by lawns surrounding the public buildings of the older part of Wailuku, and nestled beneath spreading monkeypod trees that provided much-needed shade. "I think he's part of the Pirate King's crew."

"I'm guessing he's the connection between the pirates and the Chang human trafficking operation. If we can get a lead on his whereabouts, maybe we'll get a lead on the Pirate King's latest hideout," Bunuelos said.

"That's a stretch. And are we really calling this perp the Pirate King? It's not only cheesy, as Torufu said, it romanticizes him. That Manifesto video was a total crock." Lei's neck heated up as she remembered the man's rant on YouTube. "This guy is capitalizing on the suffering of his people and painting himself as a cultural hero—and he's nothing but a murderer and a rapist wearing a costume."

"Tell that to the fan group that's made him his own Facebook page." Bunuelos shook his head as he worked his phone. "They call themselves the Pirate Horde."

"These guys are literally cutthroats," Lei said. "I think we need a press conference or something. We need to talk about how this perp brutally murdered Chaz Kaihale, who's *Kanaka Maoli*, as well as Peterson, Janssen and the captain from the *Golden Fleece*."

"Maybe some of the ladies would be willing to share what happened to them on-air," Bunuelos said. "The women saw and experienced way too much. Perhaps Ms. Gutierrez. She was raped and almost died, and she's part Hawaiian."

Lei frowned. "That's something that bothers me. If he's doing this for some misguided cultural payback, why would he kill Chaz? And rape Gutierrez, not just the *haole* women?"

"Rhetorical question, I hope," Bunuelos said. "I've got no freakin' idea."

Lei glanced ahead and to her left—the graciously planted community entrance to Wailuku Heights, Harold Chang's neighborhood, was just ahead. "I want to swing by an address before we go to Lahaina."

HAROLD CHANG'S house crowned one of the Wailuku knolls like an ancient Chinese temple. Curling, traditional rooflines marked each corner of the sprawling edifice, and a garden of elaborately trimmed hedges and plantings set off statues of Chinese dragons.

"He's not bothering to hide his wealth," Lei said as they pulled up a curving turnaround made of bricks inset with poufs of velvety grass. "This is pretty fancy."

"You'll get no argument from me. That Buddha alone cost more than I make in a year." Bunuelos pointed to a life-size black marble statue placed beside the flight of stairs leading to double front doors done in scarlet and black lacquer.

They ascended the wide stone steps, and Lei pulled a silken tassel that protruded beside the doors. Chimes rang musically deep inside the house. A moment later, one side of the door opened, framing a pretty young woman dressed in a traditional black-and-white maid's uniform, complete with a ruffled cap. "Yes?"

"We're here to speak with Mr. Harold Chang," Lei said. She and Gerry held up their cred wallets. "Maui Police Department."

"I'll be a moment." The maid shut the door.

Lei glanced around and spotted the dome of a surveillance camera in the ceiling above them. "Someone's watching us."

"That's no surprise," Bunuelos said out of the side of his mouth. "Got to be all kinds of security at a place like this. What are you trying to do with this stop-by, anyway?"

"Shake the tree and see what falls out," Lei said.

Bunuelos rolled his eyes.

The door opened again. This time a short, portly Asian man dressed in a long, plum-colored smoking jacket over black satin pajama pants stood in the doorway. "Can I help you?"

Lei and Bunuelos held up their IDs. "We sure hope you can. Are you Mr. Harold Chang?" Lei gave her sweetest smile, complete with dimple. "I love your outfit!"

"Oh." Chang shuffled his feet and she spotted fuzzy slippers. "I'm not dressed for guests."

"We won't take but a moment of your time," Lei gushed. "Please, Mr. Chang. We need your help!"

"Well, of course, anything I can do for the Maui Police Department," Chang said, tightening the belt of his robe.

"We just need to talk with you about a warehouse. I'm sure it's some mistake, but someone said you were the owner?" Lei rattled off the address of the warehouse where the container had been altered to ship the women overseas.

Chang's face drained of color. "I have no idea what you're talking about." He grabbed the frame of the door to steady himself. "You'll have to contact my attorney for any further questions." He stepped back inside the house and slammed the door so hard the bell pull was jostled, and the door chimes pealed.

Lei glanced at Bunuelos, and the smile that curved her lips was very different than the one she'd shown Chang. "Bingo."

"Well, something's sure rattled now that you shook that tree," Bunuelos said. "Hope we didn't spook him into making a move."

"I hope we did," Lei said grimly. She could feel a spot burning between her shoulder blades as she walked down the steps.

She could always tell when someone had a gun on her.

CHAPTER THIRTY-SEVEN

THE HOUSE that Keo's mom said he hung out at was an address adjacent to a run-down park on the south end of Front Street, Lahaina's busy thoroughfare.

Lei and Bunuelos had picked up some takeout and checked in with Captain Omura and Torufu en route about their progress. Torufu was on his way to try to pick up Felipe Chang for questioning, and a couple of uniforms had been dispatched to surveil the Chang warehouse for any activity.

"Those Minit Stop spam *musubi* are so *ono*." Bunuelos wiped his mouth with a paper napkin as Lei drove along the Pali Highway, sneaking peeks at the ocean.

"Yeah. That's the problem." Lei patted her stomach. "I'm going to have to get in a run after this."

"No problem for me." Bunuelos flexed a wiry arm. "I'm all muscle."

"Ha. Your wife must appreciate it, or you wouldn't have so many kids."

"Tell me about it." Bunuelos shook his head. "I'm trying to talk her out of number six."

Lei drove past the dilapidated building, casing the place, and parked a few houses down. "Let's watch the address for a little while, see who comes and goes."

"Roger that." Bunuelos took out a small pair of binoculars from the glove box and scanned the property.

Lei donned a plain cotton ball cap, tugging the brim down to shade her eyes. "Anything moving?"

"No, but I can see the back door opening and shutting. Some kind of gathering is going on in the back yard."

Lei took out her computer tablet and launched a search on the address. "The property is owned by the same corporation that owns the Chang warehouse. Harold Chang is behind whatever's going on in there."

"House is a dump," Bunuelos said. "Roof's got a baby tree growing out of the gutter, weeds everywhere, peeling paint . . ."

"Well, they wouldn't want it to look too nice on the outside. I bet this is an interim spot where they let the kids hang out and get comfortable—groom them. Let's go see what we see." Lei checked her weapon, made sure her badge was clipped in plain sight to her belt, and shouldered her small backpack as she got out of the truck, beeping it locked. Bunuelos did a similar ritual.

"Let's just split up and go around the house to where the people are in back," Lei said. "Don't give them too much time to disappear."

"Roger that."

She and Bunuelos each went around an opposite side of the house.

Broken glass and old beer cans and bottles littered the ground as Lei moved carefully forward. A scrawny cat scuttled into dried-out bushes in front of Lei as she approached the sound of voices, raised and laughing, along with thumping music.

Young voices.

Lei peered around the corner of the house at the outdoor party going on.

A foldable plastic table on the weedy lawn was piled high

with pizza boxes and Chinese food containers. A big plastic thermal drink container held down one end of the table, a hacked-open watermelon the other. All around the yard, young people drank out of red plastic cups, played Hacky Sack, and talked and laughed in little knots as a portable stereo belted out rap music.

Lei stepped out from behind the house. "Hey."

The effect was instantaneous. As if a light had hit a nest of cockroaches, the kids dropped the cups and scattered.

Bunuelos jumped out and grabbed a couple that charged his way. "Where are you kids going so fast?"

Lei caught the nearest teen she could get ahold of, a girl in a ratty Quiksilver hoodie. The girl screeched and fought, twisting inside the sweatshirt. She almost escaped—until Lei got a handful of her dreadlocks and knocked her to her knees. "Relax. We just want to ask you a few questions."

Bunuelos cuffed one of his captives to a drainpipe on the house, and led the other over to where Lei was putting cuffs on the one she'd captured. "Man, you'd think they had a guilty conscience or something."

"I didn't see any adults, did you?"

"No." Bunuelos picked up one of the half-empty cups, sniffed. He shook his captive, a slender boy with green hair. "Spiked punch and cutting school. Your parents are going to love the call from us."

"Let's take these two inside and see what's going on in there." Lei tugged the girl to her feet, clicking her tongue as a pack of cigarettes fell out of the hoodie. "I'll take these. They'll kill you, you know."

The girl answered with a string of expletives and a gob of spit that almost got Lei.

She shook the girl and pushed the teen toward the back door. "You're not making a friend here, you know. Gerry, can you check that the house is clear?"

"Yep." Bunuelos drew his weapon and did a quick pass as Lei kept their captives under control. "Nobody in here."

The inside of the house was as trashed as the exterior: trash cans overflowed beside a sink full of dirty dishes, and sand and dirt marked the floor and furniture. Lei and Bunuelos put the kids on an ancient tweed couch in the living room. Bunuelos watched them as Lei checked through the house, getting a sense of it. Only the back bedroom, with a big bed dressed in black satin sheets, seemed really livable. *Bet Keo Avila slept in that bed—and not by himself.*

Lei sat down in a rump-sprung armchair across from the teens. "First person to talk gets to go free. No call home, no trip to jail for underage drinking."

"I'll talk," Bunuelos's captive piped up. The kid was doing a rap culture imitation, wearing oversized pants that slid off his hips and puddled over his Nikes. He pushed a sheaf of dyed hair out of his eyes. "Ask me whatever you want."

"Snitch," the girl hissed. "We'll get you, Rat."

Bunuelos, positioned behind the kids, squeezed her shoulder at a pressure point. "I think you need a time-out in the bedroom." He marched the girl to the room with the black satin bed, thrust her inside, and shut the door. She promptly began shrieking for help, peppering her invective with curses, so he opened the door again. "Want me to put a gag on you?"

The girl shut up as Bunuelos advanced. "I'll be quiet."

Meanwhile, Lei had her notepad out. "What's your name?"

"Owen. Owen Mancuso."

"Whose house is this?"

"We call him Uncle Keo." The boy's eyes darted fearfully toward the confrontation between Bunuelos and the girl.

"Where is Uncle Keo?"

"Don't know. He's usually here. He has parties here."

"How long has he been gone?"

"A while."

"Not good enough. Tell me more."

"Keo's a cool guy." The boy finally met her eyes, and his were pleading. "My parents will kill me if they find out I was here and not in school."

"So not all of you are runaways."

"Only some of us are. Pammy, the girl in the bedroom. She's a runaway." He lifted his chin defensively. "She and Aaron, the kid outside."

Lei made a note of the names. "Why would a cool guy, an adult, live in a place like this with a bunch of kids?"

"Keo says he was a runaway too. He says he wants us to have a good future. He has a job as a deejay, and he practices with us. We tell him if his stuff is good for his gigs." The boy's chin trembled. "Please. Just let me go. I won't come here again."

"When was the last time you saw Keo?"

"A couple of weeks ago. When he was hiring kids to work on a ship."

Lei's attention sharpened. "What kind of ship?"

"He didn't say. But he wanted guys—bigger, older guys than me. Said they were going to . . . be pirates." The last part of this sentence was lost as he mumbled into his shirt, his hands twisting inside the cuffs.

"What? Did you really just say 'pirates'?" Lei raised her brows.

The kid narrowed his eyes. "They're doing it. They're attacking ships. I saw it on the news."

Lei sobered and nodded. "Yes, they are. And when the Coast Guard catches them, and they will, those boys will be accessories to murder, rape, and piracy—no joking matter. What I'm surprised by is that such hard criminals are looking for runaway kids to be a part of their crew."

"I'm not like that. Not a criminal, I mean."

"I can see you're not, Owen, and no matter what that girl said, you're doing a good thing by talking to me. Saving lives, even.

Now, do you know the names of any kids who went with Uncle Keo for this job?"

Lei noted down the names he gave, then met the boy's eyes. "You need to know something. Uncle Keo is a real lowlife. He's a recruiter. His job is to lure kids in, and then, once he knows you're vulnerable with no one to help you, he gets you to a place where you're locked up and shipped overseas, and sold as a human slave. I want you to tell anyone you can get to listen to you to stay far, far away from this house and anyone like him, an adult that's pretending they're a friend."

Owen's eyes had widened. He bobbed his head in agreement. "That's heavy. "

"You have no idea." Lei took out her handcuff key and unlocked his bracelets. "You've been warned. Now get out of here and tell the others."

Owen jumped up and headed for the door. "Thanks, Auntie."

Lei's heart gave a little squeeze. "Don't let me see you anywhere near here again."

He nodded, and disappeared.

Bunuelos shook his head. "Hope we did the right thing letting him go."

"I've got his name if we need him again."

"What if he lied?"

Lei snorted. "Not that kid. Now that one you've got locked in the bedroom . . . Pammy's another story. And I don't like how quiet it's gotten in there. She's up to something."

CHAPTER THIRTY-EIGHT

LEI AND BUNUELOS tiptoed to the bedroom door. Lei took up a position beside the door as Bunuelos unlocked it quietly and shoved it hard, hanging back in the doorway.

The door flew inward with force, and whacked into the wall. A lamp crashed down where Bunuelos would have been had he been entering. Following the missile of the lamp, a handcuffed Pammy leapt through the door in a whirl of blue jeans and tangled hair. She crashed into Bunuelos, who wasn't where she'd expected him to be, and struggled to get around him.

Lei sprang in from the side and caught her by the arms. "Nice try, sistah."

"Screw you, cop!" Pammy snarled.

"I don't think these two are going to talk right now," Lei told Bunuelos across the girl's thrashing body. "Let's just take her and the other boy to jail."

"You can't do that! We're minors!" Pammy shrieked, trying to bite Bunuelos.

"Sure we can." They wrestled Pammy through the house as Lei called for a backup unit. Bunuelos tied her feet with bungee cords from Lei's truck when she continued to try to kick and bite. They loaded her prone, struggling body into the back of Lei's truck until the MPD cruiser arrived.

Aaron, observing all of this from his place cuffed against the house's drainpipe, chose to get into the back of the cruiser without a struggle.

"Book them on charges of underage drinking, truancy, and resisting arrest," Lei instructed the responding officers. "Check for any outstanding warrants after you run their prints and get their full names."

Once the teens were safely stowed in the back of the vehicle, Lei told the officers out of earshot, "We'll come interview them later. But for now, these two need to think we're locking them up and throwing away the key."

"Gotcha, Sergeant."

"And can you put in a request for a daily drive-by to this address? We want to shut down this spot as a gathering point for runaways," Bunuelos said.

"Definitely. Yes, sir."

Lei and Bunuelos watched the cruiser as it drove away. Bunuelos turned to Lei. "Now what?"

"Now we see what has been going on with Torufu. But first, let's shut this place down as a hangout for these kids." Lei got a roll of crime scene tape out of the back of her truck. They locked the windows and doors, and sealed the house with the tape.

Back in the cab of the truck, Bunuelos got out his phone and put it on speaker. They got a sitrep from Torufu as they headed back to Kahului. "No activity at the warehouse so far, and Felipe Chang's last known address was a bust. I'm heading back to the station," Torufu said. "How'd you guys do?"

"Got a better idea of how the Chang human trafficking operation worked," Lei said. She glanced across Bunuelos at the sparkling blue sea off to her right. The Pali Highway between Lahaina and Kahului, with its sinuous curves and vista views of the sea and sky, was one of Lei's favorite drives on the island. "We have a couple of runaways on ice to interview later. Hopefully they have some more info that will be useful in shutting down that particular operation."

They agreed to meet up at the station later and regroup, checking in with the Coast Guard on how the search for the pirates was going.

Lei's phone beeped with an unknown number even as Bunuelos ended their call. She put in her Bluetooth and answered it. "This is Sergeant Texeira with the Maui Police Department."

"Hello. Am I speaking to the detective in charge of the Peterson murder investigation?"

"Yes, you are."

"Very good. My name is Blair Cunningham, and I'm John Ramsey's attorney. I'm calling because he would very much like to speak with you."

Peterson's shady partner was calling? "Then I very much want to speak with him," Lei said. "I'm on the way to my office. I'll call you back in half an hour."

CHAPTER THIRTY-NINE

"WHO WAS THAT ON THE PHONE?" Bunuelos asked, as Lei navigated a bend in the road that revealed another stunning vista of sea and sky, this one including the lavender smudge of Kahoʻolawe in the distance.

"John Ramsey's lawyer. Ramsey's the guy who benefits most from Peterson's death." Lei pushed down the accelerator and put her cop light on the dash. "Let's get back to the office ASAP. I want to review my notes from my interview with him."

"But Peterson's murder was a coincidence," Bunuelos said. "I mean, not a coincidence because these yachts were targeted somehow. There had to be a way the pirates knew about them, and we haven't uncovered that yet. But coincidence in the sense that he's just another victim, like Janssen, the Norwegian billionaire."

"I have a feeling none of this is random. The pirates have to know where and when a rich target yacht will be passing—they have to choose their attack points carefully. The problem has been that the attacks have been coming so fast and creating such a mess of leads to follow, that we can't catch up. Think about this . . . how did the pirates know we were onto their hideout?" Lei frowned at a slow-moving rental car that didn't pull over for her signal. She hit her siren, too, and that finally got the tourist out of her lane. "I'm just thinking out loud here . . . but wouldn't it make sense for there to be an informant somewhere key, who fed the Pirate King the identities and routes of rich target vessels? Maybe that informant also tipped him off that the raid was planned on the sea cave on Kaho`olawe."

"But how are we going to find a mole 'somewhere key'?" Bunuelos made air quotes, his face scrunched with stress. "I don't like this at all."

"I think we need to talk it over with Aina Thomas," Lei said. "At least put the idea out there. I should probably float it by my superiors at the FBI, too."

"The likeliest place for this mole would be the Coast Guard. Do you trust Petty Officer Thomas?"

Lei glanced at Bunuelos. "With my life."

"Well, Thomas dove in and saved a woman he's got a crush on so he could be a hero . . . but that doesn't mean he isn't dirty."

"Aina Thomas doesn't have a crush on me!" Lei's cheeks and neck heated in that betraying blush she'd struggled with her whole life.

"He does. And it was mutual a while back from what I saw. Torufu and I were wondering if you and Stevens were going to make it through that whole Honduras thing, and you can believe Thomas was hoping you wouldn't stay together."

"You guys were talking about us?" Lei's hands tightened on the wheel. "I'll admit it was a rough patch for a few years, but I would never have cheated on my husband."

Bunuelos raised his hands. "You wouldn't be the first to find some comfort elsewhere when things were tough at home. All I'm saying."

"Well, how about you guys mind your own business and make sure *your* ladies are happy," Lei flared.

Bunuelos chuckled. "You tell Stevens, come talk to me if you guys ever need some marriage advice, particularly in the bedroom."

"We've got no problems there, Gerry." Lei's face hadn't cooled down a bit. "Now can we get back to talking about the freakin' case?" She was close enough to the station now that the traffic had increased considerably, and she slowed to get through a red light.

"Sure. Just sayin' that Thomas is not off the list, least as far as I'm concerned." Bunuelos took out his tablet and booted it up. "I think part of what's got us confused is that we're basically dealing with two cases—the human trafficking ring operating out of Kahului Harbor and Lahaina, and the pirates."

"But we know that Keo Avila, the human trafficking recruiter, is connected to the pirates directly because we have his fingerprint at a scene," Lei said.

"I get that. But I think we need to take a step back strategically and do a bit of analysis." Bunuelos tapped his chin with a forefinger. "We've just been running around following every clue as it crosses our path. Maybe we're trying to hit too many things at once. What's causing the most harm right now? *The pirates.* Catching them will eliminate new victims. Once we have them, we can go after the various parts of the human trafficking operation."

Lei frowned at the road ahead, loosening her death grip on the steering wheel. "But we're really not in charge of that part of the operation. The Coast Guard is."

"And that's not going particularly well, is it? I think we should pull in the FBI, officially."

"I agree." Lei pulled into Kahului Police Station at last. The ugly gray bunker of a building had begun to feel like a refuge over the years. She drove through the large parking lot peppered with MPD cruisers and civilian vehicles alike into her assigned parking spot under the familiar rainbow shower tree, and turned off the cop light on the dash. She turned to Bunuelos. Usually his brown eyes were bracketed by crinkles of good humor, but today his expression was serious as he met her gaze.

"You make some really good points, Gerry. As soon as I take this call, let's see what the Captain says about bringing in the FBI. You're right. We should be taking the lead on finding the pirates. But in the meantime, let's find out what that jerk Ramsey has to say."

JOHN RAMSEY WAS DRESSED with hipster style in a silky maroon button-down and a pair of skinny jeans visible in the video call on Lei's monitor. "Hello, Sergeant Texeira. This is my attorney Blair Cunningham."

"We spoke on the phone," Lei said, inclining her head toward the man beside him, dressed more conservatively in a gray suit. Lei was conscious of her frizzing, disordered hair and that her tank top and cotton jacket had been worn for too many active hours and were far from fresh. "What's this about? Why did you want to speak to me alone?"

"We'd like to broker an immunity deal," Cunningham said.

"That isn't something I can do on my own," Lei said slowly. "Those have to be approved by my captain and the district attorney." She cocked her head, narrowed her eyes. "This means you have some information about the case that implicates you."

Ramsey sat down abruptly behind his desk and dropped his face into his hands. "Yes."

"We talked once already. Why didn't you bring this up then?" Lei softened her voice deliberately. "It takes courage to do the right thing. I'm so happy you've reached out."

"I . . . heard from Emma Peterson." Ramsey spoke thickly through his hands. "I've always admired her. What happened to her and the girls . . ." His shoulders shook.

Cunningham cleared his throat. "Mr. Ramsey would like an agreement that, in return for the information he's about to give you, he is not charged in any way."

Lei's scalp prickled with anger but she kept her voice warm and soft, ignoring the lawyer. "Wow. You must have some really good information, Mr. Ramsey." She paused and waited until Ramsey finally glanced up at her from red-rimmed eyes. "What do you know that could get justice for these women? That could save lives? Because these pirates are deadly and no joke. We just fished another corpse out of the sea and there are several more we haven't found yet, out there somewhere. We freed four victims from their latest attack who were raped and abandoned, locked in a shed inside a cave without food or water. Left to die after their assault in total darkness! And we have good reason to believe they're planning another attack, as we speak." *A bit of exaggeration, but likely true.*

Ramsey appeared deeply miserable. "I want to tell you, but I can't."

"Not without that agreement," Cunningham chimed in.

"I can tell you right now that I won't be able to get such a blanket agreement—or any agreement, frankly—without some idea of the information you've got to trade."

"I know how to contact the Pirate King," Ramsey blurted.

Lei sat back and narrowed her eyes. "Let me guess. You contracted a hit on Peterson. It's turned out to be a lot more of a bloodbath than you bargained for, and you've grown a conscience."

Ramsey turned to Cunningham, his mouth ajar in shock. "I didn't tell her that!"

"Call us back when you have that agreement in writing." Cunningham ended the connection with a stab of his finger.

CHAPTER FORTY

AN HOUR LATER, Lei sat down with Bunuelos, Torufu, and Captain Omura in the conference room. A video monitor piped in screens showing Special Agent in Charge Ben Waxman on Oʻahu, and the Maui District Attorney.

Omura opened the meeting. "We thought it was time to officially reach out to the FBI. This case is likely to go outside of our county jurisdiction, and we already know it crosses state lines with the involvement of Ramsey in Washington. With the addition of the *Golden Fleece,* an internationally registered vessel, and the Janssen Norwegian family as victims, there may even be international connections."

"I understand." Waxman, who bore a striking resemblance to Anderson Cooper, inclined his head. "I'd like you all to meet Special Agent Bateman, our tech specialist." He turned the camera to include a seatmate.

"Yo. Howzit. How can we help?" Bateman had a young, forgettable face and wore a rumpled suit with a bolo tie.

"*Aloha,* SAC Waxman, Special Agent Bateman. As lead on the case, Captain Omura has asked me to bring you up to speed," Lei said. She went through the events as quickly as she could. "We've reached a delicate point where we suspect there may be a leak in the Coast Guard; the raid on the pirate's hideout was a bust, and they must be receiving advance tipoffs about these yachts to grab them up so efficiently. We'd like your support and resources to help."

"That certainly seems appropriate. Please send over a copy of your case file and we'll go from there," Waxman said.

"Do you need online support?" Bateman asked.

"Definitely," Lei said. "I actually reached out to Sophie Smithson, one of your former agents, for help early on. She got us great background that gave a lot of momentum with the Peterson murder. But we need the same sort of background workup on the Norwegians and the *Golden Fleece*, in order to uncover a motive for his murder—because we had a break in the case today. John Ramsey, Peterson's partner, as much as admitted that he hired the Pirate King to kill Peterson. He's come forward and is trying to broker a deal with our DA to give us more information."

Lei, her partners, and Captain Omura had finished a meeting with the district attorney prior to adding the FBI into the call; the immunity agreement was at least roughed out.

"You're telling us these victims weren't targeted for the richness of their yachts, or as a hate crime, the way the Manifesto implied?" Waxman's brows had gone up.

"We're not sure of any of that yet." Omura leaned forward, tapping her nails together. "Can you send over an agent to support us, not just help long-distance? We could use more boots on the ground. I've had to recuse two of my detectives from the case already."

"Yes. I need a few hours to check in with my staff and see who's available," Waxman said.

"If I might request Ken Yamada or Marcella Scott, or both." Lei had spent a brief few years working as an FBI agent under Waxman's leadership, and had become close with both of those agents.

"Noted." A smile lurked at the corner of Waxman's mouth. "We'll be in touch." The FBI window on the screen went black.

The District Attorney inclined his head. "Good meeting. I like being in the loop. I had my girl fax over our offer to Ramsey. It's not complete immunity, but it's reduced charges. A starting point."

"Good. Because I want to get what this guy knows ASAP," Lei said.

"All of your speculation about motive hinges on this idea of murder-for-hire," Omura told Lei. "Don't get out in front of your-self too far. This could turn out to be a dead end."

"I know."

The meeting broke up and Lei hotfooted it to the fax machine. She grabbed the paper and tugged on Torufu's sleeve. "Bunuelos deserves a break. Send him home, and come to my cubicle. We'll fax this to Cunningham and interview Ramsey together."

LEI TOOK a minute before the meeting with Ramsey and Torufu to go to the bathroom and freshen up. A glance outside told her that the day was nearly over, but it had seemed so long already. *She simply had to go home after this and see the kids!* Not to mention a shower and a home-cooked meal would be nice—Stevens had texted her a picture of the meal her father had prepared for the family: one of her favorites, teriyaki chicken and rice.

She wedged a trash can in front of the door to slow down any other female staff coming in, and took off her jacket and shirt. She performed a crude bath in the sink, washing under her arms and splashing water up her face and neck, taking casual inventory of herself as she did so.

She was staying trim, but nursing Rosie had taken a toll on her breasts. Her olive skin with its freckles was still firm, but there were lines around her eyes and on her forehead now, and even a thread or two of white in the curling dark brown mass of her hair.

"Lookin' every day of thirty-five, lady," she said aloud. "And those dark circles from stress and no sleep aren't making you any prettier."

Her reflection didn't reply.

Her fingers brushed over a half-moon of scar near her collarbone—a perp had bit her there, but he hadn't lived to do anything more. She'd taken more than her share of damage over the years in this job, and considering that, she was looking damn good.

Lei used a couple of handfuls of water to tame her hair into a fresh ponytail. She put on deodorant and then pulled her top back on, wishing she had remembered to restock the stash of clean shirts in her locker. On went the shoulder holster and her crumpled jacket. With the addition of a little concealer to brighten her tired eyes and some lipstick, she was ready to face that snooty lawyer Cunningham and that slimeball Ramsey, and bring her A game. The Peterson girls, and their dead father, deserved nothing less.

CHAPTER FORTY-ONE

RAMSEY WAS SITTING at his desk in Seattle much as he'd been before, his face pale and creased, his hair disordered, when Lei's video call to him went through. A half-empty snifter of amber liquid in front of him told Lei what he'd been doing since they last talked. Even as Lei watched, he threw back the remainder of his stiff drink.

Cunningham, standing behind Ramsey, tapped a paper he held. "We got your fax. I thought that we should push for more, but my client agrees to your offer of reduced charges. We've already signed and returned our copy."

"Good." They'd agreed Torufu would be "bad cop" for this interview, as Lei had already spent time building a sympathetic bridge to Ramsey. Torufu had taken off his jacket, the better to intimidate with his tatted-up arms in a short-sleeved shirt. "John Ramsey. You have the right to remain silent. Anything you say can and will be used against you in a court of law. I won't tell you the part about an attorney, because I see you're covered on that end."

"Gentlemen, this is Detective Torufu, one of my partners on this case," Lei said. "Thanks, Detective, I think we're ready to roll, having spent a good deal of time agreeing to the legal necessities."

She made eye contact with Ramsey through the video screen. "Thanks so much for doing the right thing. Please tell us about what brought you to reach out to us today."

"I got a call from Emma recently. She was distraught. She was still in the hospital, and the girls had left with a social worker for foster care. She told me what happened, about the attack, and—what they did to her and Joanie, and their female crew member." Ramsey shook his head, covered his eyes with a hand.

"Yes, I heard her story too. And I also helped rescue her and the girls from the shipping container where they'd been held by human traffickers. I took the Peterson girls to the hospital and supported them through the rape kit process with Joanie, and got their statements." Lei allowed her voice to tremble. "Those young women will never be the same."

"None of that was supposed to happen." Ramsey met Lei's eyes with his bloodshot gaze. "I just wanted Pete out of the way. It was supposed to appear an accident, so the insurance would pay out and Emma and the girls would be taken care of. But that guy . . ." He seemed to run out of words. His throat worked.

"You hired the pirates to kill Peterson," Torufu growled.

"Pirates, no way! I did an online search. You know, on the Darknet." Ramsey's face flushed. "I'm not proud of it, okay? Pete used to be my friend. But he was getting more and more fanatical about the project. He wouldn't let me back out or sell my part of it. I was going to be chained to this environmental nut forever, when I could have made millions and still helped the world!" Ramsey held out his glass to Cunningham. "Refill, please."

"I can see how frustrating that would be," Lei soothed.

"It was! You have no idea. So, I found this guy on the Darknet who advertised 'high seas interventions for the right price.' I knew the family was renting that yacht and I figured the assassin would make sure he'd fall overboard or something." Cunningham handed Ramsey the glass and he sipped, pushing a hand through his hair. "I reached out to this guy. He sent me a link to a chat room. We agreed on a price, and I sent him the family's itinerary. I told him what I wanted: no bloodshed, make it look like an accident. I had no idea he'd turn out to be the freakin' Pirate King!"

"It's like you unleashed the kraken." Lei tried to lighten the mood, hoping to keep Ramsey talking. "You didn't mean for all this horror to happen. We get that. But you told us you had information that could help us stop the Pirate King. A Darknet site and an untraceable chat room aren't that helpful."

"No, I have more info." Ramsey took a fortifying gulp of his drink. "I started to worry this guy might come back to blackmail me. I wanted my own insurance on him—he knows me, I know him, we're even. Like that. So, I had a tech guy who works for me track everything we did. I didn't tell him who the guy was, of course, but he was able to determine the owner of the account I wired the payment into." Ramsey blew out a breath. "I know the Pirate King's name and where he lives—and it's on the Big Island."

CHAPTER FORTY-TWO

LEI PICKED her way on stockinged feet through the house to the shower. A soft nightlight in the living area illumined the room enough for Lei to navigate a minefield of Legos and Conan's dog bed. The alert Rottie had woken at the sound of her key in the door, but only lifted his head from his paws and gave a soft whine of greeting as she passed. She stroked his head. "Good boy. No barking when it's just me." She dropped a treat she'd dug out of her purse onto his bed as a reward.

Lei shed her clothes in the bathroom and sighed with relief to be under the rainlike fall of warm water in the shower. It had still been another couple of hours after Ramsey's confession for all the paperwork and arrangements for the man's voluntary surrender to be processed. He and his lawyer were on a flight to Maui now for his surrender in person.

Captain Omura had ordered her to go home for a union-required break, now that they'd obtained an actionable lead on the Pirate King for the FBI, Coast Guard, and their team to follow up on. She was more than happy to do so, and had almost nodded off at the wheel as she navigated the windy, overgrown road toward their compound in Haiku.

She'd grabbed some fast food as she passed through Kahului, so immediate needs of the body were all taken care of as she slipped into a silky sleep tee and slid into bed, trying not to wake Stevens.

He was already awake, and reached out a long arm to draw her into her special spot along his side. "Hey. You're home." He kissed the top of her head.

"Yeah. Got a mandatory twenty-four hours off," Lei mumbled, rolling onto her side so she could pillow her head in the notch between his neck and shoulder. She slid her hand under the light T-shirt he wore to sleep in, playing with his chest hair, and slid a leg up over his thighs. "I've missed you."

"I've missed you, too. Your grandpa's doing good so far. You can catch up with him on the phone tomorrow."

"Oh good. Gave me so much peace of mind to have you handling things."

"Don't forget our parents. They kept the house and kids going."

"I know." She sighed, his warm, solid presence melting her stress. "I'm so grateful. For everything."

Lei didn't remember falling asleep, but the next thing she knew, something wet and raspy on her cheek brought her hand up sharply. "Ew!" She pushed the dog away.

Kiet giggled as Conan backed up and woofed. "It's almost lunchtime, Mama. Daddy sent us in to wake you up."

"Guess I better get up then." Lei sat up. "You sicced him on me, you rascal! Get up here so I can give you a hug."

Kiet climbed up onto the bed and snuggled into her. Lei stroked his thick hair and squeezed his wiry body close. A sensitive child who'd struggled with anxiety in the past, he was doing well at the moment, and she loved to see his mischievous side. She tickled his ribs, making the little boy laugh and squirm. Conan barked with excitement. "Okay, okay. I'm getting out of bed."

The boy and dog romped off, and Lei heard Kiet's piping voice in the kitchen telling Stevens that Lei was on her way. He must be cooking, because delicious smells wafted through the open door. Lei's belly gave a hungry rumble as she tossed the comforter aside and padded over to the dresser.

She glanced at herself in the mirror—her damp curls had dried in a riot around her head, but she didn't have to go anywhere for a whole blessed day. She tugged on a pair of sweats and a T-shirt and bundled her hair into a knot on the top of her head with a rubber band as she walked down the hall into the kitchen. "I smell something amazing."

"Brunch for the family." Stevens had his back to her as he scrambled a yellow mountain of eggs in their big cast-iron skillet. "Wayne and Mom are coming over in a few. We'll eat outside at the picnic table."

Rosie, sitting in her high chair, let out a high-pitched squeal. "Mama!" She banged her hands down on the plastic tray. "Up! Mama!"

Lei hurried over and carefully hugged her daughter, trying to avoid the egg mashed all over the baby's hands and arms. "How's my darling? Eat just a little more. Mama will help." She sat down and picked up Rosie's spoon. "Open wide, here comes your bite!"

"Kiet, can you set the table?" Stevens handed a stack of paper disposable plates to his son.

Kiet took the items. "C'mon, Conan, we'll go get Grandma and Grandpa."

Lei wiped Rosie's face with a nearby dishcloth and addressed Stevens's broad back. "Can I help?"

"Nope. Got it handled."

"Then I'll get this one dealt with so we can enjoy the meal."

"You know she's going to want to sit at the table and eat all over again."

"Probably." Lei grinned at her daughter. "You're a bottomless pit, aren't you, sweetie?"

Soon they were all seated around the picnic table outside.

"Time for grace." Wayne bent his head and led them in a simple blessing of the food, then Stevens gestured to bowls of eggs, pancakes, bacon and Portuguese sausage, and papaya and pineapple slices. "Eat up everyone. I wanted to just say thanks to you, Wayne and Mom, for helping out with the kids while we were dealing with so much recently."

"We're glad to have the time and energy to do it," Ellen helped herself to the buffet. "Why do you think we live right next to you?"

"It's really worked out so well. And that's why I hope you'll still feel the same that we'll be adding my grandfather to the family compound," Lei said.

"He's agreed to sell his house and come over, after the scare he had with his fall," Stevens said. "He has enough in the bank for us to buy him a tiny house so he can have his own space as long as he's able."

Wayne and Ellen both nodded. "We thought that would be the best solution," Ellen said, "Since there are so few assisted living facilities on Maui. Does he need a caregiver?"

"Yes, right now, but he should be back to independent by the time he moves over," Stevens said. "If not, we can hire someone—he has the resources for that, at least part-time, and he could generate ongoing money by renting or selling the Punchbowl house which is paid for."

Lei gazed at her father. "Dad. Soga's your father-in-law, and he and my grandmother were so bitter for so long about your marriage. He's told me he's let the past go, but have you? Is it okay to have him here, on the property?"

Her father's gaze was warm and direct. "I understood where he was coming from with his anger toward me—but all of that is in the past. Soga is welcome in our home, in our lives. He is *ohana*—family. And family takes care of family."

CHAPTER FORTY-THREE

MORE THAN TWENTY-FOUR HOURS LATER, strapped into her seat in the eight-passenger FBI chopper, Lei couldn't help having a huge grin as she looked around at her companions. *Nothing quite like going on a raid with some of your favorite people in the world.*

The pilot and an FBI sharpshooter, Agent McKendrick, occupied the two front seats, Torufu and Bunuelos the next three with a gear bag between them, and Lei was sandwiched between two of her friends, FBI agents Ken Yamada and Marcella Scott, deployed by SAC Waxman to help with the case.

During the time she'd been off-duty, the FBI had ramped up the investigation with the name and location Lei and Torufu had extracted from Ramsey, and planned a multi-agency takedown of the pirates. A combined FBI and MPD SWAT team preceded them in another chopper, the Coast Guard had already moved into ocean position, and Big Island PD were blocking escape on land.

They were all headed for the Pirate King's likely location, a remote valley on the towering northeastern shore of Hawaii, under cover of darkness. Official maps showed the area as uninhabited, but it was owned by a corporation: Waikoa, Inc. Ramsey had given them the single name of Kabo, owner and CEO of that company.

Satellite imagery had revealed a small, sheltered bay with an unpermitted cement block bunker perched on the ridge above. Satellite images had been used by the team to plot the raid—they'd studied the structure; its entrances and exits. The only land access was a narrow dirt road. Close-ups of the bluff above the bay showed a perilous series of ladders leading to a sea cave.

"That's where they're hiding their craft," Commander Decker had said at the planning meeting. "We'll block their ocean escape. The FBI will storm the building by air, and Big Island PD will hold them by land. They'll be sitting ducks, trapped in their hideout."

Lei privately hoped they wouldn't have already fled like in the last raid. There'd been no time for her to even follow up about a possible leak in the law enforcement personnel going after the pirates.

"I don't know if you've ever been to Waipi`o Valley," Ken's voice came through her helmet, echoing in the comm unit. "It's gorgeous. Sophie and I had a super intense case there."

"I've been to Waipi`o, of course. You forget—I started out with Hilo PD," Lei said. "But this location isn't in the valley itself, is it?"

"Nearby. A couple of ridges over," Bunuelos chimed in from the front. "This whole side of the Big Island is steep cliffs and valleys."

They'd reached Hawi, a northern point, just a sprinkle of lights on the dark bulk of the island. The demarcation of the wet versus dry sides of the island was starkly apparent in daylight; baked-golden slopes ascended to heights, where water-bearing clouds caught on the ten thousand foot slopes of Mauna Loa.

But at night, it was all just shapes of dark and darker, lit by the occasional light of civilization and a faint moon glow on the water far below.

They circled the edge of the island and headed toward cliffs, rising with height and splendor on their right.

Everyone was dressed for the raid in emblazoned protective

vests and helmets. Lei had already checked that her standard issue Glock 40's magazine was fully loaded and made sure her little ankle rig was also ready. A couple of clips of extra ammo weighed down her vest pockets. Beside her, Marcella counted the rounds in her ammo clip, then shoved it home in the semi-auto pistol she favored. "Too bad it took pirates to bring us all together again," Marcella said.

"Any excuse for a reunion, right?" Ken gave his handsome, triangular grin. "I miss working with you, Lei."

"We gotta get together more often," Lei agreed. "After this is over, I want you both to come to the house for a meal before you head back to O`ahu."

"Most definitely." Marcella was as beautiful as ever; she reminded Lei of the actress Eva Mendes, with her lush curves and luminous smile.

Lei was glad she had taken a Dramamine earlier as the chopper bucked, hitting an updraft from the island. This larger chopper was more stable than the small Bell Jet Lei was more familiar with, but still it swayed and bounced as the pilot drew a line low along the cliffs.

"Radio silence from here on out," the pilot said. "We're within scanner pickup range of the target."

Lei's heart rate accelerated. She practiced calming nose-breathing deliberately, even as the helicopter dropped and danced in drafts off of rugged lava cliffs that plunged from dramatic heights down to a churning ocean. The smaller valleys that would eventually open up to the major chasm of Waipi`o were cleft by waterfalls, some of which spilled from the bluffs, silver feathers in the moonlight. Others gleamed at the backs of the gulches like veins, almost hidden by jungle.

The Pirate King's house hunkered like a gray barnacle on the top of the bluff next to the little bay Lei recognized from the satellite photos. Ahead of them, the SWAT chopper hovered over the building and dropped its team down a rope onto the roof.

She was glad they had other orders.

Lei scanned the water and spotted a Coast Guard craft, just outside of the bay and invisible from the house's line of sight. As they passed the building and turned inward onto the land, the dirt road leading to the house was dimly visible—a potholed, muddy mess screened by overhanging trees. She couldn't see any activity there, but the island's police would be blocking the road's access to the main highway while hanging back—just as the Coast Guardsmen were, letting FBI's Strategic Weapons and Tactical take the lead.

Their chopper dropped down beside a prefabricated metal barn, likely a storage area. Satellite thermal imaging had shown the barn to be empty of personnel, but the house was occupied, and likely there were more hostiles in the cave below.

Lei and her compatriots got their night vision goggles on, exited the chopper, and it lifted off again. Agent McKendrick already had a vantage point near the road picked out; he quickly surged up into the branches of a huge koa tree. Lei turned to face the house, the barn at her back, getting a sense of the area. She was assigned to cover the barn, and she was the odd one out as Ken and Marcella ran to the right of the house, running low and using cover, while Torufu and Bunuelos went left in the same manner.

Their roles were to secure the exits around the building as SWAT tackled the hostiles from the inside, and a smattering of gunfire from the direction of the house told Lei the sweep was well underway.

Lei trotted around the barn, doing a quick survey for the best spot to hunker down.

The roof appeared intact, but the whole structure was rusting in the heavy Big Island rains, beginning to sag into a lowering dip of ground. The barn was equipped with two large exterior doors and one small one. Lei tried the small one, startled to find that the push handle moved under her hand and the door opened easily on oiled hinges.

A mildew smell assaulted her nostrils along with the distinctive smell of the sea. She peered around. The NV goggles weren't great for detail, but it didn't much matter because most of the space was filled with boxes holding unknown contents. An entire half of the barn was filled with pieces of salvaged parts and equipment from boats. Lei spotted the name of the *Golden Fleece* emblazoned on a furled sail. "This is where they store the loot," Lei murmured aloud, moving around the junk. None of it appeared to be of much commercial value.

On the other side of the mountain of salvage, Lei spotted a small, two-man heavy duty Rhino all-terrain mini-truck, parked facing the doors. "Those tough bastards can go anywhere. This is an escape vehicle," Lei murmured, the hair rising on the back of her neck.

Someone was going to come for this vehicle. All she had to do was wait. She pulled back behind a refrigerator-sized box near the door to ambush anyone coming in.

She didn't have to wait long, but she'd chosen the wrong spot to wait for her quarry.

CHAPTER FORTY-FOUR

LEI HEARD a soft scraping sound coming from the ground near where the ATV was parked.

"Shit," Lei hissed. *They had a tunnel!*

She felt her way forward to the pile of salvage, picking her way on tiptoes around it as she heard a murmur of voices and light oozed through the pile of junk. She reached the edge of the pile, staying hidden, and peered around it.

Two silhouettes had climbed up out of a square hole in the ground directly behind the ATV. One of them shone his light around the space. The beam was so bright that it seared Lei's eyeballs as it momentarily struck her, blinding her behind the NV goggles.

She froze.

The light moved on. "It's clear," he said.

Lei dropped her goggles to hang around her neck—with the laser-bright flashlight beaming around, they were more of a hindrance than a help.

The other silhouette ran forward to roll back the door.

Lei raised her weapon and opened her mouth to call out, but

the one holding the flashlight spoke. His voice was guttural, foreign-accented. "We should'a fuckin' been warned."

"Yeah." The one at the door rolled it open. "But they might have got to him." This voice sounded young and American. The rusty metal door hardly made a squeak as it rolled open on a well-maintained track.

The young man ran back and got into the ATV. The other man got in the other side. The driver switched on the lights, and the brightness flared.

This was her chance! They wouldn't be able to see her, and she could see them clearly, backlit silhouettes framed as if in a photo, by the roll bar of the ATV.

"Freeze! Police! Hands in the air!" Lei bellowed.

"Go!" the accented voice yelled, as he spun in his seat and fired a fusillade of bullets from an automatic that Lei hadn't been able to see him holding.

Lei hit the ground shooting at them.

The Rhino roared into life and leapt forward.

Lei continued to fire at the silhouettes, even as the automatic sprayed around her.

The Rhino was already through the door and out into the dark when the guttural-voiced man fell out of the vehicle with a harsh cry, rolling on the ground.

Lei fired the rest of her clip at the ATV, and heard it swerve and screech. She jumped up and ran to the door of the barn, and watched in satisfaction as the mini-truck rammed into the tree the sharpshooter was in, flinging the unbelted driver out of the open vehicle onto the ground.

"Put your hands on your head!" Agent McKendrick yelled at the driver from above. *What a surprise that voice must be!* Lei pulled her goggles up and peered through them—she could just make out a shape on the ground, his arms like pale green noodles as he lifted them on top of his head. "Roll over on your belly!" McKendrick commanded.

Keeping behind the barn as cover, Lei reloaded a fresh magazine, and dropped the goggles around her neck again. She took her flashlight off her belt and lifted her weapon, approaching the perp she'd shot cautiously and keeping the light on him.

The man who was likely the Pirate King lay sprawled on his back on the hard-packed dirt. His mouth was open on a scream that had never ended, and his dark eyes were wide and fixed. A spreading blood pool beneath him soaked the solid ground like oil.

Lei kicked the man's automatic weapon, a Kalashnikov, away from the body with her foot. She touched his neck with two fingers, checking for a pulse.

Nothing.

Six foot, muscular, with thick matted hair and skin so dark it absorbed the light.

Kabo, the Pirate King, was not Hawaiian.

She eyed the Polynesian tribal marking that encircled one of his arms. She squatted, picked up a twig, and gently scratched at the tattoo. It peeled away easily.

"Fake," Lei muttered. "Just a publicity stunt." Whoever this guy was, he wasn't *Kanaka Maoli.*

Lights came on around the driveway. The battle in the house was resolving.

Lei left the body and trotted over to secure the other prisoner as Agent McKendrick stayed in the tree, alert for any other attempted escapes.

Lei recognized Keo Avila immediately as she approached the man lying on his belly. His handsome face was crumpled with pain. Blood gleamed on the back of his shoulder in a greasy slick under the harsh lights. "You shot me, bitch," he moaned. "I can't move my arm."

"You're lucky to be alive." Avila's weapon was out of reach, but she kicked it further away and frisked him briskly, removing a knife and another pistol. Avila moaned as she cuffed him and zip-tied his legs.

"I bet the whole 'Pirate King as political activist' was your idea, you little sociopath," Lei said. "Kabo didn't even sound American. You coached him!"

"I want to make a deal," Avila panted. "I know something you'll want to know."

"Yeah." Lei squatted beside the prone young man. "Who's the mole? Who's been feeding you and Kabo intel?"

Avila jerked. "How did you know?"

"I figured it out. Tell me his name."

"No. I want a deal. It's all I've got to bargain with . . ."

She was so damn tired of all these deals. *Why couldn't just one of these perps be sorry for their awful acts and do the right thing?* But this guy was a psychopath. He'd never had a conscience, even according to his mother.

Her body screening the sharpshooter's view from above, Lei leaned on the bullet wound in Keo Avila's shoulder. He squawked.

"Tell me the name, and I'll get you first aid."

"No, I can't!"

"You won't, you mean." Lei leaned on him again. This time Avila passed out, going limp as a dishrag. Thinking of Avila's loving mama and her confusion over his lies and cruelty, thinking of all the runaways this man had lured into metal boxes to be shipped overseas, Lei didn't even feel sorry.

Lei removed a small canteen from her belt and poured some water into her palm. She splashed it on Avila's face. "Wake up. You were giving me a name."

"You'll give me something if I tell you?" The young man blinked puppy dog eyes at her. Cute dimples and long lashes hid his black heart.

"I absolutely will, starting with uncuffing your arms and giving you some emergency first aid—and more of this water." Lei dribbled a little liquid into his open mouth. He gulped thirstily. "You've lost a lot of blood. The EMTs can't come until the raid is fully over, and who knows when that will be? You could bleed out by then."

"Everything okay down there?" McKendrick called. "Need some help subduing him?"

"Nope. Just got a few questions for this guy," Lei called, and leaned on Avila's shoulder with her elbow.

Avila squeaked like a mouse being stepped on. "Okay! I'll tell you. It's Decker in the Coast Guard. Decker's getting kickbacks from the Changs. He lets us know when there are rich targets headed our way, and he makes sure the patrols and inspections of cargo miss our containers."

"You're talking about the Chang human trafficking operation, right? But the pirates are a new thing."

"Yeah. I've been working for the Changs for a couple of years now. Kabo reached out to me. He was new to the area, wanted to get established." Avila shut his eyes. "It was just going to be short-term."

"No, it wasn't. You were going to keep working with that killer as long as you could get away with it. You were building a whole new operation with you as middleman, bringing Kabo together with the Changs. But hey, a deal is a deal." Lei unfastened his cuffs. Avila moaned with relief as his arms dropped to his sides. She cut away his shirt with her combat knife, took out her emergency medical kit, and slapped a pressure bandage over his wound. She rolled him onto his back, and stuffed his folded shirt under the wound. "Don't move. Your body weight pressing on this is decreasing the bleeding."

"Okay." Avila panted in shallow breaths, pale with pain.

Lei refastened the cuffs on Avila in front. "Did you know that Kabo was a contract killer? That's how we ended up getting onto him."

Avila cursed. "He never said anything about that. Just that he wanted certain ships. Decker gave him the info and then . . . the whole thing was way more than I bargained for. I told him it was going to bring too much heat, we had to lie low between jobs, but he wouldn't listen."

Lei glanced toward the house.

The gunfire had stopped. She turned her radio back on, and it crackled with voices reporting in, calling for help, and reporting pockets of resistance, particularly down inside the sea cave, where a standoff had developed.

Lei addressed McKendrick. "Special Agent, can you cover this guy for me? Pretty sure the man down is the Pirate King, and he's dead. I've got this guy treated and secured."

"Roger that. Got him and the driveway covered," McKendrick said.

Lei gave the man a little salute and stood up. She prodded Avila with her toe. "Remember. Don't move. Keep pressure on the wound."

Avila groaned in answer. *Probably going into shock.*

She had to reach someone with the name she'd been given, in case something happened to her.

CHAPTER FORTY-FIVE

LEI WASN'T sure what was clear near the house, so she returned to the barn. In its sheltering cover, she took her phone out of the zippered pocket inside her vest and thumbed to the number of the only man she could think of that might have the authority to order an investigation of a Coast Guard commander: Special Agent in Charge, Ben Waxman.

She still had SAC Waxman's cell number from her FBI days, and he'd be monitoring the raid. "Texeira. Your team is in the middle of an op. Why are you calling me?"

"I'm at the site of the op." Lei slid her free hand into her pocket and fingered the smooth curve of the bone hook. "I've got some information you need to know."

Her eyes scanning the house, alert for danger, Lei told Waxman about Decker. "You're the only person I could think of that might have enough authority to order an investigation into him."

Waxman cursed softly. "You're never boring to work with, I'll give you that, Texeira. I'll get the wheels turning to deal with this. Don't tell anyone but Captain Omura. We need to keep this as confidential as possible."

"Got it, sir." Lei ended the call with a sigh of relief. She then called Omura and briefed her on what she'd done. "The Pirate King is dead, and Keo Avila is wounded, but secure. I've been out of touch with the team, though. How's it going?"

"There's a standoff in the cave below the cliff," Omura said. "Radio in your position to your team, and see where they need you."

"Got it." Lei hung up. She radioed in to Torufu and Bunuelos, but there was no reply to any of her hails.

She went back to the koa tree and called up to McKendrick. "I can't get a signal. Do you have a sitrep?"

"The pirates have a signal jammer going down in the cave, but my headset comm is working outside the cave," McKendrick said. "Your team is down on the rocks below the house. The pirates inside the cave are refusing to surrender. They're waiting for word from the Pirate King."

"Well, they're not going to get it," Lei said, glancing over at the man's sprawled body. "He's dead. I shot him."

"That's what I told them."

"How about I take a picture of his body? And maybe a video of Keo Avila, his second-in-command, telling them to stand down? We can show it to them." Lei was already up and walking. She flicked on her torch and scanned the Pirate King's body. "He's wearing some kind of pendant." A gold medallion with a hole pierced in it, threaded on a leather thong, rested on Kabo's chest. Lei tucked the phone between her shoulder and ear as she took off the simple hook-and-eye clasp and palmed the necklace. "I can bring his medallion down as proof, too."

"Worth a try. It's been a long day," McKendrick said.

Lei studied the pendant in the light of her flashlight as she walked toward Keo's prone body.

What had appeared to be a medallion was actually a gold coin with markings worn faint by time. The hole in it appeared to have been hand-drilled. "Pirate treasure," Lei muttered. "Maybe a source of inspiration for him."

Keo Avila was panting shallowly, alarmingly pale when she reached him. "I'm cold." His teeth chattered. Lei glanced at the crude dressing—*it hadn't stopped the bleeding*. This was more than shock, and she needed him alive!

"Dammit!" Lei called to McKendrick. "Avila's a valuable witness. He's injured and I'm afraid he won't last until the standoff is over. We need an ambulance. Can you get word out through your comm?"

McKendrick barked out codes and passed on the message that FBI SWAT had authorized an ambulance to be allowed in, if Lei and McKendrick covered them.

"Copy that." Lei was gratified to hear the wail of an approaching ambulance making its way down the rough dirt road in their direction.

"Mr. Avila." She squatted to pat the young man's cheek. His eyes fluttered open. "I need you to tell your people that Kabo is dead. They think they have to keep fighting."

Avila's eyes rolled—it was hard to tell how much he understood.

She clumsily thumbed to her video feature on her phone. She turned it on, slapping Keo's cheek lightly. "Please, Mr. Avila. An ambulance is coming. You can do this. Tell your people what you saw. Tell your people about Kabo."

"Kabo is dead. It's over," Keo whispered. His eyes rolled back. He passed out again.

Lei checked his pulse—slow and sluggish. Hopefully he'd make it long enough for the medical team to stabilize him.

She conferred quickly with the sharpshooter and took up a defensive stance, covering the road. She stepped back from Avila as the ambulance rumbled into view and backed up toward them.

The EMT team jumped out of the back of the vehicle and

quickly hooked Avila up with an IV and loaded him on a gurney. As soon as the vehicle drove off, Lei headed straight for the cliff. *She had to take that proof of death down to the sea cave and end the standoff.*

CHAPTER FORTY-SIX

Lᴇɪ sᴜᴄᴋᴇᴅ in her breath involuntarily as she reached the cliff's edge. The way down to the sea cave was invisible from the exposed precipice on which she stood.

The faintest edge of dawn was coloring the horizon with mauve, just enough that she could see the ocean's churning surface seemingly hundreds of feet below. She slung the pirate gold around her own neck for safekeeping and grabbed hold of the ladder, a utilitarian metal one that reminded Lei of the one Stevens had at home for climbing onto the roof—only it had been bolted onto the rock face.

She wasn't usually squeamish of heights, but when Lei gripped the ladder and shook it, the whole thing wobbled, and the black water below seemed a mile away. Her head swam. "Shit."

Had the rest of the team come down this rickety thing? She glanced around and spotted the thin dark lines of ropes dangling off the cliff. But she didn't have any climbing gear, not even gloves . . . *the ladders must work if the pirates used them.*

First she'd try to get the photos and video to her team. Lei checked her phone and selected SEND to Marcella, Torufu and

Bunuelos, just to spread them around in case anyone else's phone was working better.

SEND FAILURE came back seconds later. "Dang it."

Lei faced the ladder. Sucked in a breath. Let it out slowly through her nose. "I can do this. I can be scared as hell and still do this." She turned around, gripped the edges of the ladder, and stepped backwards out into space.

The ladder wobbled and hummed in the wind as she climbed down, taking her time, keeping her gaze only on her feet and hands. Her hair whipped her face as it fought to escape her pony-tail. The metal was slippery and rough on her hands, smelling of rust and salt and stone. The pirate gold swung back and forth on the outside of her vest. Each tiny thump as the medallion bumped her chest seemed to reverberate through her.

Lei ran out of steps. One foot reached out into space, and her supporting foot slipped. "Oh shit." She spared a glance downward.

The next ladder was just double the length of one rung away. She reached further, found her footing.

This ladder was rustier, and damp from blowing sea spray. *The one near the bottom was going to be even trickier, but if she fell off, at least wasn't so far. . .*

"You got this, Lei!" Torufu was shouting up from below, his hands cupped around his mouth. "Slow and steady wins the race!"

At last, other human contact! Encouraged, Lei speeded up and finally reached the bottom. She jumped the last few feet to land on the black lava at the base of the cliff. "Well, that'll get my heart rate up."

"Just wait until we have to go back up," Torufu said. He grabbed her in a quick side hug. "Knew you could do it. Now that you're down, I'll tell you that we all rappelled." He pointed to the rope and sling apparatus still in place, just on the other side of the ladder.

"I saw that." Lei shook her head. "No thanks."

SWAT Captain Hiro approached. "I heard you have a photo and

video on your phone, but nobody's received it."

"Take my phone." Lei handed it over to the FBI negotiator, a wiry little man with intelligent eyes who trailed Hiro like a shadow.

She followed Hiro, the negotiator and Torufu into the mouth of the cave, a huge rock-lined opening large enough for a full-size boat to enter. Waves splashed against the walls, obscuring other sounds as Lei picked her way along a worn boardwalk into the cave. Once inside the lip, powerful lights pointed in their direction blinded her, and she could hear the rumble of a generator run by the pirates in the distance.

The pristine white shape of the *Golden Fleece* rode at anchor, along with a speedboat and a couple of large inflatables with huge outboards on them. She nodded a greeting to Bunuelos, who'd come alongside her, and joined where their team had taken up a position on one side of a large stone embankment. "Where is the Coast Guard?"

"We don't know," Captain Hiro said. "They were supposed to cover the opening, maybe even make a run on the pirates from their craft, but our signals don't seem to be getting through."

That, or Decker was deliberately ignoring their calls for help. Lei bit her tongue on speaking the words aloud.

The negotiator had one of the pirates on a walkie-talkie, and Lei listened in. "We've got some important news for you. You've been insisting you won't back down until you hear from your leader—and you won't, because he's dead."

The radio crackled with a reply. "Prove it."

"We have proof for you. Nobody's phones are working in here, so someone has to come get this phone. We have a picture of Kabo, dead, and a video of Avila telling you to surrender."

A short pause. "Send someone halfway with a white flag. Unarmed, carrying the phone. We'll send someone halfway too, to verify the proof." Another short pause. Then, "We want the person who killed Kabo."

Captain Hiro frowned. "I don't like it."

The negotiator addressed Lei. "They want you."

"I'll go," she said. "And I'll show them this, too." She tapped the medallion dangling on her chest. "It's Kabo's necklace."

"All right, then." Hiro nodded. "We'll keep you covered every step of the way."

"You guys have shooters in position and they're sending someone too." Lei tucked her hand into her pocket and gripped the bone hook. "I'm sure it will be fine. We need to end this thing."

The Captain nodded tersely. "We do."

The negotiator spoke into the walkie. "We agree with your terms. Our representative will come with the phone for you to view, carrying a white marker."

Lei's heart rate speeded up. "I can't believe I'm doing this." She rubbed her sweating hands on her pants.

Torufu squeezed her shoulder affectionately. "Remember when we deactivated bombs together? This is like that."

"I don't remember being very good at it," Lei muttered, but felt strengthened by his grip anyway. "Nobody tell Stevens I volunteered, okay?"

"You got it," Hiro said. "I'm ordering you to go."

Bunuelos had been searching for something white, poking around in their gear bags. Not finding anything, he stripped off his body armor and uniform shirt, and then tugged off his white undershirt tee, handing it to Lei. "Sorry if it's a little ripe."

Lei hugged the shirt, touched. It was still warm from his body. "You're a good friend, Gerry."

"You don't see me volunteering, so I gotta do something." Bunuelos picked up his vest and zipped it back on. "Put the shirt on over your vest. We want as much of you covered as possible."

Lei tugged the white shirt on over her bulky vest with Torufu's help. She put on the SWAT helmet he handed her with its built-in comm.

The stone embankment had a short ladder on their side. The

Captain had been communicating with two sharpshooters, already in position, and he returned, carrying a small white reflective flag on a flexible rod. "You don't need that T-shirt, but it can't hurt to have you overly identified. The negotiator will announce that you're coming over to the pirates' side. Head up the ladder and wave the flag before you get to the top, where they can see it. When the negotiator tells you they've acknowledged you, climb over. You should meet their representative halfway down the walkway. You can't see if from here, but it's much like this one."

"Okay." Lei handed the Captain her weapons except for her belt knife. She lifted the pirate's medallion out of her neckline and made sure it was visible outside her vest and tee. She touched the medallion on its thong—touching it felt meaningful, as if it brought luck. Hopefully *good* luck.

Lei climbed the steps as she had been directed, waved the flag, and at a shout to proceed from the other side, she made her way over the embankment, pausing for one last look at her friends' upturned, anxious faces.

Climbing down the stone embankment on the pirates' side, she was still blinded by the floodlights they'd turned in her direction, but the wooden boardwalk laid down along the inside of the cave was the same as the other side. Lei advanced along the boardwalk, waving the white flag on its flexible pole, feeling as exposed as if a bull's-eye were painted right on her chest.

A backlit silhouette approached. Lei couldn't make out much about the figure except that it was male and bulky.

She stopped at what seemed like the halfway point and lowered the flag, waiting until the pirates' rep stood in front of her. He wasn't dressed as she'd expected, in one of the "Hawaiian" costumes; he wore an all-black coverall, and his face was hidden by the mirrored visor on his helmet.

"Where's the proof of death?" The man's voice was muffled inside the helmet.

"Here." Lei tapped the medallion around her neck. "This is

Kabo's gold necklace. And here. A photo of his body." Lei slid the phone out of her pocket, woke up the screen, and held the phone up.

He took the phone and stared down at it.

"There's a video, too. Keo Avila is on it, telling you to surrender," Lei said. "Just scroll to the next photo."

"Is he dead, too?" The man was wearing gloves, and the phone wouldn't respond to his swipe.

"Keo? No. He's wounded, but he'll be fine." Lei moved as if to take the phone back. "Let me do it."

"I don't need to see the video, then," the man said. "I know what I need to know." He turned to leave.

Lei darted forward and knocked the man's visor up, revealing his face. She took a step back, her eyes widening in genuine surprise. "Commander Decker! How did you get in here?"

"You shouldn't have seen my face." The man's normally robust complexion was pale and greasy. His eyes were bloodshot. "There's another entrance. An underwater cave that leads to the back of this one. The Coast Guard has already taken the pirates. They were just kids—runaways." He paused, his mouth working. "I'm going to have to kill you, now."

"Don't bother. It's too late. Keo Avila told me you're the mole." Lei felt a cleansing rage heat her from within, making her gaze fearless and hot. "I know who you are. So do the FBI and MPD."

A long beat went by as Decker absorbed this. His dark eyes reflected a cold hopelessness. "Then I hope your sharpshooters don't miss." He pulled a weapon, aiming at her. "Or you'll be coming with me."

No time for regrets or what-ifs or bargaining. The resolve in Decker's expression told her all she needed to know—death was at hand, for one or both of them.

"Take him!" Lei screamed, and dove headfirst off the boardwalk into the black water splashing on the rocks.

CHAPTER FORTY-SEVEN

L\EI's headlong leap barely cleared the white foam marking the rocky edge of the water. The impact of the dive smacked her helmet and struck her body as if the ocean were solid—and then, cold water embraced her, soaking through layers of clothing and the heavy vest, filling the helmet and gurgling in her ears. Lei kicked and swam forward under water, trying to put distance between herself and the shootout she heard above as a distorted thunder.

Deep under water, Lei unlatched the helmet, tugged it off, let it go. She couldn't get the vest off with the white tee on over it. She was weighed down, but not like when she'd worn that backpack filled with equipment. Even with her boots and the vest on, she could still swim.

Lei broke the surface when her lungs were screaming, and looked around.

The huge lights were out, and the cave was plunged into darkness except for moving flashlights along the boardwalk area. Voices bounced off the cave walls, but the gunshots had ceased after that first fusillade.

They probably got Decker.

But had the Coast Guard commander been telling the truth about the pirates already being subdued? *No way to tell.* To be on the safe side, she should get back to the police-controlled side of the embankment before she tried to get out.

Lei's booted feet and vested body were so heavy that it took all her strength just to dog-paddle and keep her face above the water. Fortunately, she seemed to be caught in a current that was heading in the right direction. The rip carried her parallel to the rocks, out toward the mouth of the cave.

Lights played over the dark, heaving surface around her. Maybe they'd see her . . . "Help!" she called, but her voice was lost in the cavern. Direction and sound were hard to discern in the cave.

More echoing shouts.

Lei treaded water, riding the current over to the side of the embankment where she'd started. She paddled in close to the rocks, and used a wave's force to push herself up onto them. Clinging to a slippery stone surface, scrabbling with her boots for purchase, she managed to yell "Help!" but her voice was drowned by the surf.

Lei slid back down the rock, losing her grip, and felt the sting of a sharp protrusion on her hand—the rock's side was covered with a bank of *opihi,* a limpet with a sharp, pointed shell that was a popular local delicacy.

The next wave pushed her up again. This time she dug her boots' toes into the rough ridge of *opihi,* pushing herself all the way to the top of the rock.

"Help!" she yelled louder. "Help!" She hung on with all her might, resisting the pull of the receding surf.

Moving lights.

More yelling.

"Help! I'm here! Help me!"

A flashlight pinned Lei in its beam. Minutes later, Torufu hauled her up the rocks and onto the boardwalk by the back of her vest.

"You look like a drowned rat," her partner grumbled, but she felt his big hands trembling as they ran down her arms and legs, checking for injuries. "Are you hurt?"

"No. Just wet. Did you get Decker?"

"We got him. Slimy sellout bastard."

"Oh, thank God." Lei's legs gave out. She sat abruptly on a handy rock. "Did you get the pirates, too?"

"There was no one on our side of the cave but Decker. The Coast Guard had already taken the remaining pirates, when they entered through an underwater tunnel and ambushed them. Apparently, Decker told his team to hold the prisoners while he updated us on the situation, so they had no clue what he was doing. Decker was holding us off with nothing but those big lights, an automatic weapon, and his lies. If he was still alive, I'd want to kill him all over again." Torufu was fierce in the harsh flashlight beam.

Bunuelos ran up. "You're alive!" Her smaller partner threw his arms around Lei in a big hug. Water oozed out of the vest like squeezing a sponge.

"Help me get this off," Lei said, and he did.

Torufu pointed to the soaked tee Bunuelos had pulled off over her head. "That's how I saw you on the rocks. Could hardly hear you calling."

"Glad you gave it to me, then, Gerry." Lei's teeth chattered. Her hand came up to touch the medallion—and she gasped. "The pirate gold is gone!"

"Now that's a line straight out of a B movie." Captain Hiro had arrived with the negotiator in tow. "You did good, Texeira. Glad you're in one piece."

"Decker wanted you to shoot him," Lei said, still patting her pockets. "Once he knew he'd been made, he committed suicide by cop." *Was the Pirate King's medallion really gone?* "I think we should dive for that medal. It's evidence."

"We can ask the Coast Guard, but we don't need it," Bunuelos said. "We've got plenty to close this case, with the pirates and Keo Avila in custody."

"Okay," Lei said, but she was still scanning the rocks and the black water for the necklace, missing its weight around her neck. "That medallion had something about it. Maybe it's better that it's at the bottom of the ocean."

"I'm *glad* you lost that thing." Bunuelos shuddered theatrically. "Bad juju." He kissed the rosary around his neck and crossed himself. "I felt it the minute I saw it."

"Have Stevens buy you something pretty now that this is all over," Torufu chimed in. "I agree. That necklace is better stored in Davy Jones's locker." His big square teeth flashed. "I've always wanted to say something like that."

"With Kabo gone, we'll never know where the pirate gold came from—because dead men tell no tales." Lei tried to keep a straight face. "Think I got you beat with a cheesy line, Torufu."

Torufu snorted, and Bunuelos rolled his eyes. "Let's get home before one of you grows a peg leg or an eye patch."

CHAPTER FORTY-EIGHT

Two days later

LEI KNOCKED on the door of Dr. Caprice Wilson's suite at the Maui Beach Hotel, a no-frills older establishment blocks from the police station in Kahului, for her post-shoot debrief. She smoothed her curls, frizzing from the wind and humidity, and smiled as the psychologist opened the door.

"Hey, Dr. Wilson."

"I see this is one of those occasions when we're not on a first-name basis." Dr. Caprice Wilson gestured. "Come into my office for the day."

"I always feel like I should call you that when we're working."

"Not a bad way to keep our boundaries in place," Dr. Wilson agreed. "I'll call you Sergeant Texeira, then."

Lei put her hands on her hips and surveyed the suite. "This is nice." A rattan couch and loveseat formed an L facing a glass-topped coffee table. A wet bar and a desk held up each side of the room, and a pair of sliders framed a view of the hotel's pool surrounded by well-groomed palm trees, with Kahului Harbor in the background. The day was overcast and blustery, so the pool's surface was wind-ruffled, the palms gyrated, and the area was pleasantly empty. "I'm glad to be meeting here rather than at the station."

"Why do you think I do it this way? I'm contracted to perform psychological assessments and counseling services for the police department, but I'm not an employee. Sure, I could use one of your departmental interview rooms with its bad chairs, ugly lighting and smell of fear, but I like to set myself up for good results."

Lei smiled. "Works better for me too."

Lei took a spot on the loveseat. Dr. Wilson sat kitty-corner to her on the couch. She produced a clipboard. "I'm going to take notes, but as usual they will be vague. This is your formal shooting debrief from the incident on the Big Island." Dr. Wilson's clear blue eyes met Lei's. "What do you want to tell me about first?"

Lei stared down at the knees of her familiar jeans. "I think I'd like to start with one of the things that has bothered me most about the case: Keo Avila, and his role in all of this. I guess I want to understand how a good-looking, bright young man from a loving family could go so badly wrong."

"Tell me more."

"I met his mother. Sweet lady. Said he was the product of her first marriage. She was so confused by his behavior. She said he'd shown a lack of conscience from an early age."

"Generally, sociopaths are a combination of genetics and environment. I can tell you were impressed with his mother . . . but did she say anything about his father? And where he spent his formative years? There was probably more there than initially meets the eye. There usually is."

Lei glanced up into Dr. Wilson's penetrating blue eyes. "You're right. I had the impression that he came to live with her after she remarried. But I don't know. Something for a psychologist to explore, and I'm no psychologist."

Dr. Wilson smiled. "You're better than you think you are. All good psychology begins with an open mind and a curiosity about what drives people. Switching gears now. I've read the case file, but I'm still a little fuzzy on the details of the Pirate King and Avila, and how they fit together. Tell me about that dynamic."

"From what we can gather, Kabo was a Somalian foreign national. He was wanted in his home country for piracy. He was also a contract killer, advertising his services on the Darknet and trying to expand his business. He bought property on the Big Island under his shell company, and came over, supposedly setting up a boat tour business. Avila has filled in more details in return for further concessions, and has told us that Kabo reached out to Harold Chang, who was doing a nice little side business trafficking runaway youth out of Kahului Harbor. Harold smelled expansion, and put him together with Avila."

Lei paused, gathering her thoughts, and went on. "That turned out to be a very bloody partnership. It was Avila's idea to market Kabo's activities to the public as a sort of vigilante justice Hawaiian warrior. He coached Kabo on the culture and the costumes, but it's actually Avila himself in the viral Pirate King video, because Kabo's skin tone and accent would have given him away as a fake." Lei got up, feeling agitated, and paced back and forth in front of the sliders. "Then, with Avila's help, they recruited some gullible young men as their crew. When those young men were apprehended by the Coast Guard in our raid, they all testified that, after they took down the first ship and saw the level of violence, they tried to rebel and escape. Kabo and Avila beat them into submission."

"Sounds like what old-time sailors used to endure. They kidnapped young men for crew, a process called press-ganging."

"Exactly. Avila says he never meant for things to get so out of hand, that he couldn't rein Kabo in. He knew that the level of violence was going to 'bring too much heat'." Lei made air quotes with her fingers. "But at no time did Avila show any remorse for what they did to the men by brutally murdering them, or for what they did to the women."

"That young man's a psychopath, all right. Kabo was, too." Dr. Wilson shook her head. "I'm sure you're wondering how the Peterson girls are doing. Joanie has a long way to go, but her mother is surprisingly resilient, and the other two are making progress. They all, along with Ms. Gutierrez, have gone to a special trauma recovery program in Switzerland . . . on Ramsey's dime."

"Oh, I'm so glad to hear that. I haven't been as involved with the victims from the *Golden Fleece*, but I hear they are making progress too, with a special program at Tripler Hospital." Lei sat back down. "Yeah, John Ramsey and his attack of conscience were the turning point in understanding what was driving the choice of targets that the pirates went after."

"That brings me to Commander Decker. How did he get involved? He seems to have been key in all of this."

Lei sat back. She took the bone hook out of her pocket and stroked its sinuous curve, enjoying the organic feel of it, the way it warmed in her fingers. "Decker got into it the way people usually do . . . through debt. According to the FBI's investigation into his financials, he'd been taking payoffs from Chang for years, turning a blind eye to the human trafficking activities. He just got in too deep to get out, even when things had gone to such an extreme level. He faked the standoff in the cave in order to find out if he'd been blown—and when he knew he was, when he had that confirmation, he committed suicide by cop." Seeing the despair in Decker's eyes, realizing he was prepared to shoot her too in order to reach that ultimate solution—that memory felt etched into her psyche. She grounded herself by squeezing the bone hook, hard. "One of the hardest things has been seeing my friend, Aina Thomas, devastated by the betrayal of his commanding officer. I'm not sure he's going to get past it."

"It's always hard when we discover our heroes have feet of clay," Dr. Wilson said.

"We all have feet of clay. It's just a matter of degree."

"Would you take a bribe? Would you let criminals get past you?" Dr. Wilson's eyes invited confession, as they always had.

The moment Lei had leaned on Avila's wound, using pain to force out Decker's name, was burned in Lei's mind, too. "One of my husband's favorite sayings is, 'we're all just one decision away from stupid.' But right now, speaking to you at this moment, I can say no, never, not today."

Dr. Wilson smiled. "That's all any of us can ever promise. Just for today, I'll do the right thing. But enough days of doing that will add up to a lifetime."

CHAPTER FORTY-NINE

Two months later

LEI BENT over to remove a pan of homemade cinnamon rolls from the oven, and felt a sting on her bottom. She spun just in time to see Stevens taking aim again with a dish towel.

"Hey!" She whacked him with the pot holder she was holding. "You brat! Everyone will be here in a minute, and here you are, horsing around!"

"My favorite sight ever—my wife in tight jeans, getting something tasty out of the oven." Stevens's usually serious blue eyes sparkled. "How could I resist?"

Lei turned back to the stove. "I know I'm not much in the kitchen, but when I put my mind to it . . . I can be truly exceptional. In any area."

"No one will argue with you there, Sweets."

Lei pulled out the pan of hot rolls, waving it back and forth under his nose. "I was going to let you sneak one, but now you have to wait until the Father's Day brunch is underway."

She set the pan on the stovetop to cool, picked up a bag of white icing, and squeezed frosting over the rolls.

Almost done, Lei chewed her lip nervously, glancing out the window to where her grandfather Soga's brand-new tiny house was parked. The front half of the little three-hundred-and-fifty-square-foot house, mounted on a trailer, was draped with a concealing tarp, but she could see all of the tidy wooden structure clearly from her angle at the kitchen window.

She had already moved the temple statue from his front yard to stand near the entrance of his house, and had staked out an area for his ornamental Japanese sand garden. Stevens had made room in his workshop for her grandfather's lantern making, and had shipped over his tools and materials already.

Everything was as prepared for Soga's arrival as they could make it.

Stevens put his hands on Lei's shoulders and squeezed. He kissed the top of her head. "Stop worrying. He's going to love it."

"But Grandfather hasn't seen how small it is," Lei said. "It's one thing to see a picture, and to talk about it on the phone. It's another thing for him to arrive with his suitcases, having left everything behind, and find out that this is all there is."

"No one forced him. He said he was ready to downscale, to live close to us, to be a part of the family for as long as he had left. It's going to be fine."

"But maybe I shouldn't have made his arrival into a Father's Day event, with a brunch and all of our friends coming over. I shouldn't have put on all this pressure. He might feel like he has to pretend he likes it . . ." Lei couldn't seem to stop her anxious churning. She set the icing bag down with shaky hands. "I just want him to be happy."

"I know you do, and I love you for it." Stevens turned Lei, pressing her against him in a strong hug. "*I* think it's going to be fine, but if *you* want to worry, you're welcome to do that."

Lei pulled back in his arms to gaze up at him, smiling. "You know just how to handle me, don't you?"

"Years of study have yielded *some* insights, thank God." They kissed.

A brief knock at the door was all the warning they had before Pono entered, his Oakleys on his forehead and his arms wrapped around a large red *ti* leaf plant in a pot. "Brought the old man some good luck for his new house."

Lei's longtime partner finally seemed to be regaining some of his good humor two months after the loss of his close cousin. Tiare and their two teens followed him in. Each of them was carrying a tray piled high with fresh *laulau*.

"Where do we put the food?" Tiare asked. "Oh, Lei, it smells so good in here. Cinnamon rolls? So *ono!*"

The next hour was a blur as Lei and Stevens greeted their extended *'ohana'* of friends: Gerry Bunuelos, his wife, and their five kids; Abe Torufu and his fiancée, Captain Omura; Jared, Stevens's brother, and his wife Kathy. Elizabeth Black, Lei's favorite social worker, had brought over three foster boys that Lei had rescued on a case a few years before, with various girlfriends in tow. Marcella, her husband Marcus, and their son Jonas had come over for a getaway weekend, and Dr. Caprice Wilson had made it, too, on Maui after giving a training for the MPD.

The living room was a babel of talk, snacking, drinking and reconnecting as they waited for Wayne, Ellen, and Soga to arrive from the airport.

Conan gave his "friends approaching" bark and the gate beeped its opening tone on the wall monitor. Kiet ran in, vibrating with excitement, and grabbed Lei's arm. "Grandfather Soga and Grandpa and Grandma are here!"

Lei had been holding Rosie on her hip to keep the little girl from getting into anything, and she set her down. Rosie toddled toward Kiet, yelling with excitement. "Gapaw!"

"Yeah, Gapaw is coming." Kiet grabbed Rosie's hand, tugging her toward the door. "Let's show Grandfather Soga how good you're walking!"

Kiet and Rosie led the way out onto the porch, and all of the guests filed out behind them. Talking and laughing, Lei and Stevens's friends ranged along the railing of the house's wide covered verandah as Wayne's extended cab F-150 rolled up the driveway to park in the reserved spot marked by an orange road cone right next to the house.

Wayne opened the driver's side door, and the whole crowd yelled, "Happy Father's Day!"

Wayne threw a *shaka* sign, and waved. "Happy Father's Day to all of you dads, too!"

"What a surprise!" Ellen got out of the back seat of the truck. "Looks like a party!" She opened the passenger door for Soga. Kiet, holding Rosie's hand, approached his great-grandfather with Lei close behind.

"Rosie's walking!" Soga only had eyes for his great-grandchildren as Ellen opened his door wider. He swung his legs around to get out, and Ellen handed him a cane. "What a good boy for helping her, Kiet."

"Rosie wanted to show you," Kiet said. Rosie had gone shy, plugging her mouth with her thumb as she stared at Soga. She took another step, hit a bump in the grass, and sat down abruptly on her padded bottom. Stevens scooped the baby up before tears could fall.

Lei advanced to help her grandfather down from the high floorboard of the truck. "We thought we'd throw a welcome and Father's Day party to greet you at your new home, Grandfather." She'd been over to see Soga on two different weekends since he'd been convalescing from his hip replacement, but she still wasn't used to how frail he seemed since the surgery. She supported him as he found his feet on the driveway, and kissed his seamed cheek. "Welcome home. Happy Father's Day."

Soga's dark, unreadable eyes were suspiciously shiny. "You didn't have to make such a big thing of this, Sweets." He'd picked up using her nickname some years ago, and she loved hearing him say it.

"But we're so honored you've chosen to come and live with us." She took his arm. "Let's go see your new house before we start the party."

Everyone else, talking story, trailed behind the two of them as Lei and Soga walked slowly across the neatly mowed lawn.

The dwelling, covered with a tarp, appeared to be a big brown lump as they made the turn around the mango tree.

Kiet, thrilled with his special role in the surprise, ran forward and grabbed a corner of the tarp. He ran with it, pulling the synthetic fabric down and away. The tarp slithered off, revealing an adorable little wooden house on its own wheeled platform.

Everyone burst into clapping and cheering.

The metal roof was red, and so was the front door. Soga's old brass knocker, freshly polished, gleamed against the bright color. Windows on either side of the door glittered with cleanliness, and the edge of a white curtain shone inside like a glimpse of petticoat. The house's walls in golden stained pine seemed to glow in the sun.

It was pretty, and new, and very, very small.

Soga leaned heavily on Lei's arm. She glanced at him, just in time to see his eyes overflow as he stared at the little dwelling.

Her stoic grandfather was crying!

Were they tears of joy, or of sorrow at what he'd given up? Maybe a little of both . . .

"It is perfection. *Kanpeki,*" he said. "All I need."

"Oh, good," Lei sniffled. She hugged her grandfather. "I know you mean it when you speak Japanese about something. Let's go inside, and you can see how we furnished it with what you sent over."

Soga was settled in his new abode, resting. The party was a noisy backdrop filling the house as Lei and Kiet approached Wayne. "We have a surprise for you, too, Dad."

"What? No need." But Wayne cooperated with good grace as Kiet tied a blindfold on him and led his grandfather over to sit on the bench of the outdoor picnic table the family often used for meals, now groaning with the half-eaten food of the brunch buffet.

Wayne's work-worn hands plucked at the knees of his jeans, and his craggy face was wreathed in a grin visible beneath the bandanna. Ellen came over and set a hand on his shoulder, and she was smiling, too.

"You said this is a Father's Day surprise—but the longer this takes, the more worried I'm getting," Wayne said.

"Just a little longer, Dad," Lei called, wrestling a large, loosely wrapped bundle out of the shed where it had been hidden.

Stevens came over to give her a hand. "Hang on, Wayne. It'll be worth the wait."

"You're going to love it, Grandpa!" Kiet yelled, holding onto Rosie, who was trying to lunge forward and grab the package as it approached.

"I know I haven't always been the best dad. I hope you guys aren't going to dump a bucket of toads on my head or something," Wayne said.

"No! We're so thankful for all the ways you two help out around here," Stevens said as Lei set the bulky package at Wayne's feet. Faint squeaks and rustles came from inside.

Lei untied the blindfold. "Open it, Dad."

Ellen laughed. "Oh my. What's in there, honey? I think you better just get your nerve up and see."

Wayne glanced down, blinking. "I have a feeling that my life is about to change forever."

"Open it, Grandpa!" Kiet jumped up and down with excitement. Beside him, the family's big Rottweiler whined, snuffling at the package, his stump of tail wagging.

Wayne pulled the loose wrapping away from a plastic dog kennel with Kiet and Rosie's help. Pressed up against the wire mesh, pink tongue reaching through the wire and tail lashing, a yellow lab pup strained to reach her new master.

"Oh hell. There goes my heart." Wayne laid a hand on his left chest. He gazed at Lei, his brown eyes wet. "Sweets. This is too much."

"I thought you deserved a chance for a parenting do-over, since you were gone for most of my childhood." Lei's eyes prickled too. "Shoots, this is a teary day."

Kiet knelt in front of the kennel's door, sticking his fingers in so that the puppy could lick them. "What are you going to name her, Grandpa?"

Wayne opened the wire mesh door. The plump golden puppy leaped into his arms, licking his face and lashing him with her tail. "I like the idea of a "do-over," too. We'll call her Dove, for short."

They all crowded in to pet her until Dove wet herself with excitement.

"I think she's had all she can handle." Wayne stood up with the puppy tucked against his side. Dove settled, resting her muzzle on his forearm as if she'd always had a place there. Wayne pulled Lei close in a hug with his free arm. "I don't deserve this, but I'll take it—thank you, Sweets."

"You've more than earned a thank-you from us." Lei rested her head on Wayne's shoulder, the golden pup sandwiched between them. "But love isn't about deserving, Dad. It just is, and it covers a multitude of sins."

"Thank God for that." Wayne kissed Lei's forehead, just like she remembered him doing when she was a little girl.

Turn the page for a sneak peek of book 14 in the Paradise Crime Mysteries, *Wrong Turn*!

SNEAK PEEK

WRONG TURN, A PARADISE CRIME MYSTERIES
NOVELLA, BOOK 14

AUNTY ROSARIO NARROWED her eyes at her niece and adopted daughter, twenty-one-year-old Lei Texeira. "You'll be careful? Mexico can be dangerous."

"Too careful, like I always am," Lei snorted, rolling a T-shirt neatly and tucking it into her duffle bag. "Glad I have Kelly to loosen me up."

Rosario fussed with a row of bird nests atop the bureau. Lei had been collecting them on their nature walks since her aunt had brought her, at age nine after her mother died, to the little bungalow on D Street in San Rafael, California. "I wish you girls had a boyfriend with you."

Lei turned to face her aunt, opening her mouth to challenge her guardian's sexist comment—but Rosario's cheeks were pale, and her brown eyes shadowed with worry. "Oh, Aunty." Lei dropped the shirt into the bag. "We'll be fine." She walked over to give the short, plump woman a hug, resting her cheek on her aunt's silver-streaked, curly hair. "Don't worry. I'll call you as soon as we reach the resort at Cabo San Lucas."

Rosario wrapped her arms around Lei's slender body, and squeezed. "It's the first time you've left me since you came."

Lei pulled back from her aunt. "Really?"

Rosario dropped her arms. "Really."

"Then it's past time I got on the road. I'm probably the only person my age who's never been anywhere without her guardian."

"Just—be careful."

"Don't forget—I've applied to the Hawaii police academy, Aunty. I'm going to be a cop. I can take care of myself, and Kelly too." Lei resumed packing, reaching for her sensible one-piece swimsuit. "I'm more worried about leaving *you* here. This neighborhood has been going downhill." A series of break-ins nearby had put them on high alert. "Those robbers don't seem to care that people are home when they break in."

"I can't imagine anyone would break into this house." Rosario flapped a hand dismissively. "I know everyone on my street, and everyone knows me because of the restaurant. Momi and Deke will be checking in on me, too." Aunty Rosario ran a popular Hawaiian food restaurant nearby. Rosario's business partner, Momi, and her husband were like extended family. Rosario looked at Lei. "But I do have an idea I think you'll like, for when you get back."

"Oh yeah?" Lei shoved a pair of jeans into the duffle and zipped it up. "If it's something to keep me from moving to the Big Island, Aunty, I'm sorry but I've made up my mind. I need to return to—where it all began."

"I know, Lei-girl." Rosario straightened the bird nests one more time, and sighed. "I understand why. With your father in jail and your mother dead of the drugs—I know why you need to go back to Hawaii and be a part of making things better there. It's good for you to go on a little vacation, have fun like girls your age do; I worry, that's all." She looked up and caught Lei's eye. "But I thought of something that could help us when you get back."

A car horn tooted from outside the house. "That's Kelly!" Lei exclaimed. "I have to go, Aunty." She grabbed the duffle and headed for the door.

Rosario stopped Lei, resting her hands on the young woman's shoulders. "Don't you want to hear my idea?"

"Of course, Aunty." Lei made herself hold still, stifling her impatience. "Tell me."

"I think we should get a dog. A police dog. People can adopt animals that didn't make it through the K-9 training program."

Lei frowned. "I don't know. Sounds like a lot of responsibility. Let's talk about it in ten days." She kissed her aunt's forehead. "Love you, Aunty! I'll be back before you know it."

Lei hurried out of the bedroom, down the hall and out the front door, waving to her pretty blonde friend waiting in the red Mustang convertible parked in front of the house. "All right, Kelly. Let's get this party started!"

Continue reading *Wrong Turn*: tobyneal.net/WTnwb

ACKNOWLEDGMENTS

Aloha, dear Readers!

Thanks so much for joining me, Lei, Stevens, and all of their wonderful *ohana* for *Razor Rocks*, #13 in the *Paradise Crime Mysteries*!

I thought I was done with the series with book 12, *Bitter Feast*, but after several years and ten thrillers with Sophie (the *Paradise Crime Thrillers*), I realized I craved the little glimpses I got of Lei and her family as Sophie's adventures brushed up against Lei's world . . . So, with the help of my Facebook reader group, Friends of Toby Neal Books, I came up with an idea for a new mystery —*PIRATES!*

Who doesn't love a good pirate adventure?

Well, me, it turns out. Researching pirates, I was truly horrified to find out how brutal they can be, and no laughing matter. I'm even more grateful to the Coast Guard for all they do to keep our Islands safe! That said, I do not have an "expert" reader from the Coast Guard to keep my joint investigation honest, so if I made errors in how that went forward, I apologize.

I also want to thank my team for all their help, and most of all YOU, my faithful readers, who keep me excited to come to the page again and again, bringing these characters to life to teach us just a little about life, love, and solving murder.

I am working on several exciting projects. Look for *Wired Ghost*, #11 in the Paradise Crime Thrillers with Sophie, in the months to come. If you haven't tried the Wired mystery/thrillers where Lei's friend Sophie solves crime with her faithful dog Ginger, they might be just the thing to tide you over until I get to the next Lei book, tentatively titled *Pistol Creek*. I'm also working on a follow-up memoir to Freckled, tentatively titled *Open Road: a Memoir of Love, Travel, and the National Parks.*

And if you liked *Razor Rocks, please leave a review.* Even a few words help others discover the series, and they mean more than you know to this particular author. Some days, when the writing gets hard, reading reviews and knowing people want more is what keeps me going.

With much aloha and thanks,

Toby Neal

FREE BOOKS

Join my mystery and romance lists and receive free, full-length, award-winning novels *Torch Ginger & Somewhere on St. Thomas.*

tobyneal.net/TNNews

TOBY'S BOOKSHELF

PARADISE CRIME SERIES

Paradise Crime Mysteries
Blood Orchids

Torch Ginger

Black Jasmine

Broken Ferns

Twisted Vine

Shattered Palms

Dark Lava

Fire Beach

Rip Tides

Bone Hook

Red Rain

Bitter Feast

Razor Rocks

Wrong Turn

Shark Cove

Coming 2021

Paradise Crime Mysteries Novella
Clipped Wings

Paradise Crime Mystery
Special Agent Marcella Scott
Stolen in Paradise

Paradise Crime Suspense Mysteries
Unsound

Paradise Crime Thrillers
Wired In
Wired Rogue
Wired Hard
Wired Dark
Wired Dawn
Wired Justice
Wired Secret
Wired Fear
Wired Courage
Wired Truth
Wired Ghost
Wired Strong
Wired Revenge
Coming 2021

ROMANCES
Toby Jane

The Somewhere Series
Somewhere on St. Thomas
Somewhere in the City
Somewhere in California

The Somewhere Series
Secret Billionaire Romance
Somewhere in Wine Country
Somewhere in Montana
Date TBA
Somewhere in San Francisco
Date TBA

A Second Chance Hawaii Romance
Somewhere on Maui

Co-Authored Romance Thrillers
The Scorch Series
Scorch Road
Cinder Road
Smoke Road
Burnt Road
Flame Road
Smolder Road

YOUNG ADULT

Standalone
Island Fire

NONFICTION
TW Neal

Memoir
Freckled
Open Road
Coming 2021

ABOUT THE AUTHOR

Kirkus Reviews calls Neal's writing, *"persistently riveting. Masterly."*

Award-winning, USA Today bestselling social worker turned author Toby Neal grew up on the island of Kaua`i in Hawaii. Neal is a mental health therapist, a career that has informed the depth and complexity of the characters in her stories. Neal's mysteries and thrillers explore the crimes and issues of Hawaii from the bottom of the ocean to the top of volcanoes. Fans call her stories, *"Immersive, addicting, and the next best thing to being there."*

Neal also pens romance and romantic thrillers as Toby Jane and writes memoir/nonfiction under TW Neal.

Visit tobyneal.net for more ways to stay in touch!
or
Join my Facebook readers group, *Friends Who Like Toby Neal Books,* for special giveaways and perks.

Made in the USA
Las Vegas, NV
07 April 2022

47004849R00173